Death Is Lookin' For Elvis

Doug K. Pennington

COPYRIGHT

Elvis is in your jeans. He's in your cheeseburgers. Elvis is in Nutty Buddies! Elvis is in your mom!"

~Mojo Nixon ("Elvis Is Everywhere," 1987)

.

To my Father, J,
A lover of reading and of mysteries.

.DEATH IS LOOKING FOR ELVIS

A Dane Cooper Mystery

CHAPTER 1

"It is very simple, Mr. Cooper," Abner Lipps said, in a troubled southern accent. "My wife and I conceived our son at Graceland back in 1991, and we believe he is the reincarnation of Elvis Presley. He came to New York a little over seven months ago and we haven't heard from him in over a month now. He just seems to have disappeared and we want you to find him."

That Tuesday, January 12th, had begun simply enough. On my way to the office that morning, strolling down 8th Avenue, I ran into a woman I knew in high school. I hadn't seen or even thought of her in over sixteen years. I suddenly remembered she had briefly been the girlfriend of a good high school buddy, whose name I couldn't recall.

"Dane Cooper," she'd said, "What a coincidence to see you after all these years. I was just talking to my shrink about you this morning."

She walked away without explanation. There was definitely something in the air that morning and I must have breathed it in.

The man seated before me was Mr. Abner Lipps. He was balding, wearing black-rimmed glasses, a fat gold wedding band and a gold watch. He was square-jawed,

1

the only thing square on him. He had a happy-looking round body, a bulbous nose and a cheerful Santa Claus belly. Even the dimple in his chin seemed humorous. But all of that was contradicted by his brooding dark eyes and rigid posture. Even so, he reminded me of a big Keebler cookie elf who was having a bad day at the factory. His dark blue woolen sport jacket, burgundy turtleneck and dark gray pants suggested some conservatism, although I had my doubts, based on his reference to his son being the reincarnation of Elvis Presley.

We were in my office in Manhattan on 8th Avenue between 45th and 46th Streets, in what is known as Hell's Kitchen. At the turn of the century, this neighborhood had a gritty reputation for violent gangs. In the 1920s, rumrunners controlled illicit liquor. In the 1950s, gang wars between the Irish and the Puerto Ricans were immortalized in the Broadway play and movie, *West Side Story.*

Today, for good or ill, Hell's Kitchen has enjoyed a real estate building boom—with the accompanying sky-high rents—and impressive structures such as the Hearst Tower, The Link, a luxury 44-story glass tower condominium, and various broadcast and music-recording studios.

My building is a prewar, 5-story brick structure overlooking 8th Avenue. It houses a cranky old elevator, a cranky old security guard, various attorneys' offices, a jewelry importer/exporter, a dentist and an astrologer. Yours truly is the only private detective, which explains why most of my fellow occupants give me a wide berth on approach, as if they have many secrets and many skeletons in many office closets.

Behind my desk, dreary January light flowed in from a picture window, but it lacked warmth and inspiration, and

I needed both after last night's party at O'Toole's. It's an Irish bar on 8th Avenue at West 44th Street. I was celebrating with my old NYPD partner, Pat Shanahan. His wife, Jean, had just given birth to their third child, a daughter named Jacinta. There he was, Pat at the center of that crowded bar, red hair ruffled, a big fat grin on his broad freckled face, his chipped green eyes shining with happiness and pride.

He hoisted his beer mug high, and cheering detectives from Midtown North and some uniformed cops, along with some fine-looking women from the neighborhood bars and shops, shouted out "To Pat! Hear! Hear!" After burgers, corn beef sandwiches and more beer, Pat and I arm-wrestled. He's big-boned with sturdy strong arms. I'm lean and taut, and with my long arms, I can get good leverage. Ten minutes later, our faces were beet red and glossy with sweat. At fifteen minutes, it was called a draw. The party thundered on until 1am.

It wasn't that I was hung-over, necessarily, but I did need something to hang on to, like a big cup of coffee, which I hadn't collected yet because I'd forgotten to go to the ATM. I was out of cash. When I walked into the office to ask my secretary, Helen, for a loan, she pointed me toward Mr. Lipps, who was looking grave and impatient.

"Can you help me, Mr. Cooper?" Abner asked, his voice brittle and anguished. "Me and my wife, Lucille, are just beside ourselves with worry."

I reached for my yellow legal pad and pen. My right arm was still sore and twitching. "Mr. Lipps, when you called yesterday, you said you heard about me from Aleta Fisher, is that right?" I asked, hearing the faint whimper of the Bill Withers' song, *Ain't No Sunshine When She's*

Gone, lilting from my little radio on the floor near my desk.

"Yes, she recommended you."

Aleta Fisher was an on-again, off-again girlfriend. Mostly off right now. She was also a psychologist and astrologer, who had an office right down the hall from me. Most of the time I found her unpredictable, unnerving and unavailable.

"Where do you know her from?" I asked.

"Lucille is an acquaintance of Aleta's father, who lives in Texas. Lucille is originally from Texas."

"Where are you from, Mr. Lipps?"

"As I said over the phone, Mr. Cooper, we're living in Knoxville, Tennessee. Now, let me tell you why I know my son is the reincarnation of Elvis."

I threw up a hand, like a stop sign. "I don't really need to know anything about that, Mr. Lipps."

"But I must tell you—it's important I tell you—it explains so many things."

I suppressed a sigh. I could not suppress a frown. "Okay, Mr. Lipps, if you must."

"Back in 1991, Lucille and myself had just gotten married. We both loved Elvis so much—had only Elvis' songs performed at our wedding. I was dressed in a white suit—just like the one Elvis performed in when he was in Las Vegas. My wife had her hair done up just like Priscilla. I brought a picture with me."

Mr. Lipps reached into his jacket pocket and withdrew a 5 x 7 color photograph. He handed it over proudly. I struggled to look interested. It was a portrait of a gushing, white neon-hot couple, standing before a shiny red Cadillac. Mr. Lipps was much slimmer. He had a pompadour hairstyle with sideburns to his chin and he was flashing a broad toothy smile that suggested country cool.

He wore a white suit, white boots and electric red shirt with a mile wide collar. Lucille had a black bouffant hairstyle, bright red lips, a small face filled with giddy delight, and a frosting white wedding dress, bedecked with bows and flows and lace.

"So we traveled to Graceland for our honeymoon. We found a secluded spot one late afternoon and, well, we conceived our boy right there on that hallowed ground."

Abner leaned forward, taking me into his intimacy. "Do you know when Elvis was born?"

"No, Mr. Lipps, I'm afraid I don't."

"January 8, 1935 at 4:35am. Our boy, Elvis, was born on January 8, 1992, at 4:38am. Now you may say to yourself, as others have done, that we planned it that way. But we didn't, Mr. Cooper, I swear we didn't. We didn't even think about it until a month or two before he was born."

I suppressed a yawn. "Remarkable."

"Elvis picked up his first guitar when he was two years old, and don't you know that he was playing that damn thing by the time he was two and a half. The first song he ever played all the way through was *Love Me Tender*."

His eyes got misty. "It was so beautiful. So damn beautiful."

"Mr. Lipps, when did you last see your son?"

He didn't seem to hear the question. "He learned every song that Elvis ever played and he was such a good performer, Mr. Cooper. You just can't imagine. Well, I know I'm a proud father, but when he performed at our little church he just charmed everyone. When he was in elementary school, he sang Elvis and twisted his little hips just like *the* Elvis, and had all those teachers under a damn spell. When he got to high school, he was simply dazzling. Did an Elvis impersonation that just knocked your socks off! He was the most popular kid in that school! Girls fell all over themselves around him! They used to call the damn house, day and night. Drove my poor wife half crazy. But we loved it! Loved every damn bit of it! What a son, Mr. Cooper! What a son!"

"Where is your wife now, Mr. Lipps?"

He sank back into his chair with a deep sigh. "She's just heartsick—just unable to rise up from her bed, back in Knoxville."

"You said your son came to New York about seven months ago?"

"Yes."

"Why? Why did he come to New York?"

Mr. Lipps went into a full bull-dog bluster. "The damn kid wouldn't listen to me—wouldn't listen to reason—wouldn't listen to either one of us! I tried to tell him he had no business going up there to see that girl! And we didn't even know who she was, who her family was, what her name was or how old she was! I wanted him to go to Nashville—that's where his future is—that's where he can get back into the big-time—get on back to fulfilling his destiny—Elvis' destiny! He is wasting his life, wasting his future, wasting all my efforts to get him back on his destiny track!"

I started distancing myself from this case. It was just way too wacky for me. I stood. "Mr. Lipps, I don't really think I'm the right person for this particular case."

He grimaced, as if I'd back-handed him across the face. "I don't understand... This is not a case, Mr. Cooper. This is my boy we're talking about. This is Elvis."

"I appreciate that, Mr. Lipps, but my caseload is pretty heavy right now."

I expected fist-pounding anger and argument. Instead, he looked back at me wounded, stricken, like a poor old dog.

He squinted up at me, with misty eyes. "Aleta Fisher said you are an honorable man, Mr. Cooper. She said we could trust you. She said you were the best at what you do. She said you are lucky and you are smart. Now that's good enough for me, Mr. Cooper. Hell, that's how I made my millions. Please, Mr. Cooper, help us. I own two carpet outlet stores in Georgia. I also have one new car lot and two used-car lots. I have partnerships in two restaurants. I am a rich man and I will pay you for your time, Mr. Cooper. I will pay you anything you want to find my boy. Now, if you think this whole Elvis reincarnation thing is just a little bit too strange for you, then you just forget about that part of it. You just put that right out of your head and pretend that I never said one word about it, because I know, and I have met, people who just aren't comfortable with this kind of thing, Mr. Cooper. Okay. So be it. So damn be it! Throw it out! Toss it in the fire, so to speak! Forget it!"

His eyes leaked tears. His voice cracked with emotion. "Instead, you just think about a father—a father who loves his son with all his heart—a father and mother who are lying awake at night—walking the floors at night and praying to God on their knees at night, that their one and only son, their one and only child, will come back to them. The days are spent in heartache and regret, Mr. Cooper. The nights are spent in repentance and soul-searching. I am convinced and I am persuaded, by my own disturbing thoughts and the troubled words of my wife, that Elvis might be in trouble. Now I will do whatever I deem necessary to help me get my boy back. Whatever I deem necessary."

Mr. Lipps wiped his moist eyes and then, in a brittle, earnest voice he asked, "Will you help us, Mr. Cooper?"

I felt strongly that Mr. Lipps was not only a passionate man and gifted salesman, but he also possessed a great talent for the dramatic arts. But as I searched his face and watched him squirm uncomfortably in his chair, I also saw a sincere man who, at that moment, was struggling to achieve dignity and grace. Opening up to me had probably not come easily for Mr. Lipps, despite his Broadway caliber performance. I also appreciated the fact that Mr. Lipps had money. That always helps *my* performance.

I eased back down into my chair and folded my hands on the desktop. "When was the last time you heard from your son, Mr. Lipps?"

He cleared his emotional voice. "Friday, November 30th, right after Thanksgiving."

"You didn't hear from him at Christmas?"

He didn't look at me. "No."

"Did you try to call him?"

"Yes. Lucille and I tried several times, but his cell number had been disconnected. Hell, I would have used the cellphone tracking device to find him if he still had the damn phone."

"Prior to November 30th, you had a New York address and phone number for him?"

"Yes."

"And you spoke with your son frequently? Once a week? Twice a week?"

"Lucille called him regularly two times a week. I spoke with him at least once a damn day! Sometimes he wasn't there, so we left messages. Sometimes he called us back and sometimes not."

"Have you tried to contact him through any of the social media: Facebook, Twitter?"

"My wife is into all that. Elvis hasn't posted anything since that time. Nothing! Why do you think we're so troubled, Mr. Cooper?"

"Did you check the local hospitals?"

"Lucille and me have called hospitals, checked all these missing person databases on-line; we've called this one, that one, and the other one. We are stumped and scared, Mr. Cooper. Just stumped and scared for our boy."

"Mr. Lipps, did you and your son have an argument on November 30th that caused him to stop calling you?"

"Yes," he said, meekly.

"And what was that argument about?"

"It was about what it is always about! I wanted him to come home! I wanted him to leave that whoever-it-is-girl and come on back home so we could get his career started. I have contacts in Nashville, I have big connections in the recording and TV industry, Mr. Cooper. I could get him on those TV talent shows. I begged and I pleaded for him to come back home where he belongs."

"And you have no idea who the girl is? The one he came to see in New York? A first name, number?" I asked.

"No! He's never introduced her. I've begged and I've pleaded, Mr. Cooper. I have begged and pleaded."

"Where did he meet her?"

"In Knoxville somewhere. Hell, I don't know. He said she was just passing through. She lives here in New York. Says he just met her and that was that!" Mr. Lipps shook his head vigorously. "That's what I've been trying to tell you, Mr. Cooper. Lucille and I do not know anything about this girl. We don't know how old she is, where she's from, nothin'. Elvis kept the whole thing, her whole identity, his whole relationship with her, a damn secret. Now he cuts us—his own family—off. I just don't understand it."

Mr. Lipps shot up and paced the office. He moved with the grace of a box-turtle, shuffling across a country road.

"Mr. Lipps, why did you wait until now to find your son?"

His voice dropped an octave. "He just had a birthday, January 8th. His birthday is the most important day of the year to me and my wife. Elvis knew that. But that's not all, Mr. Cooper. My wife's birthday was three days ago. He never forgot Lucille's birthday. Never. He loved his mother more than anything else. I believe he would have called her, no matter what, if he'd had the opportunity. When we didn't hear from him, I knew I had to do something. I knew it right then and there."

"Your son just turned 20?"

"Yes."

"Have you filed a missing persons report with the police?"

"No. I thought about it, but... well, Lucille and me have done so much searching and we just don't think the police would really do that much. So, we made a decision. I flew straight here from Knoxville, got into a taxi at LaGuardia and came right to your office."

"Does your son have any medical problems?"

"None. Healthy as a horse."

"Has he ever been arrested?"

"No. Tickets for speeding, that's it."

"Does he do drugs?"

"Hell no! He hates drugs! Never!"

"Is he close to any family members—an uncle, aunt, grandparents? Maybe he went to stay with one of them?"

"I called them all—every damn one of them. At Christmas, they were all asking about him. I tell you, they're all upset about this, just as we are."

I dropped my pen on to the legal pad. "Mr. Lipps, I have to tell you that it's possible you're just wasting your time and money. Your son may just want some space for awhile. Most kids go through that. I did. Elvis will call you when he wants to. Maybe it will be soon or maybe in a few months."

Mr. Lipps lifted his chin in defiance. "I'm not taking that chance, Mr. Cooper. No sir."

I waited. "Elvis has taken very deliberate and careful steps to disappear. And it is clear, based on what you've told me, Mr. Lipps, that he does not want you to know where he is."

"Fine, if after I talk to him and see him, face to face, that's how it turns out, then fine, I'll live with that. But I need to know that he's okay. I've got to hear that from him and hear it face to face, just father and son!"

I picked up my pen again. "Did you ever visit your son here in New York?"

"We wanted to—we begged him—but he said no. He said he needed his privacy. I told Lucille I was going to come up here anyway and check him out, but she stopped me several times. She said let the boy have his space for a while. All right, it's been awhile! So here I am."

"During your telephone conversations with him, did he ever mention any names, neighbors, places where he was working; anything like that?"

Abner turned and reached into his jacket pocket. He took out a piece of folded white paper and approached me energetically. "On the plane, I did remember a name he told me once and I wrote it down, anticipating that you would probably ask me this very question."

He handed me the paper. I opened it and read the name Buddy Blue.

Abner sat down and leaned forward, folding his chubby fingers. "Elvis said that this guy was a real good musician."

"Anything else?"

"Said he was from Texas and was looking to make a name for himself in country music."

I scratched my nose. "So why does Elvis come to New York? I mean, New York is not exactly the country music capital of the world."

"I asked Elvis the same damn question. He said, he was just passing through."

"Was Buddy Blue a neighbor? Roommate?"

"I don't know. Elvis didn't say or I don't recall."

"Mr. Lipps, you said your son was the most popular kid in school. Does he have any good friends back in Knoxville he might be contacting? Maybe a good buddy or a girlfriend he's calling or sending regular text messages or emails to?"

"His best friend was Carter Davis. He's away at college, down in Florida. Florida State. Hell, I wanted Elvis to get some college, but he wouldn't hear of it; he was into his music, then. Until he met that damn girl."

"Do you have a number for Carter Davis—his address?"

"I know his home address and number by heart. But, like I said, he goes to school in Florida and I don't have that number. I called his parents before Christmas to see if they could ask their son if he knew where Elvis was. They called me back and said Carter hadn't heard from him since before Thanksgiving. I didn't believe them, of course, and I told them so. I begged them to give me Carter's phone number, but they refused."

I handed Abner a piece of paper and pen, and asked him to write down Carter's address and home phone number. He did so and handed it back to me.

"Is there anyone else you can think of who may have kept up a relationship with Elvis before and after high school?"

Abner's lips tightened—his face darkened. "There were a lot of kids who were jealous of Elvis—jealous of his looks and talent. Even some of his teachers had it in for him. Hell, I was going to wrestle one of those damn teacher rascals myself when he called my boy names."

"And who was that? What was the teacher's name?"

"Well, that don't matter."

"It does to me, Mr. Lipps. What was his name?"

"He is Rod Faulkner. He was the gym teacher."

I massaged my stiff neck. "Mr. Lipps, I think if you keep checking around with some of his high school friends, you'll find that Elvis has been in communication with at least one or two of them and they'll be able to tell you where he is and how to reach him."

Abner nodded absently. "I did that, of course, Mr. Cooper. I called every one of the kids who I knew had been friends with Elvis. Lucille called all of his old girl-friends. None have heard from him. Not a damn one of them! At least, that's what they told us."

"What was the fight with the teacher about? The one you were going to wrestle?"

Abner looked away. "It was nothing—no damn thing at all."

"One thing you should understand, Mr. Lipps. If I take the case, the client tells me everything leaves noth-ing out and tells no lies. If I find out there has been a lie, I keep the retainer and walk away. What was the fight about?"

Abner took a deep breath and then blew it out of his burbling lips. "He said Elvis was screwing his wife... the music teacher."

"Was he?"

"No!" Abner said, sharply. "Absolutely not. No way! We took Elvis to church every damn Sunday from the time he was born until he was 16 years old. He loved gospel music—sang gospel music and read his Bible every day. Now I asked him directly if he had ever been with that woman and he told me it was all just a lie. A fabrication! There was absolutely nothing going on and never had been!"

I scratched my head, wishing Aleta Fisher had kept her mouth shut. "Okay, Mr. Lipps, look, here's what I'm going to suggest. Give me a couple of weeks to look into this and see what I come up with. By then, I'll be able to tell if I can do anything for you."

Abner lit up. He rubbed his stubby hands together in triumph. "Okay, all right. Sounds fair. Now, what's all this going to cost me?"

"My standard fee is $250 an hour plus any travel or photographic expenses or other pocket expenses. For any out-of-town investigations, I charge $550 a day, plus expenses. I usually require a minimum retainer equaled to 50 percent of the estimated cost of the investigation. I also like a minimum nonrefundable retainer of $450. I give written reports."

Abner extended his meaty hand and we shook.

"My secretary, Helen, will set you up with the paper work. I'll need all the information you can give me about your son: full name with middle initial, Social Security number, date of birth, recent photo, the last address and phone number you have for him and any credit card and driver's license information. I need as much information as you can give me, including user names and passwords of his social media accounts."

Abner looked down at the floor. "I hesitate to tell you this, Mr. Cooper, but I've been having a lot of dark feelings about all this. I just can't seem to shake them."

He started for the door.

"What was the music teacher's name and address, Mr. Lipps?"

Abner turned, alarmed. "I hope you're not going to go down that damn road."

"May not have to, but I'd like to have it just in case."

Abner licked his lips nervously. "That happened when Elvis was 18 years old! It has nothing to do with anything. In my opinion, Mr. Cooper, she's a dangerous woman, if you know what I mean."

"I'd still like her name, Mr. Lipps."

Abner's jaw tightened as his large ears flushed red. "She's a temptress and a beguiler, Mr. Cooper. If you do talk to her, be careful. She's also a deceiver."

"I'll be careful. I can be discreet."

Abner struggled for a moment. "I hope so, Mr. Cooper. I really hope so. Her name's Darcy-Lynn Roberts. She's divorced. Divorced from that damn gym teacher. I hear she's still in Knoxville, but I don't know where and I don't want to know where."

Abner stared at me for a long moment. I saw a haze of overwhelming pain in his eyes.

"Are you going to be in town long?" I asked.

"No... I'm going straight back to Knoxville on a late afternoon flight. I don't want to leave Lucille alone for very long. The doctors don't really know what's the matter with her. Of course, how can doctors diagnose a damn broken heart? You can't see that sort of thing with all that expensive medical equipment. But I can see it. I can see it in her swollen eyes. I can feel it—" he said, jabbing his fist into his chest a couple of times for emphasis—"here in my chest. I can hear it when she cries herself to sleep at night. Find him, Mr. Cooper. Find him as fast as you can."

He turned and shuffled away toward reception.

CHAPTER 2

Two hours after Abner Lipps' exit, I stepped out of my office into what I call reception. This is the domain of Helen Manheim, my secretary general. The room has high ceilings, blue and white walls, a water cooler and a couple of sturdy plastic chairs, with cushions made of premium red felt. The floor has a dark blue woolen carpet, with only three or four coffee stains on it that I've learned to ignore, because I made them.

Helen had framed and hung some wide posters, depicting tropical islands with quiet palms, shimmering emerald water and broad white beaches. We were both hopeful that these images encouraged a touch of class or, at the very least, a touch of the exotic.

Helen is Charlie Neff's mother, the cop who co-owns the building; another reason I settled here. Helen is leaning somewhere between 55 or 60 years old. She is a gruff, short and round, woolly-headed woman, who believes in hard work and hard cold cash. She does not much believe in humor, as it wastes her valuable time.

We met at a Wall Street brokerage firm, when she was working as an office manager. I was still a Homicide Detective with the NYPD, investigating the murder of a tall leggy secretary, who had worked with Helen. We'd hit it off, meaning that she thought I was a smart-ass with attitude and I thought her a sour, nasty woman who was a wizard at juggling schedules, information and personalities. Nothing and no one intimidated her: not size, rank or urgency. She barked orders like a drill sergeant and everyone, including her boss, snapped to attention. You could almost see them put an open hand to the side of their temple, salute and shout, "Yes, Ma'am!" So, Helen was the logical choice when I went private and, fortunately for me, she was ready for a change and her son just happened to be co-owner of this Hell's Kitchen building. "He knows people in the real estate business," Helen had said, with a conspiratorial wink. "You know what I'm sayin', Dane?"

Helen's stubborn mouth suggests a love of argument, and much of that argument is often pointed at me—like a gun. She has lost none of her zest for life or for late middle-age defiance. I simply think of her as a reluctant saint with a serrated edge.

I went to Helen and waited. She sat behind her beloved Dell computer, pounding away at the keys, head held high, perfect posture, as if she were playing a classical piece by somebody whose first and last names elude folk like me.

"Were you ever an Elvis fan, Helen?" I asked.

She stopped typing and looked up, insulted. "Were! What the hell do you mean, were!? I don't care what anybody says, Elvis will live forever! His music will be around long after Mozart, that crazy deaf guy Beethoven, and some of those other long hairs are forgotten."

"So you are an Elvis fan?"

"Hell yes!" she said, swelling with pride. She looked up with dreamy, drowsy eyes. "When he sang a song, you thought you'd died and gone to heaven. Nobody can touch him—none of these clowns they call super stars today. They're all pathetic, croaking amateurs."

I hated to spoil her mood, but I still hadn't got that coffee and time was a wastin'.

"Do you share your opinions about Elvis with your grandkids?"

Her self-righteous expression fell into annoyance. "Little brats don't give a damn—don't know anything about history and what makes this country great!"

I handed her the photograph of Elvis Lipps. It was a professional black and white headshot, obviously taken for delivery to agents and producers in the acting and music business. He wore a black leather jacket over an open white shirt, showing a smooth chest. His hair was stylishly cut and stiff, but a little curl hung, like an inverted question mark, over his forehead. There was some contradiction in the lean, angular face. It revealed the bold confidence of a young man who expected recognition and success. But his dark eyes held a look of uncertainty and reserve that added a vulnerable charm. The smile was slightly forced and there was a calculated quality to it, as if he hadn't yet found his own true smile and was copying someone else's.

"What do you think of that guy?"

Helen took the photograph and glanced at it. Almost immediately, her eyes enlarged. It was the expression of someone who was remembering an old naughty secret.

"This boy is handsome!" she exclaimed.

"Do you think he looks like Elvis?"

She gave me a wonderfully absurd look. Then, cocking her head to one side, she studied it. "Well... you know, I have to say that there is the same kind of energy in the eyes—and the hair's like Elvis'. And he's got some of Elvis' rakish charm and vulnerability."

"He's our new client."

"He's the kid!?—Abner Lipps' son?" she asked, with awakened delight.

"Yes, ma'am."

"Whoa! I wouldn't mind finding him. Put me on the case, I'll find him in 24 hours."

I took the photograph from her. "It's a deal."

"With his looks, he should be easy to find."

"Mr. Lipps thinks he's the reincarnation of *the* Elvis."

"Bullshit! What kind of a nut case is he?" She snatched the photograph back and took another look at it. Her voice softened, her body relaxed, as she slipped under the spell of the alluring image. "He does have that something though... That same something that Elvis had."

"Tantalizingly handsome, a reporter once said of Mr. Presley," I said. "I Googled it."

Helen nodded in complete agreement. "Yep. Yeah. He has that. Hell yes, the kid's got it! But I'm not saying he's the reincarnation of Elvis!" she snapped.

"Yeah, well, for starters let's try our many data bases and see what we can find out about him, even though he just turned 20 and probably won't register much. DMV might show something. He might have recently ex-changed his out-of-state driver's license and we can pull his address from that. Maybe you can call your son and see if he could pull Elvis' old cellphone records to see if he pinged some towers in and around Manhattan. And, as a bonus, Helen, if you find Elvis, you can invite him over for coffee or something."

Helen barked out a laugh. "Hell with the coffee. The *something* for sure."

I grinned and made a turn to my office. "His father gave me his son's credit card number and last known address here in New York. I'm going to call the company and give that a shot. I hit the jackpot six months ago in the Kaufman case. Maybe lightning will strike twice."

Helen slipped on her glasses. "What about Facebook or Twitter? Come on, this kid would be posting every five minutes."

I gave her the yellow lined page that Abner had scribbled on. "The father says the son hasn't been social lately. He's hiding out somewhere."

Helen nibbled her lower lip. "Dane... Have you thought that maybe this kid is dead?"

"Yes, I've thought about it. Let's do all the computer digging, if you know what I mean, and see what turns up. He's had to leave a trace somewhere."

"Why did the kid move up here anyway?" Helen asked.

I stopped in the doorway. "The age-old story, Helen. A girl. He met a girl."

Helen shook her head. "That's one lucky girl."

Back at my desk, I called the Star Struck Deli and ordered a large black coffee, a bagel with cream cheese and grape jelly. After devouring it and consuming a Rolo, I called the credit card company and gave them the schpiel that I, and others in my noble profession, have used before, often with success.

It was a light, female, feathery voice that answered the phone—friendly, but businesslike.

"Hello, my name is Elvis Lipps and I'm declaring bankruptcy. Can you please let me know how much I owe you?"

She asked for all the numbers and I glanced at my legal pad and rattled them off, slowly.

I waited and reached for another Rolo. Oddly enough, coming from my radio was *the* Elvis Presley singing *Are You Lonesome Tonight?* There was something disconcerting about it—I didn't like the coincidence.

"Hello, Mr. Lipps? You show a zero balance."

"Really. All paid up, huh?"

"Yes."

"You know, that's really strange. I mean, I don't remember ever getting a statement. Did you send it to the right address?"

"Have you recently moved, Mr. Lipps?" she asked.

"Yes. What address did you send it to?"

"Mr. Lipps, can you please give me a date of birth?"

"Sure. January 8, 1992."

"Can you please give me your last two addresses?"

I rattled off the Knoxville address and Elvis' last known New York address, 98½ Riverside Drive Apartment 9B, New York, New York, 10024.

"Mr. Lipps, we sent your last statement to that same address on December 2 of last year: 98½ Riverside Drive Apartment 9B, New York, New York, 10024. Is that your new addr...?"

I interrupted. "I see, well, thank you very much."

I hung up. It was never that simple. I allowed myself one last Rolo for the day, while I leaned back in my chair, laced my hands behind my head and pondered what I would say to Elvis when I found him.

CHAPTER 3

At four o'clock on January 13th, Wednesday afternoon, I stepped out of the subway station at 79th Street and Broadway and walked west toward Riverside Drive. The wind off the Hudson River was cold and blustery. It was a quilted dark gray and white sky, with high-soaring birds that didn't seem to be in a hurry to get anywhere. On the ground, everyone was in a hurry: cabs, people, dogs straining on leashes, a postman grumbling and hustling into the biting wind.

I passed apartment windows that still displayed Christmas decorations: blinking colored lights, a Frosty the Snowman smiling and waving, plastic orange candles aglow, all still trying for warmth and cheer, long after the spirit had dissipated into the barren and relentless January chill. The cheery phrase "Happy New Year" had already faded into the blah subtext of "Happy Same Old Thing."

I was on my way to Elvis' last apartment, hoping that the doorman or the super would be able to tell me where he'd gone. Helen had come up empty online. She'd also struck out with our contacts at the cellphone companies. DMV records revealed he hadn't exchanged his Tennessee license, but did show a couple of speeding tickets, like his Pop had said. Voter Registration came up zip.

On Riverside Drive I turned north and started toward 82nd Street. An attractive woman deliciously bundled in a brown fur coat approached, not gracefully. Her black Great Dane, who had the look and bearing of a Wall Street billionaire, was walking her—dragging her along. The dog gave me a look of derogation, as if I had no business being anywhere near him or in the neighborhood. She glanced down at my left leg limp as she passed. I nodded, and she smiled, but alas, the dog was in charge and I just didn't fit into his busy agenda. He yanked her across the street toward Riverside Park.

The limp was an old wound, received when I was a NYPD Homicide Detective. I got shot when my old partner, Shanahan, and I came face-to-face with a murderer and rapist, who decided to make a stand. We got him, and he got me in the left leg. It seldom bothers me now, only whenever I go into a department store to shop or whenever I think about registering for the New York Marathon.

Just before I stepped into the prewar building, I felt the odd sensation that I was being followed. Something in my inner ear isolated a noise that was vaguely different from the usual and expected city sounds. The footsteps were close—too quiet—too hesitant and cautious. I did a sideways glance, but saw nothing. I paused at the entrance, adjusted my topcoat and entered.

The prewar had the usual brown pattern marble floor, stained-glass windows and wood-paneled lobby. The lighting was amber and moody, like cognac. The doorman, dressed in blue and brown, was perched on a stool reading a newspaper and sipping coffee. I strolled up, identified myself and presented Elvis' picture.

"Do you remember this guy?" I asked. "He lived in 9B."

The doorman was Hispanic, and he was friendly. He had the expression of someone who wanted to please—wanted to make a friend. "Elvis! Yeah! Can't forget that name, man. I mean, Elvis!" he said, spreading his hands and slanting me a knowing look. "But that guy, he used to live here. About five or six months. Kind of cocky-like, you know what I mean? A little bit of a bullshitter. But okay."

"When did he move out?"

The doorman thought for a minute. "Oh... maybe four or five weeks ago."

"Did he leave a forwarding address that you know of?"

"No. I mean, he didn't leave nothing with me."

"Does he still get mail here?"

The doorman shrugged. "Maybe. I leave that up to the postman. Come to think of it, I don't remember seeing the mailman, Albert, put mail in that mailbox. Now that's kind of strange, ain't it?"

"Was Elvis subletting the apartment?"

"I don't know. It's a co-op, you know. It's owned by some guy, but a Mrs. Johnson lets people stay there. I've never seen the guy... the owner."

"Is Mrs. Johnson up there now?" I asked.

"No. She don't live here. I've never seen her, but I know that she has people stay here."

"What's Mrs. Johnson's first name?"

He shook his head. "I don't know. I just know that she calls sometimes and says that she's gonna have somebody staying here for a while. She sounds real nice on the phone."

"Is there someone staying in the apartment now?"

"No. There ain't been nobody up there for a couple of weeks now."

"The co-op board doesn't mind that all these people are coming and going, and Mrs. Johnson doesn't own the place and isn't living here?"

He lifted his shoulders slowly and let them drop. "Guess not. Maybe she pays a little extra to the owner, you know. I mean that's how the world works, ain't it? It's a real nice apartment. One bedroom. Overlooks Riverside Park and the Hudson River."

"What's the name on the mailbox?"

The doorman scratched his head. "Hey, let me check that out."

He drifted over to the bank of metal mailboxes and used his index finger to search. "Let's see... ah... that is 9B...Papania. Victor Papania."

"Have you ever met Mr. Victor Papania?"

"No... Never really thought about that. I just know that Mrs. Johnson always calls."

"Do you remember any other names of people who stayed in that apartment in the past?"

"Well, there was another guy who stayed there for about three months. Al or Oscar Radkey or Ratcliff, maybe it was Owens, something like that."

God love him, but for a doorman, his mind was a busted steel trap.

"Then there was a guy... he was from California, I remember. Oh, yeah, his name was Rusty."

"Last name?"

"That was over a year ago. I don't remember."

"What about a guy named Buddy Blue? Do you remember that name?"

"No."

"Did you ever see Elvis with anybody else?"

"Yeah, he was with this girl a couple of times, just before he moved out."

"Did you get her name?" I asked.

"No."

I reached inside my topcoat and took out my little notebook and pen. "What did this girl look like?"

The doorman reached for his coffee and took a thoughtful sip. "Well, she had short spiky hair, built nice—big tits—sexy, you know. Like, tight clothes. Black boots. She looked real hot. Maybe she was in her 20's. She was hangin' all over Elvis and he was really eatin' it up."

"How tall was she?"

"Maybe 5'7", with the boots. Now that I'm thinking about it, she really seemed a little drunk or something— maybe on drugs or something. She was kind of goofy and shit. But Elvis always had some girl with him."

"Did you overhear anything?"

"Not really. Sorry. I was just too busy."

"Had you ever seen her before?"

"No."

"Did you ever hear Elvis call her by name?"

He scratched the side of his nose and looked toward the ceiling. "You know what? He introduced me to her, I think. Like maybe her name was Jennifer or Jenny or no, maybe it was like Tiffany or Sheri. Damn! I don't remember what he said her name was."

"Did you help Elvis move out? Carrying boxes or bags?"

"Just a little…"

"Did he tip you when he left?"

"No. Elvis didn't tip. That's one reason I didn't help. He kind of struck me as a rich kid's son, you know. Had it easy his whole life. Expected something for nothing."

"Do you know if there is anyone else in the building who Elvis was friends with?"

"No. I didn't really see him that much."

I looked toward the elevators. "Did Mrs. Johnson give a nice Christmas tip?"

He brightened. "Oh yeah. I've been here two years and she always tips real good. Always comes in a blank envelope with my name written on it. I hear she tips everybody real good, especially the super."

"Do you recall if Elvis, or any of the others who stayed in that apartment, ever spoke to you about Mrs. Johnson?"

"No. I even mentioned her name to Elvis a couple of times, you know just to make conversation, and because I was a little curious, but he wouldn't talk about Mrs. Johnson at all. It was like he was nervous about it or something."

"Is there another doorman I can speak with? Maybe he works a different shift and got to know Elvis and the girl?"

"Luiz comes on at 5 o'clock, but he's only been here for about a month."

"What happened to the previous doorman?"

"He moved back to Bangladesh, where his family is."

"What about the super? Can I speak with him?"

The doorman hesitated for a moment, then reached for the house phone and dialed a number.

It was a short wait. I checked my email and phone messages. The super came to the lobby and refused to speak to me about Elvis, even though I pulled the parent sympathy card. He was a heavy man, who carried heaviness in his eyes and slumping shoulders.

"Are you a parent, sir?" I asked, with an earnest tone.

"Yes, but that's none of your business."

"Well, sir, Elvis is missing and his parents are worried sick. Being a parent, I'm sure you understand. I'm just trying to help them find their son. Can you help me?"

"No, no... You've got to go now."

"Do you know who owns 9B? Could I speak with him?"

He ignored all of my pleadings and asked me to leave. He said that he respected his tenants' privacy, was responsible for their security, and that doorman should have never spoken with me. After he said this, he gave my friend the doorman an ugly glance and escorted me out of the building.

I waited for five minutes and then went back inside. The doorman's nervous eyes immediately slid away from me. I put $50 and my card on top of his newspaper. I asked him to call me the next time anyone moved into that apartment. He remained silent, but he took the money, nodded and smiled.

I got back to the office at around 6 o'clock and Helen had already left for the day. I went into my office and answered a few emails before going through Darcy-Lynn Robert's file that Helen had collected and printed for me. Darcy was still living in Knoxville.

I dialed her number and waited. Four rings later, a woman's breathless voice answered.

"Hello."

"Is this Ms. Roberts?" I asked.

Silence. "Yes...who is this?"

"Ms. Roberts, my name's Howard Taylor and I'm calling from Atlantic Digital Studios in New York City. I'm the Director of Employment Services, and Elvis Lipps listed you as a reference."

More silence. "...Listed me as a reference?"

"Yes, that's right."

Her voice softened. "What job is he applying for?"

"Publicity, marketing."

"What does your company do?" she asked, with a still cautious southern accent.

I'd used this ruse before and had done my homework, just in case someone knowledgeable in this business would ask such a question.

"Multimedia. We do multimedia, Ms. Roberts."

That didn't satisfy her doubt and curiosity. "What exactly does that entail?"

"We do audio—you know, music and voiceovers for TV shows. You've probably seen many of our shows on cable: The History Channel, Discovery and ESPN. We do some other things, as well, but that's a big part of it. With Elvis' looks and confident personality we believe that he will be an excellent addition to our publicity and marketing departments."

There was that silence again. Had I really been calling for a reference, I would have scratched Elvis' name off the list right then, based on Darcy-Lynn's many silences.

When she finally spoke, her voice had relaxed some, though it was still tentative. "What would you like to know? Mr. Howard, is it?"

"Mr. Taylor. Howard Taylor."

"Excuse me, Mr. Taylor. How can I help you?"

"Mr. Lipps wrote that you were his music teacher in high school."

"Yes."

"Was he a good student?"

"Yes, an excellent student."

"Was he reliable, trustworthy and hard-working?"

"Yes."

"Was he well-liked by his fellow students?"

She hesitated. "They respected his talents."

"In your opinion, Ms. Roberts, does Elvis possess leadership qualities?"

"Yes."

"Was he always on time for class?"

"Well… like all high school kids, he could be a little late, sometimes, but he would often stay after school and help out with things."

"What types of things, Ms. Roberts?"

She stammered. "You… you… well…you know, putting sheet music away, straightening the chairs…"

"Did Elvis ever get into any trouble that you know of?"

"Trouble?"

"I'm sure you understand, Ms. Roberts. We have to be very careful about the people we hire, especially in this business. Was he ever involved in drugs or alcohol abuse?"

"He comes from a good family, Mr. Taylor—a religious family. As far as I know, he never got involved in drugs or alcohol."

"Are you still in the teaching profession?"

Her voice got small. "No."

"What profession are you in, Ms. Roberts?"

She took on an edge. "I believe we're talking about Elvis and not me, Mr. Taylor."

"Of course, excuse me, Ms. Roberts. As I mentioned, we do have to be very careful about who we hire, and sometimes, we find it helpful and revealing to learn as much as possible, without intruding of course, about the person who is recommending a potential employee to our company."

Her voice got apologetic. "Yes... yes, of course. I left teaching. I'm working part-time as a bookkeeper and am working on a master's degree in business and finance."

"So you're leaving the teaching profession?"

"Yes."

"Do you remain in touch with Mr. Lipps?"

Her voice got defensive. "I beg your pardon?"

"Since Elvis listed you as a reference, I just wondered if, after his graduation, you and Elvis have remained friends."

"You're intruding into my privacy, Mr. Taylor."

"Please pardon me, Ms. Roberts. I assure you, that is not my intention. I'm only trying to establish a recent link between Elvis and you, as a reference. Elvis may have changed since high school, Ms. Roberts. Young people can change dramatically in a short period of time. It is my job to make sure that I protect the company. I cannot recommend a potential employee unless I'm sure that they are reliable, ethical and free from any substance abuse."

She spoke fast, coldly, struggling to mask an obvious irritation. "Mr. Howard... Taylor, I was in New York two months ago and saw Elvis. I can assure you, he is reliable, ethical and free from any substance abuse. I recommend him highly for any job. Now, if you'll excuse me I've really got to go."

I spoke quickly. "Was that September when you saw him, Ms. Roberts?"

"Yes, September the 22nd."

"Ms. Roberts, just one last question. On his application, his handwriting isn't clear and we can't read his phone number. We of course want to be able to reach him. Do you happen to have it?"

I crossed my fingers and waited as she went to look it up.

"We haven't spoken in some weeks, Mr. Taylor, so I can't say definitively that this is his latest number. It's 646-749-7890." I recognized it as being the same number his father had given us and Helen had already tried with no success.

I knew I was taking a big chance now. "Do you happen to know his email address, just in case the phone number isn't current?"

"You can't read that either, Mr. Taylor?"

I tensed up. "I'm afraid not."

"Elvis' handwriting was always very clear, Mr. Taylor. I doubt whether that has changed since he graduated from high school less than a year ago. What did you say your company's name is?"

She was almost on to me. I had pushed too far. "Atlantic Digital Studios."

"Goodbye, Mr. Taylor."

She hung up.

Ms. Roberts will probably Google Atlantic Digital Studios. I was covered—the company exists—but I don't work for them. Neither does Howard Taylor.

It seemed clear at this point, that Elvis was hiding, dead or running away. Why? It was entirely possible that he had gotten himself into big trouble. I didn't have much to go on. Who was Mrs. Johnson? It surely wasn't her real name. Buddy Blue? I came up empty on my records checks, including the Musician's Union. No one with that name in New York. In Texas, there was only one man and he was 62. Buddy Blue probably wasn't this guy's real name.

If Elvis was in trouble, why wouldn't he call his father for help? If he wasn't in trouble, why was he hiding from his parents?

Who was the girl he'd met in Knoxville? Surely, somebody down there knew. Was she the sexy gal the doorman had described?

With any luck, Florida State was still on semester break and Carter Davis was still home. Knoxville, Tennessee seemed like the best place to start sniffing around and educating myself about Elvis, his friends and his past.

I did know that the Smoky Mountains were somewhere in that area and that there were "b'ars in them thar hills." Maybe I'd drop by and see a bear or two and, while I was there, I'd drop in on Carter Davis and Darcy-Lynn Roberts. That was *the* Darcy-Lynn of course—the temptress, beguiler and deceiver. Unusual to meet this type in my line of work. I hadn't met one in, oh, say one or two days.

CHAPTER 4

On Thursday, January 14th, at around 9am, I called Carter Davis at his parents' home. A woman answered. Her "Hello" was slow, warm and welcoming, like melting chocolate. It startled me, a born New Yorker who is used to the quick, curt and edgy "Hello" or the sharp, "Yeah?" "Yeah" is the sort of challenging greeting that demands a reason for intrusion—"this better be worth my time"—or it's a challenge—"don't waste my time unless you give it to me in five seconds or less." Either way, its impact is like a jackhammer on a hot summer day.

But Mrs. Davis' greeting was a trip to the bakery, where sweet smells and idle talk were as natural and comforting as sitting in a rocker next to a fire on a cold winter's eve, with a cup of hot cocoa and a book of baseball's greatest moments.

I asked for Carter Davis. She affably asked me who was calling. I heard my voice rise in pitch and pleasantness. It was unnerving and distracting. She was pulling me in to her southern, languorous style.

I said, a little more quickly, "Ben Paxton."

Her words lilted from the telephone, flute-like. A melody to be remembered and whistled. "Could you hold on for just one moment, please?"

35

"Hello…" Carter's voice was reedy and flat—tone deaf compared to his mother's.

"Carter Davis?" I asked.

"Yes, who is this?"

"I'm Ben Paxton."

I waited for his response. "Okay. Yeah?"

"I'm a writer for *New York Music Magazine*. We're doing a set of articles about music and new musicians in New York City—you know, about out-of-towners who are trying to make it in the Big Apple. We saw Elvis perform at one of the clubs a couple of nights ago and we decided to do a little article about him. I was wondering if I could come down and talk to you about him—get a little history, maybe some funny stories about the two of you in high school. Obviously, I'd want you in the article as well."

There was the silence again. Then, "Did Elvis give you my number?"

"Yes he did. I hope that's all right. He said you wouldn't mind. Getting his name in our magazine could really boost his career."

"Well, um, I don't know… I mean, well I'm leaving for school on Friday morning."

"I could be down there this evening and meet you first thing in the morning or whenever you say. Totally at your convenience, Mr. Davis."

Carter cleared his throat, and it sounded to me as if he didn't really need to. "So, Elvis is performing again?"

"You're surprised?" I asked.

"Well, it's just that the last time I talked to him, he said he wasn't doing any music. He said he was giving it up."

"That's interesting, Carter. When did you last speak with him?"

"Just before Thanksgiving."

I could have pushed a bit further, but at this point, I knew I'd find out more in person than I'd ever find out over the phone.

"Carter. Could we meet for lunch tomorrow?"

He sighed into the phone. "… Yeah, okay."

He suggested we meet downtown at a restaurant called the Tomato Head at 1pm. I told him I'd be there. We exchanged physical descriptions and hung up.

A few minutes later, I called Shanahan, at Midtown North. He'd just walked into the squad room, or so I was told by his new partner, Bob Rickson.

"Hey Dane-O. What's up?"

"Crime's up. What the hell are you guys doing about it?"

"We're beating up on old women and kids. Then we're reading them their rights."

"Good! Now I can sleep better at night."

"How's the snoop business?"

"I have a caseload of characters who are good candidates for either Bellevue or next year's Halloween parade."

"See, all that advertising in *Mad Magazine* is paying off."

"I need a favor," I said.

"Of course you do, Cooper. It's the only time you call me."

"Not true. I called two months ago with Jets tickets."

"But I couldn't go."

"And you missed a good game."

"Who did you finally go with?"

"Nevermind."

"No favor unless you tell me."

"Helen…"

"I thought she was a Giants fan?"

"She is, but she didn't want to baby-sit the grand kids that day. Look, I need you to check on a guy who owns a coop apartment 9B, on 98½ Riverside Drive. His name is Victor Papania. Helen's swamped, I'm lazy and you can get the info faster. And I need it fast."

"How about you buy me dinner some night?"

"Only if you'll dance with me after."

"I'll even kiss your ass," Shanahan said.

"Not on the first date you won't."

"I'll get back with you, Cooper."

"I'll shave my ass," I said.

"I'll bring a big camera."

I booked a flight for Knoxville, leaving LaGuardia at 6pm that same evening. It would arrive at Washington DC-Reagan at 7:06. I'd grab a new flight there and end up at Knoxville's McGhee Tyson Airport at 9:50.

After some quick research, I booked a room at the Radisson Summit Hill Hotel, which was somewhat close to Market Street, where I'd be meeting Carter.

Helen and I spent the rest of the morning discussing a couple of our other active cases, always seeming to arrive back at the incomparable photo of Elvis Lipps. I could see the stars in her eyes whenever she mentioned his name or glanced over at his file. It is true what they say about love—it is not proud. It knows no age. It makes fools of us all. As Helen spoke of Elvis, there were moments I saw the 16-year-old girl she must have been: awkward, nervous and chatty, yet stumbling through conversations, hoping not to appear silly. I'd never seen her so vulnerable. It unnerved me.

As I listened to Helen, I observed that Elvis surely had what is known as "IT." As with the other *real* Elvis, women most certainly experienced an impulsive, delicious pleasure at the mere sight of Elvis Lipps. Drawing close to him must be frighteningly daring and irresistible, like approaching a tiramisu after a long fast.

I could picture the young Mr. Lipps in a room filled with women of all shapes, ages and backgrounds. I could hear their wheezy nervous tones—feel the sexual energy burning around the room, like a wildfire, sucking the breath of blissful agony from every woman's tremulous body. I've been there—on the other side—looking at a woman with a desire so scorching that my body felt singed; the soles of my feet seemed to melt.

Rita Tucker was such a woman, and she was largely responsible for me joining the NYPD, although she never knew and probably wouldn't have cared less. But life is full of sudden changes of mind—of unexpected turns in the road that transform one's life forever.

I had an apartment in Brooklyn. I'd done two years of college but dropped out because I was bored; I was a poor student, struggling with economics and business administration. I was working with my father in construction and he was driving me nuts, God love him. My mother always said you could say anything bad about another person as long as you added, in conclusion, "God love 'em."

Rita Tucker lived alone, down the hall from me on the first floor. She was known for her numerous boyfriends and raucous weekend parties. She possessed all the positive, attractive qualities of woman-hood, and then some other dubious qualities that woman-hood might regard with a squinting, jealous leer.

One morning, blond, proud and dressed in red, she left the building on very high heels, just before I did. I followed her down the street, feigning indifference. We stopped at the crosswalk. Rita would go left. I was supposed to continue straight, toward the subway.

The red light flashed to green. She turned left. I hesitated, then followed her. Oh, what an adventure! She clicked along the sidewalk, her body a delight of movement and wonder. Her perfume pulled me along, like a floppy puppy on a leash with his tongue hanging out, wanting to lick every curve and mound of her Aphrodite-ripe body.

This is where destiny galloped in to bushwhack me. A half block later, I ran into John Blevins. We hadn't seen each other since high school. I didn't particularly like him. He talked too much, he had bad breath, and he had the unfortunate tendency to spit out words with spit. So, John grabbed me by the shoulders, then jabbed at me playfully, pulling my rapt attention away from Rita's bewitching retreating figure. Dark clouds covered the sun.

John was hell-bent on joining the NYPD and he started jabbering about it. And as Rita turned and disappeared around the corner forever, I listened absently as John demanded that I go with him, the opposite way, to talk about old high school football glories. He dragged me along the Brooklyn streets toward Manhattan, where my destiny lay ahead and Rita lay with someone else.

John and I eventually joined the NYPD.

Rita moved out a week later—late in the night I was told—because she had many creditors, including her landlord, after her. I'd often been tempted to search my many databases to find Rita Tucker, to thank her, of course, for leading me onto the path of my life's work, but I never did. I prefer remembering her as she was, turning that corner on a bright spring morning, a twitching red flame, sent to tempt me, taunt me and send me off to find Elvis Lipps.

After leaving Washington, on the flight to Knoxville, I dozed, ate peanuts and glanced occasionally at the little page of facts about the city that Helen had found on the Internet and printed out for me. I learned that Knoxville was founded in 1791 and was the third largest city in the State of Tennessee. It was nestled between the Great Smoky Mountains, the big South Fork National River and the Cumberland Gap National Historic Park. Surely there were lots of beautiful mountain streams to fish for trout in, secluded trails to hike in and plenty of good old bear watching. Too bad I wouldn't have the time to do any of those. The average temperature is 58 and the median age is 36. I'd probably fit right in, since I was only three months away from my 37th birthday.

As we were about to make our final approach, the pilot told us that it was 38 degrees and overcast. The teenage girl in the seat next me, coughed and sneezed and sniffed. She looked miserable. When I looked at her blotchy face and swollen eyes, I hoped I wasn't seeing previews of my future.

On the ground, I took my carry-on, found the car rental, got directions to the Radisson and arrived at my hotel at about 11:10pm. I hung up my suit and sport coat, my blue shirt and white shirt and tossed two pairs of socks and underwear in the nearest drawer.

Downstairs at the bar, there was a business crowd talking politics and sports. An attractive woman with a low authoritative voice, dressed in a business suit, seemed more knowledgeable about sports and politics than three men she was drinking with. I considered getting into the discussion, as I sipped my Jim Beam, but thought better of it when their conversation suddenly took a turn toward the bizarre: they began discussing which of the four of them would look better naked. Did the guys really have to ask?

The next morning, Friday, I called Helen to check in and I listened to her rant about the filthy state of the women's bathroom down the hallway. I reminded her that her son, an NYPD cop, was part owner of the building and that maybe she should talk to him. She told me they'd fought about that very thing the night before and now he wouldn't take her calls.

The Super, Juan, was a full-time drunk and part-time super, but he was cheap and friendly. I suggested she offer him a tip to clean it. That set her off on another tirade. Fortunately, her phone rang and she let me go.

I spent the rest of the morning at the Women's Basketball Hall of Fame. It had a lot of neat little interactive things to do and I was having so much fun, I almost lost track of time.

I luckily managed to find a parking place just off Market Street and walked along Market Square in dazzling sunlight and a crisp wind until I arrived at a great old rehabilitated building that was The Tomato Head. I looked at my watch. It was about ten minutes to one. I'd checked my cellphone messages a few minutes before to make sure that Carter hadn't called to cancel. He hadn't.

I entered the restaurant. It was alive with activity, loud voices and the smell of cheese and things that I associated with Italian. The place was spacious, airy and bright. I looked up to see a stamped-tin ceiling, and thought it didn't make good acoustical sense. Voices bounced, played and ricocheted. I saw a sound stage that probably supported spirited musicians on Fridays and Saturdays. I would surely need earplugs. The place was also a kind of art gallery, and there were those who were leaning in close to some of the art and discussing it, while the food was being dished out.

I looked around for Carter. He'd described himself as 5'10", 180 pounds, broad, short black hair, and he'd be wearing a dark blue sweatshirt, jeans and red sneakers.

I'd dressed in my best reporter-like outfit. Dark green pants, cream colored turtleneck, a dark brown corduroy jacket and brown loafers. I also carried a little briefcase that contained a legal pad, assorted pens and a digital voice recorder.

As I glanced about to see if I could spot him, I felt a tap on my right shoulder. I turned to face Carter Davis. He was dressed exactly as he said he'd be. I was struck by his youth. He was indeed broad, and had the body of a man, but his face was soft, reluctant and boyish. The expression in his marble blue eyes suggested he'd never given the big issues of life much thought. His stance and body language implied adolescent discomfort and unease, as if his footing wasn't sure or anchored in the world. He kept one hand stuffed deeply into his pocket. The other he offered limply, to shake.

"I'm Carter," he called out, over the crush and noisy lunch crowd.

We shook.

"I'm Ben Paxton. Pretty crowded," I added.

"Yeah. Don't worry. I have friends who work here. I've got us a table."

He pointed to the left. He started forward and I followed.

After we'd settled in at a 2-top, he waved to a girl who was seated at a table with two other girls across the room.

"You come here a lot?" I asked, taking out the voice recorder.

"I used to. Not so much anymore. But some guys I went to high school with are going to UT now, you know, the University of Tennessee. They work here. Others are actors and artists I got to know from hanging around some bars."

"Do you mind if I record our conversation?"

"Yeah, I mean, it's okay," he said, studying the recorder, nervously.

I pressed the *Play* button and placed the recorder between us. "Did Elvis come here?"

"Oh, yeah. Elvis liked this place."

Carter recommended the Cheddar Head. It was tofu and cheese. When I nixed that, he recommended The Lucy: mushrooms, carrots, walnuts and some other things that sounded suspect. I finally settled on the salmon/pesto pizza and a soda. He went for the Cheddar Head.

He got up and put in the order. When he returned, he seemed a little more relaxed, though he scratched his right cheek often and had difficulty meeting my eyes.

"I've never been to New York," he said. "I was going to go up and visit Elvis, but then, I guess he got busy and it just didn't work out."

"When did you say you last spoke with Elvis?" I asked.

Carter scratched his right cheek again. "In November. Just before Thanksgiving, because I thought I'd come up and visit during Christmas break. He'd suggested it three months back. He said we could hit the bars and clubs in the Meat Packing District."

"What did he say he was doing? I mean was he doing music?"

Carter looked away toward the three girls again. "He sounded real funny. He didn't really talk a lot. He just said that there was no way I could come up, because he was into something."

"Did you ask him what that something was?"

"Yeah. I said are you playing music some place? He said, he'd stopped doing that because he found something that was paying a lot more money. He said it was PR. So, that's why I was so surprised when you said you saw him performing."

I leaned back and smiled reassuringly. "Oh yeah, he's definitely performing. He didn't say anything to me about being in PR," I said. "He did mention that he met a woman down here about eight months ago and that's one of the reasons he moved to New York."

Carter smiled and shook his head. "Elvis was always meeting girls. I mean, they'd just walk up to him. It was really unbelievable. They'd just come up to him and start talking."

I leaned forward. "Elvis wouldn't tell me who the woman was when I asked him," I said. "Do you know who she is?"

"No. He was real secretive about it. But then Elvis is a secretive guy. But he did tell me she was an older woman and that she lived in New York. I figured she got real big on him and offered to throw some money into his career or something. And hey, why not. I said go for it, man. But don't print that. Elvis will really get pissed off if he knows I told you that. And he wouldn't want his parents to know that. I mean, it would really freak them out."

"Yeah, don't worry," I said. "What are Elvis' parents like?"

He grinned, with a shake of his head. "Oh, man... I mean, if you ask me, that's really why Elvis moved away to New York—to get away from them. His old man used to like really embarrass him in front of people—say that his son was going to be as big as *the* Elvis, talk really loud and like brag about how great his son was. All of the kids just stayed away from Elvis' home. His mother is like this freakin' nut case. She has all these little baby pictures and little kid pictures of Elvis, dressed up as *the* Elvis, you know, with the guitar and the hair. You get the idea. Their house is like one big Elvis Presley shrine. And when you talk to her, that's all she talks about. I mean, all she talks about! Elvis this and Elvis that. What movies he did, who he dated, what he ate. They must have every piece of sheet music, every 45 record and every album the guy ever recorded. That collection must be worth a fortune."

I watched Carter glance over at the three girls again.

"Nice looking girls," I said.

Carter shrugged. "Yeah, they're all right. The blond used to be one of Elvis' girlfriends."

I looked over. She had a sheep-dog haircut, full pink lips and a willing gaze. The two girls with her were less attractive. They gazed back at us curiously.

"And you're big on her?" I asked.

He lifted a right shoulder. "She goes to UT. Not my type."

"Want to invite her over?"

"No way."

"It might be fun to get her view of Elvis. Might be a nice touch for the article."

"No freakin' way, man. She's like, still in love with him. That's the only reason she's looking. She's probably going to come over and ask me how she can get in touch with him."

"So you and Elvis stay in touch by text or email?" I asked.

"We used to text but then he must have changed phone numbers or something. I've sent him five or six emails since Thanksgiving. The last two I sent, bounced back. He must have closed out his Google account too. So then just before Christmas vacation, my parents called me at school and told me that Elvis' father is looking for him and they want to know if I know where he is. I told them what I just told you."

I said, "Do you think he's hiding from you all?"

"Yeah, that's what I thought. To tell you the truth, until you called and told me you'd seen him, I was getting a little freaked out about not hearing from him. I thought maybe something happened to him."

Carter's words carried an impact.

A short waitress, with deep brown eyes and short spiked red hair, dropped off our food. We ate in silence for a few moments. The room made up for our quiet. There was thumping music, the rattle of dishes and scattered bits of brassy conversation.

"Can you give me his new phone number?" Carter asked.

The request startled me. I gave a flimsy, stupid excuse. "Yeah, sure. I mean, I didn't add it to my contacts. Stupid of me. I'll get back to you."

"Tell him to call me," Carter said.

"Yeah, sure. Carter, do you know if Elvis had any other friends that he might be contacting...? I mean, I wouldn't mind interviewing them as well, to get another perspective."

Carter took a bite of his interesting looking food, chewed thoughtfully, then spoke with his mouth partially full. "I don't think so. Most of the guys were jealous of him because most of the girls really wanted him. And a lot of kids mocked Elvis' parents, which really pissed him off. His senior year, he like mostly just hung out with me and a lot of girls."

I looked right, to the table where the three girls were eating. I indicated with my head toward the table. "Did Elvis and that blond date for awhile?" I asked.

"Pamela? He dated her maybe four or five times."

"She's attractive," I said.

He didn't look over. He lowered his voice, as if anyone would be able to hear him over the clamor. "Elvis said she was all over him. Practically tore his clothes off."

"Ah... That kind of thing happened often to Elvis?"

Carter nodded. "Definitely." He lifted a bright eye. "Why do you think I was friends with him? You know what I'm saying? We had some great dates together."

"I can imagine."

Carter licked some oozing yellow sauce from his right fingers and lay his sandwich down. He inclined forward and spoke in a soft voice, "Elvis dated two girls at once—on the same date!"

"The girls didn't mind?"

"Didn't seem to."

"And you were there?"

He nodded proudly. "I was driving the car, with this chick in the front seat. Elvis was going at it in the back with the other girls. It was wild. Well, I mean we'd smoked some stuff and drunk some vodka and stuff. I guess we were like in the zone of decadence or something."

48

"I won't print that," I said, feigning embarrassment, and remembered the alphabet soup hormones of my early youth.

Carter snapped to attention. "Oh, hey, no way, man. I mean you can't print any of that!"

Carter wasn't as innocent as I first thought. The face was—the man wasn't. I decided to try and get back on track.

"I'd like to interview some of his high school teachers. Do you know of any?"

Carter picked up his sandwich and took another bite. I was surprised by his expression. The young mischievous face clouded over, and suddenly he looked older—but not in a natural way. In the way that fear distorts the face and fills the eyes.

"Did I say something wrong?" I asked. "A bad memory?"

He chewed for time. "No... just that. Well, you can't print this either. But Elvis got into this thing with his music teacher."

"Thing? It sounds like Elvis really got around."

"Yeah... but, she started it. At least that's what Elvis said. But she was married to the gym teacher and football coach, Coach Faulkner. It got real bad. I mean, real bad."

"How did the coach find out about it?"

Carter looked up, shaken by the memory that was still fresh and vital, as if it could strike him down with the power of it. "He was tipped off. Some asshole on the football team told him."

"How did he know?"

"It was obvious whenever you saw her around Elvis. She was like all clumsy and awkward. Her eyes were real dreamy and faraway. Anyway, the coach caught them in his house, going at it in the basement Rec Room. Fortunately, Elvis heard footsteps on the stairs and he like hauled ass out of there through a window, before the coach could get to him. Coach had guns. So, I guess Coach found his wife there naked and... well, he beat her up pretty bad. The police came and everything. It was a freak show."

"How old was Elvis when this happened?" I asked.

Carter pondered the question. "I think that was February of our senior year so... he was 18."

Before I'd left New York, Helen had presented me with Darcy-Lynn's background check. In the state of Tennessee the statutory age of sexual consent is 18. Elvis was 18 years old at the time of the alleged relationship. Nonetheless, Darcy-Lynn was charged with improper relationship between educator and student, a second-degree felony. But Elvis denied having any sexual relationship with his teacher and Mr. and Mrs. Lipps did not file any charges. The local school board terminated Darcy-Lynn's position for breach of contract, with the understanding that she would be unemployable as a teacher in the future. Seven months later, all charges were dropped.

I studied Carter, considering my next question. I had been eating my pizza slowly. It was good, but as I listened, I lost the taste for the food. I drank some of the soda and adjusted myself in the chair.

"So, what finally happened to Mrs. Roberts?"

Carter took a deep breath. "Mrs. Roberts moved out and had to get a court thing to stop the coach from harassing her. She was fired from the school and she moved away someplace. She's still in Knoxville, I think. I heard they got a divorce."

"How did all this play out in the school?"

"It was all over the school, of course. I mean, everybody was talking about it. Elvis' father got all freaked out of shape and threatened to sue everybody for trying to disgrace his son. Well, everybody turned against Elvis, except the girls. He was more popular than ever with them."

"What did Elvis think about all of this?"

He picked up his white paper napkin and wiped his mouth. "He told me he really liked Mrs. Roberts. He said she was one of the nicest people he ever knew and he was really sorry he'd gotten her into so much trouble. But hey, she started it, you know?"

"Did the Coach stay at the school?"

"No. He was let go too. I heard that the house was sold and he just left town. But Coach saw Elvis once on the street before he left, and he told him he was going to kill him some day. I mean I was right there and I heard it. I was right next to Elvis when Coach said it. It was really freakin' scary."

I looked down at my hand, flexing it. "Sounds dramatic."

The memory drained Carter's face of color. "Coach meant it, too. You could see it in his bulging eyes. I think that's the reason Elvis left town. I think he was scared shitless. I mean we were both really scared."

"What's Coach's full name?" I asked.

"Coach Faulkner. Rod Faulkner. But you can't print that!"

"Of course not. Just curious. Just checking and cross-checking."

He looked at me doubtfully. Suddenly, he sensed danger—he smelled something foul. I wasn't sure what I'd said or done that suddenly changed him. Maybe he'd just realized he'd been talking too much. He looked at me differently, with sharper, wiser eyes, and I recognized that this man-child was on to me.

"Who are you?" he said, his hollow voice taking on an edge.

I played it casual. "I told you."

"Bullshit! You're going to write all of this stuff, aren't you?"

"I'm not. I promise you."

"You're going to like, make Elvis and me look like jerks, aren't you? So you can sell more magazines."

I held up my hand, as if to take an oath. "Scout's honor. I'm not. It just helps to get a lot of background when you're writing this kind of story."

Carter shot up. "That's a load of shit! I'm out of here."

He tossed down his crumpled napkin, snatched his blue Nautilus jacket from the back of the chair and stormed away. The kid was smarter than he looked. When I glanced toward the three girls, thinking I might have a little chat with them about Elvis, they'd fled.

As I paid the check, I knew I'd have to pay a visit to Darcy-Lynn Roberts. My only question was: could I play it straight with her?

CHAPTER 5

Friday night at the Radisson Hotel proved to be quiet and restless. Sleep did not come easily, and any attempt at trying to sneak up on it was as fruitless and foolhardy as trying to wrestle a big chunk of Jell-O.

I'd developed the uncomfortable feeling that this case was not going to be as simple and fleet of foot as I had originally thought. So far, all the evidence leaned toward an Elvis who'd either stumbled into some unforeseen trouble or an Elvis who'd deliberately allowed himself to tango the night away with some enticingly beautiful trouble. He'd probably planned to tango with style and verve and then flamenco away. He may have learned that there are people who have been "tangoing" with trouble a lot longer than he, and who have much faster moves than his. Mind you, it was all speculation but my nose was sniffing down that path.

I was certain though that he was hiding from something or someone, and I acknowledged the possibility that that something or someone had already found him and sent him into "that good night," to coin some poet who drank a lot and hung out down at the Chelsea Hotel. Pat Shanahan used to quote the guy's poetry, but I was never entirely convinced that Pat had memorized it correctly.

Early Saturday morning, at 7:25, I was driving west on
Sutherland Avenue watching crimson light rise and wash
the sky. I turned right onto Longview Road and drove to
the top of the hill past bare trees, some of them dog-
woods, and passed a red brick T-shaped complex. It was
a three-story building that was probably constructed in
the late 1960s or early '70s. I found a parking space with
a clear view of the entry/exit and killed the engine. I saw
a blue and white canopy over the building entrance, and a
black rubber mat walkway that led to double-glass doors.

The area was quiet, except for the occasional squirrel
that skipped by, tail flicking. Weak morning sun struggled
to filter beams through puffs of purple heavy clouds. I
looked about and noticed red earth. Unusual. I made a
mental note to ask somebody what causes it.

I sipped warm coffee and waited for a time while people, cars and SUVs came and went, cats roamed and
hunted and a distant dog barked his head off.

Finally, I gathered myself and stepped out into the
cold humid air. I took off my black mostly cashmere
topcoat and tossed it into the back seat. I adjusted my
dark blue and gray tie and buttoned my dark blue suit
jacket. In the mirror that morning, I'd combed my hair to
the left instead of straight back, selected a white shirt
instead of blue and ran a hand towel over my black Wing-
tips to go for a dull shine. I wanted to appear as busi-
ness-like and non-threatening as possible to Darcy-Lynn,
and, I wasn't all that sure what I was going to say to her.

I stretched and moved toward the entrance and
glanced at my watch. It was 8:12. I entered the building
and noticed a glassed-in office on my immediate left. It
was closed. There was a black plaque just below the gold
office sign that read: Office Hours 9 a.m. to 5 p.m. I

started down a long hallway across green carpet, and suddenly had the impression that the place had the look and feel of a hotel. I passed white walls, black apartment doors and a locked community room, and proceeded on until I reached apartment 114. There was no one about in the hallway. All was quiet—just the distant sound of muffled TV. I smelled bacon and some kind of lemon disinfectant.

I took a quick breath and rapped lightly on the door. I waited. Nothing. I knocked a bit louder, hearing my knock fill the silence. The door opened slightly—secured by a safety chain. A young, attractive platinum blond, probably mid-to-late 20s, with smooth white skin and deep blue troubled eyes looked back at me through a three inch space. "Yes...?" her small voice said.

I kept my voice even and gentle. "Ms. Roberts?"

"Yes?"

"Ms. Roberts, I'm sorry to barge in on you like this so early in the morning. My name is Dane Cooper. I'm a private investigator. I'm wondering if I could speak with you for a few moments either now or whenever it's convenient for you."

Her narrowed eyes carried a warning. "If this is about my ex-husband, you can just..."

I quickly interrupted her. "It's about Elvis Lipps, Ms. Roberts."

She looked me over, startled and anxious. Her voice grew breathless. "What about Elvis? What's happened to him?"

"Ms. Roberts, if I could just talk to you for a few moments."

"No... absolutely not! I've got nothing to say. I work on Saturdays. I have to get ready."

The door slammed closed.

I reached for my wallet and took out one of my business cards. On the back I wrote down where I was staying, the room number and my cellphone number. I bent down and slid the card underneath her door. I waited another moment or two, just in case she changed her mind. She didn't. I left.

I found a Holiday Inn down the road and had breakfast. I was out in the parking lot, striding toward my car, when my phone rang.

"Mr. Cooper, this is Darcy Roberts." It was a nervous, weary voice. "I can meet you for about a half-hour today at 12:30. I'll be at the Knoxville Museum of Art. You can ask anybody where it is. I'll be at the North Gallery, Upper Level."

She hung up.

I got to the museum early, close to noon. It's located in downtown Knoxville, on the site of the 1982 World's Fair, and I learned that it is one of America's newest museums. I drifted through the two gift shops, glancing at postcards, posters and T-shirts and at 12:25 I started toward the Upper Level.

The current exhibit was about 50 Years of Polaroid Photography (1947-1997). I glanced around looking for Darcy, and, not seeing her, I ambled along perusing the framed photographs. I remembered our first Polaroid camera. My mother went nuts, snapping everything in sight: our new television, my father's tool shed, cakes and pies, and, the ever popular pet cat, Cat Boy. Maybe I'd see a photo or two of my mother's work. Cat Boy was, after all, very photogenic.

At 12:35, I saw Darcy enter the room, looking somewhat constrained by nerves. She looked for, and found me easily. There weren't many of us. I was immediately struck by her posture. It was ruler-edge straight. She started toward me slowly, her expression tentative, as if she was considering this meeting a big mistake. Her black woolen coat was still buttoned, just in case she'd need a quick escape. As she closed the distance between us, her restless blue eyes avoided me.

Darcy was a thin pretty woman, with an aura of proud refinement. Her shoulder length platinum blond hair glistened under the museum spots, giving her an artful focus of attention. My fascinated eyes drifted over her easily. She stopped about four feet from me, staring with cold eyes, a pouty defensive mouth and slightly irritable manner.

"Is Elvis in any trouble?" she asked.

"Maybe. I was hired by his father to find him. He hasn't heard from his son since November the 30th."

Her eyes slid away from me. Her voice was hesitant and low. "Did Mr. Lipps give you my name?"

"Yes, Ms. Roberts, he did. I have also spoken with Carter Davis."

She looked up sharply, registering mild shock.

"I can assure you, Ms. Roberts, I'm only interested in finding Elvis. I don't want to cause you any embarrassment or discomfort."

She turned, pretending to study a photograph, but I could see that she was far away, perhaps blinking away painful memories.

"Ms. Roberts, when did you last see Elvis?"

She didn't look at me. "Are you from New York?"

"Yes."

She faced me. She smiled a little and became prettier, softer. Her red full lips were moist. "I really like New York. I've been there three times. I went to the opera and to the New York Philharmonic. I saw *The Music Man* a few years ago. It was such a good production. I laughed so many times."

Then the smile disappeared. She gently shoved both hands into her pockets. The room was warm and I wondered how she could stand having her coat on, buttoned to the neck.

"I'm not sure I could live there, though," she continued. "I think I'd miss the quiet and there doesn't seem to be a lot of that there."

"It's there, but like everything else in New York, you need a connection and it costs you."

"You grow up there?"

"Brooklyn. Greenpoint, Brooklyn. Yes, ma'am."

"You sound like one of my ex-students, calling me ma'am. Except, most of them weren't so polite." She looked at me—seemed to study me for the first time. "You don't look like a private detective."

"Oh?"

"You have a certain physical dignity. A disarming quality. I guess that's good in your line of work. And, you're a handsome man, Mr. Cooper."

She caught me off guard. I grinned. "Thank you, ma'am."

"Oh God, stop calling me ma'am."

We walked a little, crossing the room. "Why do you limp?" she asked.

"I was shot."

She raised a curious eyebrow. "You've been doing this kind of work long?"

"I started out in the NYPD. Went private a few years ago."

"Does it hurt?"

"Sometimes. I find it often attracts sympathy and helps business. Clients trust a detective who hobbles and looks like a gruff old pirate."

She smiled again, enjoying my response, then she drifted away, taking in the photographs of pets and their owners. I followed. "What's Greenpoint, Brooklyn like?" she asked.

"It was a working-class neighborhood when I was growing up there. Parts of it have been gentrified since I was a kid. I couldn't afford to live there now. Rents are sky high."

"Did you grow up in an apartment?" she asked.

"I grew up on Kent Street, in a brownstone. My grandparents bought it way back and my father sold it in 2005 for a good price and then they moved to Florida. My father was in construction and later became a consultant. We lived a pretty good middle class life."

"Are your parents still alive?"

"Yes, both very much alive."

We strolled and drifted.

"My parents always thought I was intelligent and sensible," she said.

"And now?"

"Let's just say that they no longer think so."

"Well, look at it this way. At least they thought it for awhile. My parents never even considered the possibility."

She turned to face me, with a faint smile. "I don't know you well enough to agree with that."

"I can see you're the prove-it-to-me type."

"Yes, I am, Mr. Cooper."

"You're not going to tell me anything, are you Ms. Roberts?"

"I don't really know who you are or if I can trust you."

"But you're intrigued or you wouldn't be here."

"I want to help Elvis, if he really needs helping. That's why I'm here. But I'm not sure you're the one who can help him, or if he even needs help, Mr. Cooper. So I have nothing to say about it."

"Call me Dane,"

"I'd rather call you Mr. Cooper. I still have nothing to say."

"What can I say or do that will change that?"

She closed her eyes. "I don't know."

"Aren't you hot with that coat on?" I asked. "You look hot."

I was hoping for the smile I got. "Yes, I am."

She released the buttons, shook out of the coat and draped it over her arm. She was dressed in chocolate brown slacks, rust colored sweater and an exquisite gold chain. The colors added a luster to her skin. I suddenly saw a new appeal in her face, full lips and elegant neck.

"Better?" I asked.

"Yes. Better... Elvis is just another case to you, isn't he?"

"I'm not sure I would put it that way."

"But you have other cases?"

"Yes. I do have to make a living."

"So you'll find Elvis, tell his parents, get your money and go on with your life."

"Ms. Roberts, if you're implying that I'm not emotionally involved with Elvis and his family, you're right. I'm not, nor do I intend to be. I was simply hired to find a 20-year-old kid and that's what I'm trying to do."

She crossed her arms. Her eyes got chilly. "I'm sure you've heard all about me, too, Mr. Cooper. You probably have a thick file of me sitting on your desk or in your computer, and you have made up your mind as to what kind of person I am. You probably shook your head when you heard Mr. Lipps and Carter Davis tell you all about me—what a horrible person I am and how I ruined Elvis' life, my husband's life and my own."

"Ms. Roberts, I've been in this business a long time. I've seen saints in hookers, in car thieves, ministers and attorneys. I've seen sinners in hookers, in car thieves, ministers and attorneys. I also look in the mirror every morning. I see a guy who needs a shave and who doesn't know who the good guy or bad guy inside really is most of the time. And, anyway, we're talking about Elvis, not about you and me."

She stared at me, carefully. She turned abruptly and ambled to the other side of the room. I stared at her, believing that her self-esteem and self-image were probably at an all-time low. It's easy to recognize the symptoms, because I'd seen them so many times before in bars, coffee shops and courtrooms.

"Quiet lives of desperation," my old English teacher taught. She had made an incredible difference in my life and in many others'. And because she was attractive and young, and because she gave me extra time after class because I struggled and was not the brightest bulb on any Broadway Marquee, an accusation was made by the sloppy, bug-eyed history teacher down the hall, that she and I were lovers. Others came forward, generously embellishing what they saw—or what they believed they saw and would testify to.

My parents were called. I was whisked before the principal into his private office. He was handsome and officious, if a bit on the fussy side. I often thought he would have made good gigolo material. But that day he shouted, ranted and accused me with an emphatic forefinger. He didn't ask me any questions or let me tell my side of the story. He'd already determined I was guilty.

I had a shorter fuse then—had not fully developed my patience and charm. I stood abruptly and punched him in the face. He dropped like a good looking beach towel and didn't get up for ten minutes. I was suspended from school for a few weeks and the devoted English teacher left town. We'd never once touched, or even gotten close to touching, although I had wanted to.

I wandered over to Darcy and pointed at the photograph of a yawning brown and white cat.

"Looks a little like Cat Boy," I said. "She was famous for her hair balls. Could whip one up in minutes." I quickly added. "Cat Boy was a girl. My father had an odd sense of humor."

Darcy stared, blankly. "Do you really think Elvis is in trouble?"

I faced her. "Yes, I do."

She glanced about to ensure we had privacy. "Elvis entered my life like a tornado and I was never the same. I fell in love with him and couldn't seem to help it. It makes me physically sick to say this, because I betrayed myself, my husband, the school and Elvis. My husband deserved more than that. There is absolutely no excuse for what I did."

"Maybe you're being a little hard on yourself, Ms. Roberts."

"Not in the least. What I did was unforgivable and I know it. My only defense, if there is any, is that I truly loved him. I did love Elvis."

"And you don't anymore?"

She didn't answer.

"When did you last speak to him or see him?"

She hesitated. "What do you know about his parents?"

"They believe he's the reincarnation of Elvis Presley, he's missing, they're worried sick, and they want me to find him."

"Elvis is very mixed up. I'm only telling you this because I believe he's trying to run away from them, and doesn't want to be found. He's sick of them and wants to be free for a while."

"Is that what he told you?"

"Yes. Many times. His father is a bully, who has pushed him into things that Elvis was never comfortable with. From the time Elvis was a child, his father has told him that he was Elvis Presley and that he must fulfill his destiny. He's dragged him to theatre auditions, local TV stations, radio stations—any place where Elvis could get some exposure. Elvis could have done well, and he did get offers, but his father always ruined it for him. He's loud, demanding and crude. He destroyed many of Elvis' opportunities."

Two pensive men and a young, distracted girl approached. Darcy stopped talking and moved on. I followed.

I said, "What if you're wrong and Elvis really is in some kind of trouble? You're not going to feel very good about it when you realize you could have done something to help."

She didn't look at me, but continued to examine the photographs. "Don't use your private detective psychology on me! I've used it too many times on teenagers."

"Did he ever talk to you about a woman named Mrs. Johnson?"

She turned, her face starched with annoyance. "Mr. Cooper, I know Elvis is okay. He's applied for a job——a

PR marketing job for a good company in New York. I received a call from HR a couple of days ago asking for a reference."

"Would that be Atlantic Digital Studios?"

Darcy blinked quickly, her face straining with thoughts. Her spine straightened. "How do you know that?"

"Howard Taylor. I believe you called him Mr. Howard a couple of times."

Her eyes enlarged only slightly in sudden realization. "You son-of-a bitch!" she said, shaking her head. "You don't really care about anyone, do you? You just want the money!"

"And you don't really care about Elvis or you'd help him. You'd rather just mope around and feel sorry for yourself. Look world, I'll beat myself up and blame the whole damn world too, because some good-looking kid screwed up my life! It's an old, old story, Ms. Roberts. It's an old act, a cliché act and I've seen it about 3,000 times. It's adolescent and it doesn't help you, Elvis or anybody else. "

I had been purposely harsh. Either she'd storm away or she'd help me. She gave me a frosty glare that soon fell into hurt and the start of tears. She struggled for her voice. "You have no right to talk to me like that!"

"He might be in trouble, Ms. Roberts. He might even be dead!"

"He's not!" she shouted.

Several Museum patrons glanced over, as did two security guards. I realized that I'd just flunked How to Conduct an Interview 101.

Darcy went limp with distress. She fell into a drooping despondency. My words had deeply wounded her.

She edged around me and left the room. I waited a moment and then went after her.

I found her outside, smoking a cigarette. The sun was bright and it added some warmth to the chilly air. I looked up at the three-story pink marble and glass building, then turned and watched distant flags snapping in the wind. I contemplated a new approach.

I inched closer to her. "In Private Detective School, they taught me how to wine and dine pretty good. I'm not bad at it as long as your expectations aren't too high. Consider it an apology for what I said back there. How about dinner? Say seven o'clock?"

She didn't look at me. "I was in New York about two months ago, November the 15th, I think. Elvis had called me four days before. He said he missed me. He said he was lonely. I told him I didn't think it was a good idea, but he pleaded with me, and in all honesty, he didn't have to plead much. He found me a hotel on Broadway and 77th Street. It wasn't much, but it was reasonably priced and it was close to Elvis' apartment on 82nd Street and Riverside Drive. He met me at LaGuardia and we went straight to my hotel."

She smoked quietly for a moment and then looked at me curiously. "Have you ever been married?"

"Once. Not anymore. Why didn't Elvis let you stay with him in his apartment? Why the hotel room?"

Her eyes got remote. "Mrs. Johnson, Elvis said."

"And she was?" I asked, cocking an ear toward her.

"He said she took care of him—but only as an admirer—nothing else."

"Did you believe him?"

"Of course not. I'm sure he's her, what's the expression, little boy toy on the side."

"Did you ever meet this Mrs. Johnson?"

"No. Something you should know about Elvis, Mr. Cooper... perhaps several things you should know about him: he's incredibly attractive, extremely clever and is a consummate liar."

"Did he tell you what he was doing? Did he mention people he was working with, friends?"

"I was only there for a day and a half. He did seem nervous—and whenever I asked him about it, he just said that there was a lot going on. Early the next morning, he got up and took his phone into the bathroom. He thought I was asleep. I heard him arguing, so I got up and went over to the bathroom door because I was concerned. He was talking to a guy named Buddy, and he sounded scared."

"Buddy Blue?"

"He just called him Buddy."

"What was he saying?"

"Things like, I can't do it... I won't be there. He just kept saying 'No' over and over. As soon as he hung up, I rushed back to the bed."

"Did you ask him anything about the call?" I asked.

She finished her cigarette and stabbed it out in one of the canisters provided. "Of course. We had breakfast in a diner close by. He just said that Buddy was a friend and he wanted to borrow some money or something. He was so nervous that he accidentally spilled a cup of coffee all over the table."

"Ms. Roberts... when was the last time you spoke with Elvis?"

She took out another cigarette, placed it between her lips and lit it, blowing the smoke toward the sky. "I'm a vegetarian, I don't drink alcohol, I don't eat sugar and I take a massive amount of vitamins. I also go to church every Sunday. I stopped smoking my senior year in college. I started again five months ago and I can't seem to stop."

"When did you last speak with Elvis?"

"Just before Christmas... he called me."

"What was the date?"

"December 12th, I think. He wanted me to come to New York. I told him I wouldn't. I told him I never wanted to see him again. I was angry, confused and hurt. He hadn't called me in almost a month. No phone call, no text, no email, nothing. Frankly, I wanted to kill him and it was the first time in my life I'd ever had such a thought. I didn't know who I was anymore. I still don't know who the hell I am."

She suddenly looked drained and exhausted.

"So you didn't go see him?" I asked.

"No. I had allowed this boy to nearly destroy my life, and I was allowing him to do it again. I had to stop it! I told him I never wanted him to call me again and I never wanted to see him again. I hung up." She trembled. "God, his mother really did a job on him."

"Meaning?"

Darcy narrowed her eyes on me. I saw restless fireworks. "Meaning, she's crazy. Meaning, that at around 13 or 14 years old, that crazy woman forced Elvis to have sex with her."

CHAPTER 6

I'd once heard a police psychologist use the words "was left psychically stranded," referring to woman on trial for the murder of her two kids. In Darcy-Lynn Roberts' case, she also seemed emotionally and physically stranded.

We were sitting in a pancake house that was nearly empty at 3 o'clock in the afternoon. I was sipping a soda and Darcy was staring off into the middle distance, looking fragile and blunted by her earlier confessions.

She only worked half days on Saturday. Her job as a bookkeeper was a flexible one and she said she was grateful for that. Darcy had visibly changed, in just under an hour, from a refined silky cool, to a wilted victim with a tight-jaw anxiety.

We had taken my car and driven along Kingston Pike. She'd accepted my offer to go somewhere immediately, quietly, and it was clear that she didn't want to be alone. In the car, her posture had fallen into a stoop, and she stared brooding, like someone who'd accepted a long prison sentence, had exhausted all avenues of defense and had lost the will to fight.

Several times I tried to start a conversation: things like "What makes the red clay red around here?" And "Who is Ross the Boss?" A reference to a hair salon we'd passed. She didn't respond. I feared I had caused something to snap inside that had been waiting to snap for a long time, and I didn't have a clue how to snap her out of it.

We'd wound up at the pancake house because I was hungry and because I wanted to find some way to reconnect with her face to face.

I had ordered a hamburger, French fries and Sprite. When the waitress turned to Darcy, she pointed at the menu, to the word, coffee.

Darcy hadn't touched the coffee since its arrival.

After I had eaten and drained my soda, I leaned back in the booth and studied her. I decided to try a different approach.

"Darcy... do you miss teaching?"

Silence.

"What kind of music do you like? Classical? Broadway—you said you liked *The Music Man*."

Silence.

"My wife, Connie, loved James Taylor, Billy Joel, and Natalie Cole. She even liked some classical music. I never even listened to music until I met her. Do you play the piano?"

She didn't respond. Finally, I asked for the check. After the waitress dropped it on the table and walked away, Darcy stirred.

"He's mad that trusts in the tameness of a wolf, a horse's health, a boy's love, or a whore's oath," Darcy said, flatly.

"Excuse me?" I said.

"Shakespeare... King Lear."

I perked up, straining for a subject that would keep her talking. "I saw Macbeth once, in Central Park. I liked it—not sure I got all the jokes though."

"I can't go back," she muttered.

"Back to where, Darcy?"

"I can't be alone in that apartment. Not now. I won't make it through another night."

"Do you have a friend or relative you can stay with? Maybe a therapist you can call?"

She twisted away, grimacing. "God, no. I can't be with them—with anyone who knows me. I can't talk to them anymore. Don't you understand?! I can't!"

I softened my voice. "Darcy... Is there anyone at work you can...?"

"...No...Well, Carol. Carol Hemmings. Sweet Carol. Silly Carol. We went to high school together. She's a good friend and she's the one who got me the bookkeeping job, but..."

"But what?"

"Carol's married to a guy who took Rod's side. Carol is a good friend, but she still thinks Rod and I can make it, if we'd just go to a marriage counselor or something." Darcy lifted a weak hand and let it drop. "She's a hopeless romantic..."

She began twisting her hands. Her face fell into agony. "I've just been such a fool."

I leaned in toward her. "Darcy, all you did was fall in love. That's all. That's nothing to beat yourself up about."

"Don't you see? I've ruined everything! Everything I stood for and believed in."

I searched for the right response. "Just give it time... a little time to get your balance back."

She shook that away, gathered herself up, then gave me a strange and hopeful look. "I know this is going to sound crazy but...can I come to New York with you?"

That jarred me. I had never even considered the possibility. I scanned her, up and down. She appeared sickened by the gravity of the moment. Seeing her moist eyes and brittle state, I was left with few options. And, no, I'm not a saint. Having her with me couldn't hurt: she was my best hope for contacting Elvis. Her question had changed the quality of the conversation. We sat in a guarded silence. She turned to face the open window, staring out into the gray face of winter.

"Look, Darcy, you can come with me—if that's what you really want—but maybe making contact with an old friend or close relative—going to see them and forgetting about everything for awhile—might be better for you."

She shrank, and I could see the dark remoteness return. She was silently screaming for help and I wasn't qualified to administer the kind of help she needed. What could I do? Leave her? Say no? Then what?

I decided not to abandon her. I decided to listen and let her unload her mountain of guilt and anger. I hoped that after a good night's sleep, she'd change her mind. And I was sure that by morning, she would change her mind.

"Darcy, you can come to New York with me if you want. You can stay the night at the hotel with me, if you want. I have two double beds, or, you can take a separate room. That's fine too. I'll call the airline and get you on my flight leaving for New York in the morning."

She looked at me, her eyes pleading. "I know I sound a little crazy. I know you've just met me and I hear my own crazy words, but I can't help it. I can't go back to that lonely apartment and I can't be alone. I hate being alone. I'm not a person who can be alone."

"Okay,... then you'll spend the night at the hotel and we'll take it from there."

She slowly relaxed, and didn't meet my eyes when she spoke. "I guess I'm past caring what people think of me. If you think I'm crazy and unbalanced, then fine, so be it. I just know that if I go back to the apartment, I'll..." She slowly lifted her eyes to mine. "I'm not even sure if I can trust you." It was more of a question.

"I just happen to be the last life preserver on your sinking ship?" I asked.

She nodded. "I suppose so."

"In New York, I hope you won't expect me to be a tour guide to Little Italy and the Bowery."

She gave me a slightly closed-off smile. But at least it was a smile.

I drove her back to the museum parking lot, where she climbed out and went to her red Grand Am. She looked back at me, uneasily, before she slid behind the wheel and started the engine.

I followed her back to her apartment and waited outside while she packed a bag, and called her friend, Carol Hemmings. She told Carol she was leaving town for awhile and asked if she would inform her boss. She said she'd call Monday and tell him when she'd return to work.

She didn't want me to come in because "the place was a mess," she'd said. After the call to Carol, I wondered if she'd called Elvis to tell him she was coming. Surely when they last spoke on December 12th, when he'd asked her to come to New York, he must have given her his number and address. I imagined that the conversation had gone something like this.

Darcy had said, "I can't do this anymore, Elvis, please don't call again."

After continued pleadings from Elvis and repetitive "No's" from Darcy, he'd probably said, "Here's my address and phone number, just in case you change your mind."

She surely wrote it down.

I paced the parking lot, strolling through columns of hide and seek sunlight, fidgeting and tinkering with my thoughts, trying to envision what my life would be like if Darcy-Lynn really decided to come back to New York with me. We hadn't discussed any details: would she stay at my apartment or find a cheap hotel nearby? For how long? Does she have any money? Will she be strong enough in a few days to return to Knoxville by herself? Will she self-destruct in my apartment if I leave her alone? Should I try and find her a therapist and get her some meds? Was she already on meds? One step at a time, Cooper, I decided.

And then there was the issue of the night to come. I did not know this woman. I did not know what she'd expect—whether being alone to her meant just being around me, having me close by, or if it meant something else entirely.

She was an easy woman to look at—a melting beauty—that stirred the heart and nearly pulled me into her unpredictable moods, because of her vulnerability. She was, after all, battling the demons of obsession, struggling not to buckle under the weight of anger, a nagging guilt and an open wound of desire. Who can't relate to that? That grassy path has been worn to dust by all of us who have sought an eternal, impulsive pleasure that surely must be love. I'd found it once—for two years—with Connie.

When Darcy-Lynn passed through the double glass doors, pulling her large dark green suitcase and olive garment bag, her posture had improved and there was less tension in her face.

Darcy did not want to take her car. She was throwing herself on the mercy of my court. As I drove out of the lot and started toward the hotel, I thought that this was the first time in my career that my interview of a subject had produced this result. Either I was improving and polishing my skills, or I'd completely jumped the track and should consider a career as a priest or social worker.

Darcy did not speak during the ride to the hotel, but her perfume was stirring and pleasant. She sat like a statue, staring straight ahead.

In the hotel room, she avoided my eyes as she worked quietly, unpacking a few toiletries, a bathrobe and shoes. I saw the fatigue take hold of her. She lay down on the near bed and shut her eyes. Her breathing slowed and deepened and she drifted off to sleep. I covered her with a white cotton blanket I'd found in the closet. She didn't stir. I watched her sleep for a moment—a silent sleeper—no sounds at all, just the gentle rise and fall of her chest. I closed the drapes, took my cellphone and went to the lobby to make some calls.

I called the office and asked Helen if she'd heard from Shanahan regarding the apartment on Riverside Drive. She hadn't, but she did say that Juan, the Super, was found passed out on the stairwell, with a mop in his hand. He reeked of alcohol and was mumbling "Boliche" (Bowling) under his breath. She'd called her son again, and again, they'd gotten into a shouting match and he'd hung up on her.

Helen pleaded with me to call him ASAP and straighten the whole thing out, because the bathroom was a "disgrace, falling into hell." Everyone on the floor was complaining, she said. I told her I'd call him as soon as I could. I also told her I'd be back in the office sometime tomorrow afternoon.

She then told me that a doorman had called for me.

I straightened and moved toward the lobby windows to get a stronger signal. "What did he say?"

"He said that the co-op board voted, unanimously, to kick Victor Papania out of the building. He said you'd know what it meant."

I did indeed.

I called Helen's son, Charlie Neff, and he bantered and complained about his mother with "the barbed wire personality." He told me he'd already made arrangements to fire Juan and have the bathroom cleaned by the 2nd shift janitor, a guy from Ecuador, who had been an engineer back home. He couldn't find an engineering job in the U.S., because he didn't have the English.

Following that conversation, I found the number to the airline, called and made a reservation for Darcy, just in case. The ticket was expensive, but I had a good month in December. Fortunately, they were able to seat us together.

After a quick Jim Beam at the bar, I went back upstairs to the room. Darcy-Lynn was still asleep. She hadn't moved. I decided that a nap was a good idea—something I'd never even consider in New York, the direct result of psychological damaging, thanks to my parents. They both believed that a nap was a heinous and detestable act.

They believed that work was the true religion and that traditional religion seldom worked. Their religion was instilled in my sister, Ellen, and in me at an early age and strictly reinforced.

A nap in the middle of the day was considered sacrilege. Punishment ranged from excommunication from the dinner table, usually on a night when my mother cooked her famous pot roast and freshly baked apple pie, to a possible cool glance from the folks as we entered the living room to take our seats before the television. Often, if we'd been caught napping, they'd overrule our favorite TV show to watch some boring thing about nature or a pathetic sitcom that even they disliked. But that was the religious law of Ma and Pa Cooper.

"Sleep is to be done at night. Day is for work," my father, the construction worker said.

My mother said, "If you have to take a nap in the middle of the day, you'd better have a temperature of 103°!"

To this day, whenever I visit them in Florida and feel a delicious nap coming on, I take the damn thing. I'm a man now, not a boy. But as I drift off to sleep, I can imagine my father pacing the floor in steaming irritation, knowing he'd never done such a thing in his time and how could he have raised up a son like me, who dared to spend good working hours sleeping!

And, while I'm sleeping, I always keep one eye open, wondering if Momma is gonna withhold that freshly baked, juicy piece of apple pie.

As I watched Darcy sleep, I gave in to a weary fatigue; but as soon as my head sank into the marshmallow pillow, my eyes were wide open. Who was this woman who slept in that next door bed? Minutes later, I must have fallen into a deep sleep.

I awakened sharply to the sound of the shower. I jerked right to see that Darcy was up.

I swung my legs to the floor and stood, finding the light switch. When I saw Darcy's purse on the floor near the night stand, I went to it. It was one of those bulky Coach handbag creations, all brown textured leather, with endless multifunctioning pockets. The shower was still running. I opened the purse, searching for an address book. I found a cellphone, cigarettes, lipstick, a small round mirror and some chewing gum.

I heard the shower go silent. I glanced sideways toward the bathroom. I unzipped an inside pocket. I saw a small book. The right size. I extracted a smooth black leather book. Success! I held it under the flood of light. The L Tab was red. I opened the page and, with my index finger, quickly scanned the list of names looking for Lipps. I heard Darcy brushing her teeth.

I saw Elvis' phone number. It was the same number she'd given Howard Taylor from Atlantic Digital Studios. The address was 98½ Riverside Drive. Nothing new. I turned over more tabs, looking for anything that might grab me, but nothing did. The names meant nothing. I turned off the light and carefully replaced the address book, pulling the zipper closed. I replaced the handbag.

I'd just managed to switch off my lamp and lie down when Darcy emerged from the bathroom, bringing a beguiling and pleasurable scent into the room. The light from the bathroom threw a yellow plank of light across my bed and I saw Darcy dressed in a royal blue full-length silk robe. She passed the foot of my bed and went to her suitcase. She swung it up on to the bed. I heard her unzip the cover.

"Sleep well?" I asked.

She looked up. "Yes. You?"

"Good. What time is it?"

"Almost seven."

"Hungry?"

"No."

"You should eat something. You didn't have any lunch."

"That's nice."

"What?" I asked, sitting up and leaning back against the headboard.

"That you said it. That you thought about it...about me."

I folded my hands and placed them behind my head. "I made the plane reservation. We're all set to go in the morning. The plane leaves at 10:15. We have a brief layover in Charlotte. We'll be in New York at a little after 2 o'clock."

"That's where I grew up. Charlotte, North Carolina."

"And you began studying the piano at five years old?"

"Six."

"Brothers and sisters?"

"Older brother. He lives in San Diego. He's gay. He designs clothes and never stays in touch. I'm afraid that both of us have been a great disappointment to our parents. My father's a Baptist minister."

I wanted to avoid any painful subjects. "How about a movie?"

I watched her take some article of clothing from her suitcase and lay it carefully on the bed. "All right."

"Afterwards, we'll eat."

"If you insist."

"I do."

"What did you say your first name was?" she asked.

"Dane."

"I have money, Dane. I'll pay you for the flight and for any other expenses."

"Don't worry about it."

"I received an inheritance from my grandfather. In his will, he said I was his favorite. Of course, he died three years ago and thought I was a good little girl."

"Darcy... none of us are as bad as we think we are or as good as we want to be."

She stopped and appraised me. "You're a philosopher."

"No. I've just met lots of people and seen lots of things. Most people are like bells. They swing good sometimes and swing bad sometimes. And that bell is always going ding dong."

She laughed a little, as she rummaged through her suitcase. "Well, anyway, my grandfather left me a lot of money."

"We'll talk about all of that later," I said.

The front desk told us where the nearest theatre was. Darcy dressed in crisp designer jeans, a sky blue turtleneck, medium heels and brown leather jacket. I wore jeans, a black turtleneck, my old Yankees Baseball cap and dark green jacket.

Her lips were deep red, blue eyes glittered as we passed under the lobby lights. Male heads turned and watched her sway. Outside in the wind, her hair scattered beautifully, and when she raked it from her eyes, she looked at me and smiled.

We decided on a comedy and I got popcorn and two sodas. She ate a little of it and I ate a lot. We settled, sipped and watched. Her perfume was astonishingly compelling. It just kept making a good impression. She was one of those quietly seductive women, who was probably unaware of her power. It was a concealed feminine energy that stealthily enveloped a man like a fine mist—subtle fingers, intimately reaching, exploring and touching. I refused to call it mystical so I blamed the whole thing on her remarkable choice of perfume. Whatever it was, Darcy-Lynn made me restless and I knew that wasn't a good sign. But I was determined not to get emotionally involved in this case. The whole thing was just too strange.

The movie made us laugh a couple of times. It was one of those formula movies, about boy meets girl, girl hates guy because he's sloppy, loud and stupid, but falls in love with him anyway because he has a cute dog and that's just the way it is in the movies.

We drove for a little while afterward, and found one of those brew pub places that every city in the U.S. has tucked away somewhere. Inside, it smelled of simmering steak. The tables were thick mahogany, the lighting dusky and the overhead music a combination of country and pop. A friendly hostess sat us away from the music and presented us with laminated menus. Darcy studied hers intensely, turning it over several times. I spotted what I wanted right away.

She ordered the angel hair pasta with vegetables, and I ordered a mug of beer and the glazed pork tenderloin, mindful that she said she was a vegetarian. She'd said she didn't mind.

The movie was our first topic of conversation and we both agreed that it was one of those films that could be Netflixed or demanded on HBO and it didn't rank a theatre appearance. Having said that, I felt better and she seemed improved.

Slowly and consciously, I think, she steered the conversation to my marriage and Connie.

"How long were you married, Dane?"

"A little over two years."

"Did you break it off or did she?"

"Neither, she was killed in a car accident."

Darcy folded her hands and lowered her gaze. "I'm so sorry. Really, I am sorry."

A swift busboy brought bread and butter. I offered Darcy the basket but she declined, so I reached for a warm roll and took a bite.

"Did you have kids?" Darcy asked.

I chewed, slowly, swallowed. "Connie was pregnant when it happened."

Darcy's face clouded over. "...Oh..." was all she said.

This was a subject neither of us wanted to continue, so we shifted the conversation to the weather, back to the movie and then to my illustrious police career. I talked and she listened thoughtfully, asking perceptive and engaging questions. Her eyes widened a couple of times at my "war stories," and I enjoyed her reactions and little chuckles of surprise. She kept asking for more, like a kid around a campfire not wanting the stories to end.

When our food came, we ate for awhile in silence, listening to the music. She didn't think much of it. "Uninspired," she said. "Most of the time I think of this kind of piped-in music as music pollution," she continued.

In the car traveling back to the hotel, she said, "I miss being married. I liked it. I've never liked being alone. You seem like the type who has always been a loner, Dane."

"I don't mind it. But I'm not a hermit."

"Do you think you'll ever get married again?" she asked.

"I don't think about it," I said. I glanced at her. Her expression was undecipherable.

Back in the room, she undressed in the bathroom and entered the bedroom wrapped in her silky robe. I was seated on the couch watching the news. She climbed into bed and pulled the covers up to her chin.

"I won't be any trouble, Dane. I promise. I'll only stay a couple of days."

I switched off the television. "It took courage to ask for help, Darcy. A lot of courage."

"I don't know. I've never thought of myself as a coward, but I certainly have been lately."

"New York's a great place for a person who loves the arts. You can hit the museums—see what's going on at Lincoln Center. You'll get your balance back. You'll be fine."

She was asleep before I finished my shower.

As I crawled between the covers and turned off the light, I felt a comfortable intimacy. I fought it, but I finally admitted that it was nice having someone else in the room—someone pretty—a woman who had probably been a wonderful wife and who'd be an exceptional mother. But she'd have to find a way to chase off her demons, and I suspected it would take her a long time.

I lay my head back into the pillow and stared into the darkness, reviewing the events of the day, coming to the conclusion that I'd never had such a day. There was no benchmark for this kind of relationship, no diagrams, no maps and no self-help books, not that I'd ever read one. So maybe I should look for one in one of those airport bookstores? Maybe I should read it and then self-help my way back to something? But what? What I was before Connie? What I want to be now, after two long years without Connie? Forget the past? Focus on the future? Try and live in the Now? The Now that runs, hides, plays and hurts and leaves you running back to that damn airport bookstore to buy yet another self-help book?

Nah, I won't read one. I'm not old enough to grow up and move beyond my hurts, fears and old loves. I want them. I want all of them. I want to hold on to every single painful and wonderful thing. I'll self-help myself along that rocky path and just play it as I see it.

I had no idea what the next few days with this woman would bring. That was an uncomfortable feeling. I hoped she wasn't going to New York to try and find Elvis. But my instincts told me that's exactly what she intended to do. She had it bad, and she was using me because she felt I was her best hope. I drifted off to sleep with the thought "Hope is a raft, bobbing on a lonely, restless sea."

CHAPTER 7

As we descended through heavy clouds, sliding over Manhattan about to make our final approach into La-Guardia, I gazed out the window and concluded that New York was the color and texture of an old gray sock. Hazy and gray. The buildings and skyscrapers were gray, the Hudson River ragged and gray, little boats and dull silver bridges, gray, the stream of cars on the West Side Highway, gray.

I'd hoped for effulgence, a word my sister, Ellen, often used. I wanted Darcy-Lynn to see New York blazing under a beautiful January fireball, the water glittering, the palaces of steel sun-polished, hundreds of windows glinting sharply. But the place had fallen into the January blahs, and I was afraid that the only sunshine I was going to see was in a bottle of Jim Beam. Unfortunately, Darcy-Lynn abstained from alcohol so I wouldn't be able to share my sunshine with her.

Throughout the flight, we'd kept the conversation purposely vague and general, covering topics such as favorite foods, favorite movies, favorite books and favorite sitcoms.

Darcy had awakened in better spirits and said, "I haven't slept this good in weeks."

But she was quiet during breakfast and hardly ate any of her oatmeal. I kept her company outside as she smoked. I could see the struggle for a bright mood in her eyes and voice, and sometimes when I spoke, she seemed engaged by a distant possibility or old regret.

I was gently surprised when she did not waiver or second guess her decision to travel to New York. In fact, she was energized by the realization that she was escaping the prison cell of her apartment and all those dark thoughts, like a refugee fleeing a war zone. She'd swarmed the hotel room readying herself with nervous enthusiasm. I wanted to ask her things: why she'd stayed in Knoxville when it held such painful memories? Had she ever heard from her husband? Did she have any close friends other than Carol Hemmings, who'd supported her during the difficult times? But all those questions would have to come later, once she felt safe and far away from anything that could seemingly harm her.

What had intrigued me was her obvious comfort in sharing a hotel room with me. I wondered how many women in the United States would be as comfortable as she, sleeping in the same room with a man she'd just met, didn't know and who, in a sense, had insulted her, bringing her to the edge of despair. She didn't seem embarrassed or overly modest as we passed to and from the bathroom and, when she'd slipped into peach silk pajamas that revealed firm, ripe breasts that drew my naughty eyes, she seemed unaware. It was almost as if we were a comfortable old married couple, although I wasn't all that comfortable. Perhaps in her mind it was all make believe. She was pretending to live the life of a married woman again because it gave her balance, and made her feel secure and safe.

Once on the ground in New York, we gathered her bags at the Baggage Claim Area and joined the line outside at the taxi stand. Once we were on the Long Island Expressway, moving in medium traffic toward Manhattan, Darcy turned to me, smiling.

"I feel so much better, Dane. I guess I just needed to get out of there. I needed to do something completely different."

"Why did you stay in Knoxville?" I asked.

She thought about it for a moment. "I don't know. I traveled for awhile. Went to the Caribbean and to England with a friend from college. She recently got married and moved to Germany. Her husband works for some corporation there. I guess I stayed in Knoxville because I didn't know where else to go. I was afraid and confused."

"Why did you decide to get out of music?"

She looked away. "I wanted to erase my past. I wanted to start fresh." She turned, forcing a bright smile. "What's your place like?"

"It's not as big as some. It's a one bedroom apartment, with a view of a brick wall."

"It doesn't matter. I'll stay out of your way."

"I didn't mean that. I just meant... well, you can have the bedroom. I have a comfortable couch that pulls out into a double bed."

"I'll take the couch."

"No ma'am. The bedroom door closes and you can have all the privacy you want."

She looked down and plucked a piece of lint off her black woolen coat. "You'll have to work of course."

"Well, this is Sunday. I'll go into the office for a few hours this afternoon, but I seldom work on weekends."

She looked pleased. "I'll treat you to dinner tonight, at any restaurant you choose, and to a Broadway show tomorrow night."

I nodded. "Most Broadway shows are closed Monday nights, but maybe we'll find one or two that are open. But I'll only agree to the above on one condition."

"And that is?"

"I know a great piano bar down in the West 40s. I want you to play something for me. Anything you choose."

She shook her head. "Oh God, no."

"Just one song. One little song."

She folded her arms, staring ahead. "... All right, one song."

I closed the apartment door behind us and we stood for a time in an awkward silence, panning my West Side, Manhattan pad. Somehow, it looked even smaller in the gray light of afternoon. I watched Darcy-Lynn give it an evaluation. She wandered to the center of the living room, acknowledging my blue brocade couch, dark brown recliner and mahogany coffee table. The carpet was brown, with little flecks of blue, the TV 32 inches and the fireplace stately, but non-functional. Her eyes strayed toward the CD player. She went to it, found my CD rack and studied my collection.

"Beethoven's Fifth and Ninth Symphonies? I'm impressed."

"Don't be. Connie bought them."

"Madonna?"

"Connie."

"Marvin Gaye's Greatest Hits. Connie?"

"Connie."

"Have you ever bought a CD?"

I went over and slid one out and handed it to her. "Reindeer Pie."

"Reindeer what?"

"Reindeer Pie. One of the Homicide Detectives at Midtown North has this little singing group on the side. A few years back, it was their Christmas album. I wanted to support them."

She looked it over. "Is it any good?"

"It's an acquired taste, I think."

I went back over to the bags. "I'll take your things to the bedroom."

In the bedroom, Darcy came in behind me and slid out of her coat. She dropped it on the unmade double bed and gave the room a once-over. She moved toward, and then parted the blue curtains I'd brought from the house in Queens, where Connie and I had lived. They were one of a few items I'd kept. Call me sentimental, but I loved waking up to them. There was a chest of drawers, a little night table and a bookcase filled mostly with biographies. Darcy ran her hand along the edge of the bookcase.

"I don't see any novels."

"Novels are basically a bunch of lies strung together. I prefer biographies. Things that really happened. People who really lived. Events you can measure. The truth."

"Novels are true in their own way. They can touch something very profound and intimate, if the writer has been fortunate enough to connect with his or her own truth."

"You sound like a teacher."

Darcy turned reflective. "I loved teaching."

I motioned toward the bathroom. "The sheets and towels are in the bathroom cupboard. I would have made the bed, but I didn't know you were coming."

Darcy didn't seem uneasy, but I was. I could feel my pulse in my neck.

"I bet my husband—my ex-husband—was one of the few men who got up in the morning and made the bed first thing. He said that unless the bed was made, he had a hard time organizing his day."

"Connie was that way, too."

Darcy folded her arms. "Of course, if I was in it, it threw off his entire rhythm, so I seldom got to sleep late."

"You can sleep as late as you like here."

She paused. "What day is it? I've lost track of time. Oh, yes, you said Sunday."

I looked at my watch. It was 3:20.

"Are you going to your office?" Darcy asked.

"Just for a few hours to catch up on some things. Will you be all right?"

She took a little breath, then nodded.

"You're sure?"

"I'll be fine. Thanks for everything, Dane. Really."

"I should be home by 7 o'clock. Call me if you need anything."

Before I left, I showed her the kitchen, where I kept coffee/tea, cups and glasses. She suddenly seemed ill at ease and preoccupied, perhaps frightened at the thought of being alone. Again, I went to the front door, with a slight hesitation, and looked back.

"I'll be fine," Darcy said. "I feel like a nap. That's a good sign. It means I'm relaxing."

As soon as I left the apartment and closed the door firmly behind me, I stopped. Feeling slightly foolish, I pressed my ear tightly against the door and waited. I heard her muffled voice—she was on the phone. I could hear a conversation. I quickly inserted my key, released the lock and pushed open the door.

Darcy-Lynn turned sharply to face me, surprised.

I pointed toward the bedroom and whispered. "I forgot something."

Then over the phone, she said. "Yes, two tickets for tomorrow night's show. Front mezzanine…"

I hurried into the bedroom, waited a moment, then returned to the living room, moving quickly to the front door. I waved, she waved and smiled, and I left.

I spent a half-hour watching the front door of my apartment building, from a safe distance away. Darcy-Lynn did not emerge.

Finally, I started for the subway, wondering if she'd called Elvis. When she was stronger, I'd confront her, nicely.

I left the subway at 50th Street and started west toward Eighth Avenue, moving through cold gray light. On Eighth, I walked toward 45th. I passed a wandering beggar with wild eyes and smelly clothes, a young mother, kid in tow, texting and dodging traffic, and Japanese tourists searching, pointing and chattering.

I stopped at a bagel shop to get some coffee. Inside there was frantic movement. Customers hollered out orders, music thumped, a red neon clock seemed to shout out the time, and a thin old man gobbled down a bagel while reading the *New York Times* Sunday Edition. It was good to be back in the City.

I entered the office and was shocked to find Helen at her desk. She never worked on Sundays. I mean, never.

"What are you doing here?" I asked, incredulous.

"Harvey and me had a big blowout. He's an asshole. Promised to take me to Peter Luger's Steak House in Brooklyn a week ago and then today he says, 'Sorry, dear, I forgot I was playing poker with the guys tonight.' I told him to kiss my ass and left. So I came here. I can always find something to do."

She was bent over one of those lottery scratch cards. She had a nickel, scraping and scratching in a fury.

"Hot damn! Forty dollars, Dane. I just won 40 friggin' dollars!"

She looked at me in a state of rapture. Rapture did not come easily to Helen, and beholding her in such an exalted state was almost frightening. She popped out her computer CD tray and slipped in a CD. In seconds, she was dancing her chunky body to the "Oldies."

"Well I'm glad to see I was missed," I said.

"The bills are paid and the women's bathroom is clean," she called out, twisting and shouting.

I left Helen to her celebration, stepped into my office and closed the door. I booted up my laptop, while I checked my phone for messages. There was a text from Shanahan from yesterday. I hadn't seen it. It read, "*Call me.*" I logged on to check emails while I found Pat's number on my speed dial.

"Back from the wilds of Tennessee?" he asked. "Wasn't Daniel Boone born on a mountain top in Tennessee?"

"So the song goes," I said. "I saw no conclusive evidence. How's it going?"

"Well, we had a little bit of drama Friday morning. Some asshole, thinking this was the Tombstone Territory, pulled a big gun outside the precinct and shot holes in the sky because he said he wasn't getting any media attention. I just happened to be outside when it happened."

"Did you duck and cover?" I asked.

"My Irish American ass was the first to hit the ground."

"A citation to come, no doubt, for having the biggest and fastest ass to get out of the line of fire."

"John Jay College called," Shanahan said. "They want me to teach a course on fat-ass ducking."

"So you've got another specialty," I said.

"Something I can do when I retire. Why did you call, Dane-O?"

"You texted me... probably about that Riverside Drive apartment thing."

"Oh yeah. Apartment 9B. I've got the info here someplace. I brought it home with me. Hang on a minute."

I reached for a pen and a legal pad, waiting.

"Dane-O. The lease was in the name of one Victor T. Papania. As of one week ago, that lease was terminated."

"Any other information on Mr. Papania?"

"Now why do you suppose I knew you were going to ask that question?" Shanahan said.

"Because you're going to ask me what this case is all about, because you have a boring life, and a partner who doesn't even like the Jets."

"So what is the case about?"

"I'm just trying to find some 20-year-old kid who, I think, probably got himself into a lot of trouble. His Mommy and Daddy miss him and want me to track him down."

"Well, you could have done this search yourself, Dane-O. You're getting lazy. Mr. Papania is forty-seven years old and is an attorney—medical malpractice, for Green, Wexler and Papania, at 61 Broadway. He's married. Second time. Has two kids. He was convicted of insider trading and conspiracy about six years go. He served a

five-month prison term. He has a home in New Ro-
chelle. 129 Errol Place. Phone 914-623-0890. Went to
law school at Boston College. He was arrested about two
years ago for indecent exposure. A woman alleged he
pulled his thing out on the boardwalk in Long Beach.
The case settled, his people paying an unknown sum.
Ten years ago, his father represented the 67th District
Assembly, which included the Upper West Side and parts
of Clinton/Hell's Kitchen. Papania, the elder, died of a
heart attack in 2009. Enough?"

"Yeah, for what I need. What would I do without
you?" I said.

"You going out with anybody these days, Dane-O?"

"I don't know. I might be."

"I like the sound of that. Maybe I'll investigate."

"I wish you would. It's confusing as hell."

"Let's do Chinese for lunch sometime, Dane-O."

"You got it.

"Say hello to Jean."

"And you say hello to that person you might be going
out with."

As I clicked through my emails, I was thinking about
Darcy-Lynn. There was no denying it, I was looking
forward to dinner with her. I wasn't sure what we'd talk
about, since we'd covered all of the "safe" subjects on the
plane. There was a part of me that didn't want to shatter
a possible romantic mood, if it presented itself, by asking
her questions about her husband and Elvis, but the other
part of me knew I'd do just that. I needed to convince
her that Elvis' life could depend on her being candid and
honest with me.

My hand kept snaking closer to my cellphone. Was
she there? Finally, I reached and dialed. Her phone rang

three times. I was just beginning to feel a sinking feeling in my chest, when she answered. A rusty, sleepy voice.

"Hello... this is Darcy."

"Darcy? It's Dane."

"Dane... is that you?"

"Did I wake you?"

"I didn't know where I was for a moment. I'm glad I'm here and not home."

"Sorry I woke you. I was just checking in."

"That's so sweet."

Her voice was low and sexy. A pillow, smoky voice.

"Go back to sleep. I'll see you soon."

"Don't forget, I'm buying you dinner tonight."

"I'm holding you to it."

I hung up and swiveled my chair around to face the window. I gazed out. A light rain was falling, gently striking the glass. I kept hearing the same phrase bounce around in my head.

"A beautiful, classy blond is sleeping in my bed. A beautiful, classy blond is sleeping in my bed."

And then I thought of Abner Lipps. I heard his voice. "What the hell are you doin', Mr. Cooper? What in the hell do you think you are doin'?"

Reluctantly, I returned to those emails, my daily summaries and snail mail correspondence. I had an email from my accountant who wanted to "apprise" me of his bill that I'd neglected to pay. That snapped me out of my daydreams. Helen didn't usually forget this kind of thing. Knowing her, she'd probably conveniently forgotten, since she'd often made it clear that she didn't like the guy. I forwarded the email to Helen. Within seconds, I heard her high-pitched lilt of expletives, alerting me to the fact that she'd received the email and was in the process of paying it.

At a quarter to five, Helen was on her way out of the office when my phone rang. I grabbed it, waving goodbye to Helen.

It was Abner Lipps.

"Any word, Mr. Cooper, about my son?"

"I've made some progress, Mr. Lipps, but I haven't found him yet."

"Is that unusual? I mean, does this kind of thing usually take this long?"

"That depends—every case is different. I am currently following several leads and I'm hopeful that by the end of next week, I'll be able to give you some definitive information."

Abner's voice got firm and sharp, like a parent getting tough with his kid. "I don't really give a damn about that definitive information, Mr. Cooper, unless it involves you finding my son."

"It's only been five days, Mr. Lipps. Like I said, when you were here in the office, I want to give it two weeks. If I come up empty, then we'll re-evaluate and decide which course of action we need to follow."

"Don't come up empty, Mr. Cooper. For God's sake, don't come up empty."

I hung up, settled back in my chair and reached for a Rolo. Abner Lipps would not be pleased if he knew Darcy-Lynn Roberts was sleeping in my bed. He would feel that I'd betrayed him.

"All just part of the job, Mr. Lipps," I could say. "It's logical that Darcy is the most likely person to know where Elvis is," I'd say, in a voice filled with smooth authority. "Mr. Lipps, I'm confident she'll lead me to Elvis in time. We just have to be patient."

From the radio came Elvis' song *Suspicious Minds*. I reached over and punched off the power switch.

CHAPTER 8

I entered my apartment to see Darcy-Lynn standing in the center of the living room, wearing a black strapless dress and matching shoes. I closed the door, feeling a little catch in my throat.

"It's Yves Saint Laurent," she said, with a cool challenging smile, as if to say, "Try and hit my 98-mile-an-hour fastball."

Her hair was up in the manner of a ballerina, revealing that aristocratic long neck. She turned slightly under the soft overhead light, and I beheld her clear white skin that had seldom been kissed by the sun, but had been blessed by the gods overseeing complexions. It reminded me of fresh cream. Her lips were deep red and parted, her eyes shining with the hint of sinfulness. Darcy was not voluptuous or earthy, though her breasts were full, body curvaceous. She was ethereal, graceful; a concept of mystery and fascination that ebbed and flowed like the sea at sunset.

"What can I say? You look, well... beautiful."

Darcy-Lynn tilted her head, touched by the complement. "I've chosen the restaurant. I hope you don't mind."

"As long as they serve food. What's it called?"

"The West Park Café."

In the taxi, traveling toward West 59th Street, my thoughts were mildly spiced with questions and uncertainties. Why The West Park Café? There were so many obvious choices. New York has a wealth of celebrity chef restaurants, famous bistros and new restaurants "all the buzz." I'd heard of The West Park Cafe, though I'd never dined there. It mostly had the reputation for trendy, expensive and eccentric. The food? No idea.

I turned to Darcy. She sat erect, serene, her slender hands resting in her lap. "Why The West Park Café?" I asked.

"I saw it advertised in *New York Magazine*. It sounded fun."

I nodded, not believing her. "Did Elvis bring you here?"

She faced me, watching me steadily, betraying nothing. "No. He told me about it."

We exited the taxi and entered The Cafe, stepping onto the neon-green-color-infused escalator. We traveled quietly up to the spacious lobby entrance and took in the surroundings. I watched Darcy's eager curiosity.

A tall, strenuously British hostess, who offered a welcome and a stiff smile, met us. She took our coats and handed them off to a coat person nearby. She spoke freely about the cold weather and Darcy's lovely dress. Darcy explained she was from out of town and would love to look the place over. The hostess dutifully led us through the surreal lobby, to the tucked-away library bar that had a collegiate feel to it. Darcy nodded and smiled as we passed the antique purple felt pool table, roaring fireplace and deep overstuffed leather couches and chairs—all strategically positioned for a snowy afternoon rendezvous.

After the quick tour, we were escorted back to the lobby. We passed the rock garden outdoor terrace, strolling with proper interest and curiosity into the Gothic looking dining hall, with exposed-brick walls, massive oak tables, mahogany paneling and 40-foot vaulted ceilings.

Darcy said it reminded her of a scene in an old movie, *The Student Prince*, where Mario Lanza's dubbed voice sang of bygone college days to his college friends in a college-type cafeteria or bar in Austria or Germany. I said I'd heard the name. I'd also heard that the guy ate a lot, got fat and was possibly rubbed out by the Mafia. Darcy thought I was making a joke and laughed. It was a rich laugh.

I viewed the place and figured it sat about 140 to 160. It had class, a gimmick and communal tables. I told the hostess that I wasn't feeling communal.

The hostess indicated toward a private table. "This way then."

After we were seated and the menus dropped, we quietly studied them. A waiter approached, carrying the pungent aroma of the officious. Standing at attention, he rattled off the specials in clear bullet points, while staring at the wall beyond us. He then turned the full glare of his attention on to us—as if he were the attorney and we the jury—and he began prosecuting the menu.

"The menu is, shall I say, often uninspired or over-inspired. I'm an honest server," he said, crisply. "Frankly, the *specials* are the way to go. As I said, I'm honest. I've learned to tell the truth and, with that truth, I can honestly say that the *specials* have been carefully prepared by an entirely different chef, whom I have known and respected for years. His food is excellent. I have tasted each *special* entree and I can tell you, truly, that the *specials* are to die for."

He concluded and waited for our verdict.

I admired his eccentric honesty. Darcy-Lynn sat in a state of astonished wonder. She struggled to answer.

I said, "Well, it is rare to find an honest server these days."

He scrutinized me to see if I was mocking him.

Darcy gathered herself. "Well... I'll have the sea bass then. The *special* sea bass," Darcy said.

"A very wise choice," our attorney waiter said.

"I'll have the steak," I said, firmly. "Not from the *specials*, but from the menu. Medium rare."

The waiter sniffed as he wrote. He gathered up our menus.

We ordered a bottle of California Red. Darcy preferred it, even though she'd ordered the fish. She said that since this evening was an exception, she'd drink wine.

Before our waiter left, he gave me a squinting look of displeasure. "Thank you."

He pivoted and was gone.

Darcy sat in pondering mystery. "Was that odd? I mean, that whole presentation thing?"

"Yes, it was odd, even for New York. Obviously, there's a bit of kitchen antagonism going on back there. I guess we'll just have to throw ourselves on the mercy of this waiter's court and hope for the best."

Jazz was playing through the overhead speakers; a raspy sax, lazily bending a tune. Loud conversation came from a communal table to our left. It was a group of the young, doing pop-culture chatterboxing.

I loosened my tie a little and eased back in my chair. "What's your ex-husband like?" I asked, casually.

Darcy-Lynn lowered her eyes. "He's a big man—your size or a little bigger. He's direct and proud, and he's a good football coach. The school had two winning years. I'm sure they hated to let him go."

"I heard he beat you up pretty bad... I mean, over the Elvis thing."

She shut her eyes against the thought. "Are you in your private detective mode now?"

"Yes and no."

She opened her eyes. "I didn't blame him for what he did."

"Had he ever done it before?"

"He was a jealous man."

"That a yes?"

"If you want it to be."

"Did you know that he once threatened to kill Elvis?"

"Yes."

"Did he ever threaten to kill you?"

"I wonder if the trout would have been a better choice?"

"So vegetarians eat fish?"

"Some do. I do. They call us pescatarians."

"He did, didn't he, Darcy? He did threaten to kill you."

She looked up, around and beyond me. She folded her hands, tightly. "If you found your wife in bed with an 18-year old student, who was known to be the most sexy and promiscuous boy in the school, wouldn't you want to kill her?"

I sighed a little. "You're awfully forgiving."

Her eyes flashed anger. "If the roles had been reversed, I would have killed my husband—on the spot—with whatever I could have gotten my hands on."

"A gun?"

"If one was handy. Yes!"

"Have you seen your ex-husband since the divorce?"

"He moved somewhere in Pennsylvania. A small town. He's teaching there. Physical Ed, I think."

"You've seen him then?"

"Yes."

"When?"

She lifted her shoulders slightly, then let them drop. "He stalked me for awhile. I had to get a restraining order."

"After the divorce?"

"Yes."

"Did he hurt you?"

"He threatened me. Said he'd kill me and Elvis eventually—in his own way and in his own time."

"How long ago?"

"Ever since he found Elvis and me together. Then, I don't know, October. Just after I got back from seeing Elvis in September. Then he threatened me again, I think in November."

"Middle November?"

Her voice took on an edge. "Yes! I guess so. Rod began leaving threatening phone calls. He would wait for me outside work and when I left for lunch he would follow me. He cornered me once in the parking lot. He said, he knew I'd been in New York screwing Elvis and he was going to kill me and Elvis. Fortunately, a co-worker, a fairly big man, came over and Rod reluctantly left. That's when I called the police and got the restraining order."

After the wine was presented, opened and poured, Darcy and I sat in a long silence. We toasted. I stole glances toward her thin creamy shoulders and the soft angles of her face. She felt my eyes and looked back. It was a look impossible to decode.

"No wonder you don't feel particularly comfortable at home," I said. "Maybe you should move away."

She folded her arms. "I'm going to leave. I should have left months ago. I'm going to move."

"Where?"

"Arizona, New Mexico. Someplace warm. I don't know, maybe California where my brother is. At least I'd be around someone I know."

"When?"

She smiled weakly. "In the next couple of weeks. I've already begun to pack. That's the reason my place is in such a mass."

"That sounds like a good move to me," I said.

"Do you like what you do, Dane?"

I shrugged. "It's what I do."

"Your mind must never get to rest. It's always trying to figure out reasons, facts and motivations. Analyzing who is telling the truth and who isn't. The why of whys, the secret of secrets, the filth of people's lives." She caught my eyes. "Am I an attractive woman?"

Once again, her directness struck like an arrow. I nudged my glass of water aside. "Yes, ma'am. Surely you must know that."

She sighed, giving me an intimate gaze. "Dane... I want to ask you something. It's not easy for me to ask. It's selfish and silly really."

"So ask."

She lifted her chin, just a little. "Can we just pretend, Dane? Can we pretend for awhile that you and I are on a high school date, or maybe we're a newly married couple who are crazy about each other? We don't have much of a past, and the future is beautiful and promising. We believe that the world is filled with innocence, and love will surely conquer all. We don't have to battle ourselves or each other, because we haven't yet learned that evil and darkness lie within our hearts. We don't yet know that despite our best efforts, evil, desire and wickedness will attack without warning and destroy all of our good and best impulses."

"So gloomy," I said. "If I carried a gun, maybe I'd shoot myself."

She smiled, uncertainly. "Are you good at pretending, Dane?"

Her words chilled me. There was that weary resignation again. A feeling that she had fallen from a great height and shattered into pieces, and all the king's horses and men, couldn't put Darcy back together again.

"You are a beautiful woman, Darcy."

"Does that mean we can pretend?"

"You may have to define that word for me as we go along. Pretend is a loaded word."

She gave me an enigmatic smile. A moment later, she looked away.

Darcy talked of high school. She'd been a cheerleader. Dated jocks, except for one nerdy "smart guy" who was "hotter" than any of the jocks because he knew poetry and Bach and had "read a lot of books about how to satisfy a woman."

I told her about my football days, how my English teacher forced me to memorize a little Shakespeare, and how my high school sweetheart married the valedictorian.

"The nerds definitely had something to offer," I said. Then added, "Now they're the guys with all the millions and most have retired, thanks to computer technology."

Our dinners arrived and we ate, laughed and drank, slowly drifting into a kind playful intimacy, succeeding in

Darcy's desire to pretend. I was aware of it and surprised by how easily I'd fallen into it. The food was surprisingly good. Darcy loved the sea bass and the steak was tender and juicy and cooked to perfection.

As we left the cafe, Darcy turned back, taking it in. She reached for my hand and held it tightly, as if suddenly insecure about something. Crowds passed, taxis edged toward the curb looking for passengers and a siren wailed in the distance.

"I hope you don't find Elvis," she said. "I want to forget all that. I want to forget I ever existed before tonight."

I looked at her pointedly. "You don't know where Elvis is, do you, Darcy?"

She shook her head, then looked skyward. "No...I don't. I should have come when he called in December. He'd sounded so frightened—I'd never heard him sound frightened. He was always so sure of himself—never scared of anything, which was a lot of his problem. He'd always had his own way and he was charming and good-looking enough to always get his own way. And when he didn't, his father was there, just in case, to see to it that his son never encountered obstacles."

We started walking East toward Columbus Circle, into the chilly night. We were still holding hands.

"What did Elvis want to do with his life? What were his interests?"

A sudden burst of wind tousled her hair. She tossed her head back, clearing her face. "He wanted to be famous. That's all he'd ever known—all he'd ever heard from his parents. I don't think he really knew what he wanted. He's too busy running about, playing with life."

"When he called you that last time, did he say anything else to you, anything that you might have forgotten, that might suggest a person a place… anything?"

"I don't know. With Elvis, it wasn't all about money. I know that. I'd asked him if he needed money and he said he was doing okay. He said he was making money."

"Did he say how?"

"No…" Her voice got bitter. "But I knew it was this Mrs. Johnson who was certainly feeding him money for…" Her voice trailed away. "If you find Mrs. Johnson, you'll surely find Elvis."

I lifted a hand as a cab drifted by.

"Back home?" Darcy asked.

"No. You owe me a song."

She shrank away in embarrassment. "Oh, no!"

I pulled her into the cab and instructed the driver to take us to Moe Black's on 47th between 8th and 9th Avenue.

The taxi drew up to a red brick building, with a black awning and white letters announcing MOE BLACK'S. I paid the driver and we got out, immediately hearing jazz spilling out onto the street.

Darcy looked at the building, apprehensively. "I can't play jazz, Dane."

"Don't worry about it. Just play what you can play."

I pushed open the heavy wooden door and we stepped into the warm breath of heat and the smell of beer and fried food. The music was feverish—high riding patterns of sharp slides, thick chords and drum raps. The bass line thumped. On the small bandstand, a trio pianist, bass player and drummer—were boiling up a brew of raw emotion.

The room was close, with open brick walls, round tables, wooden chairs and dim track lighting. The wooden floor sloped a little and was dull, scratched and worn. Hanging on the walls were framed photographs of some of the jazz "greats:" Art Tatum, Dizzy Gillespie and Bill Evans.

The room was crammed with singles and couples, charged and high on music and booze. A table of young groupies drummed their fingers on the tabletop, ready eyes fixed on the musical men.

The bar was two-deep standing, mostly with men: businessmen, body builders and artists. Two eye-catching black women touched and grinned, nodding to the sounds.

I caught Sean the bartender's eye, and waved. He was busy shaking up a cocktail with one hand and pouring brown booze with the other. He nodded at me.

"Hey there, Dane. Where have you been?"

I indicated toward the room and shouted. "Not bad for a Sunday night!"

I ushered Darcy to the edge of the bar and we elbowed in to meet Sean. When Sean McCord smiles and grabs your hand for a solid shake, you just want to give him money. He had learned long ago that in the booze pouring business it wasn't about cocktail recall; it wasn't about the superior memory or the short-stop quick reflexes or the dancing feet of the professional boxer that counted: it was the smile. It was the welcomed attention that his customers reacted to.

"People come to the bar, Dane, because it's fun," Sean once said. "They want to escape. They want to talk to the bartender about their wife, their job, their shrink, their kids. They want to meet other people and talk. So you smile and you listen and sometimes you pour a little extra.

Then it's all real friendly and they stay longer, laugh a little and maybe when they leave they feel better."

Sean was thin, narrow, graying and well into his 40s. He'd come from Dublin when he was 20 or so. He loved New York and never left.

"Good crowd," I said.

"Not bad."

I introduced him to Darcy.

"Lovely girl," he said, as he bent and kissed Darcy on the cheek.

"Looking for a table, Sean. What do you think?"

He pointed to a table, as a couple arose, edging away. "Grab it, Dane. Come see me before you leave. You want the usual, your Jimmy Boy Beam?"

"On the rocks," I said.

"Champagne for Lady Darcy," he said, smiling gloriously. "On me..."

I pulled a twenty and slapped it into his hand.

We commandeered the two-top and sat. I watched Darcy cock her head and stare at the trio through track light beams. I turned to the musicians and saw their hectic faces, shiny grins and trance-like nods as they played. The crowd was dazzled by their energy.

"They're great!" Darcy said.

The drinks arrived and we settled in. I located Moe near the stage, got up and told him about Darcy. Moe Black is not black. He's white—very white. He's an albino. He's a stocky bald man, who most people think looks like Mr. Clean. I'd known him from my detective years with the NYPD, when he owned a bar near the precinct. Moe said the trio would be breaking soon and Darcy could play anything she wanted.

For the next five minutes, Darcy twisted uncomfortably in her chair, trying to argue her way out of playing. I just kept shaking my head and pointing toward the stage.

Finally the break came. The musicians wandered off the stage and over to the end of the bar. Moe stepped up onto the stage and announced that there was a beautiful guest artist and he wanted everyone's undivided attention. The room fell into curious mumbles. Darcy slowly rose and climbed onto the stage. The chatter ceased when she reached for the microphone.

"I wish I could play jazz, but I can't. I've always admired and loved listening to it, as I have tonight, listening to these great musicians. I'm going to play a piece by Bach. It's *The Second Prelude and Fugue* from *The First Book of the Well Tempered Clavier.*"

After scattered applause, she sat behind the piano, took a staggered breath and began to play. I didn't focus on the music—it was a lot of restless notes. But Darcy shimmered like a diamond under the stage lights and played with strength and assurance. The room gathered into a hush and I gathered that she was good, because the musicians, leaning against the oak bar, nodded to themselves in endorsement.

When she finished, the room erupted in deafening applause. Darcy stood, and with great poise, bowed, then left the stage and returned to her seat.

"I feel shaky," she said, reaching for my whiskey. She drained it, then ordered another. She drank that one too.

We spoke little during the cab ride up town. The world seemed to rush past us and around us, while we sat in stillness, gazing tentatively out the windows. Occasionally, she glanced over and smiled. It was a warming smile. It was a genuine, authentic smile. I liked this woman.

Inside the apartment, Darcy hung up her coat and went directly into the bedroom. She closed the door. I lingered in the kitchen, wiped off the counters that she'd already cleaned earlier, wrapped the garbage and dropped it in the hallway for pick-up in the morning.

I heard her enter the bathroom and close the door. Then, like an afterthought, it reopened. Her head appeared.

"You can use the bedroom. I'll be in here for awhile."

"Righto."

The door closed.

I changed into comfortable khakis and a denim shirt, then relaxed on the couch and lulled my head back. I switched off the lamp and closed my eyes. The bathroom door opened and I heard the bathroom light switch click off. The bedroom lamp clicked on, spilling dim light into the living room. I heard footsteps draw near, then stop. I opened my eyes. Darcy stood before me, in white silk pajamas, top two buttons unfastened, breasts invitingly close. She stood on the cusp of shadow, her hair brushed and perfumed. She parted her lips, eyes studying me.

"It's been so long since I've felt safe," she said. "So damn long. Do you know what I'm trying to say, Dane? Do you?"

I stood. Gave her a long stare, searching her eyes. I leaned and kissed her. The smell of her intoxicated. Her lips were soft, moist, open. I pulled her close. She moved into me gently, allowing her body to sway and press. We touched and explored. I ran a finger down through the shallow cleft between her breasts and she leaned back swaying, as if listening to distant music.

We worked our way to the bedroom, holding hands, tongues licking, stripping, squeezing. I turned off the light. On the bed, she coaxed and reached. She was a gentle lover, nothing rushed, nothing urgent, no other moment. She loved with her breath, hair, nibbling lips and hands. She used the softness of her skin to tease and taunt, her full breasts to tantalize, her slender fingers to trace and grasp. Her voice soothed, then beckoned, then dared.

When she opened, we met in silence and stillness. Utterly still. Waiting. Lips opened, tongues surged and darted. Raw energy began a slow rise. We waited, hearing our breath in the darkness that was alive with quiet. The motionless joining, aroused, drew an inner fire that burned at us both. Skin was hot. We braced, searching eyes, seeing the mounting desire. Heartbeats drummed, lips tightened, muscles tensed.

Gradually, I felt her give way to motion, her body taking over—little moans of joy in my ear. I tangled her hair in my hands, suddenly feeling her magnificent power, the surge of her passion. She grabbed for me, then let go. She rose and fell, found her easy and startling rhythm. I matched her and we sailed. The storm was on us. Bodies slick with sweat. Passion raging. Bodies taut. Then a staggering embrace of flesh, breath and fire.

She shook in spasms of agony and pleasure, calling out in delight, losing control. I went with her into that dangerous-to-trust moment of amnesia.

The night swallowed us. Time released us. We slept, then awoke and loved.

When the first streams of daylight appeared, I awoke and reached for her again. She came with a new longing.

Since it was Monday, I called Helen and told her I'd be a little late. Darcy and I ate breakfast on 85th Street at a French-style Bistro. I left her a little after 9am and took the subway to the office.

I spent most of the day catching up on other cases. I'd often received calls from old friends, or friends of friends, asking me to snoop on their wives or husbands. I nearly always refused, using the excuse of case overload or "That's not really what I do." Most of these kinds of jobs were a no win. Either the client got angry and called me a liar, when I confirmed their worst suspicions, or they refused to pay the bill. Some didn't have the money to begin with and believed I should donate my time and tawdry services for their most worthy charitable cause: keeping home and family together.

So I made a few calls to "friends" and told them I wasn't the guy for them. I recommended another guy, whose agency specializes in covert wireless video surveillance. This other guy and his son work as a team. They can plant video body wire on victims and install video cameras in homes of folk whose spouse is suspected of adultery. This agency also provides the client with a full page computer-enhanced hard copy that they extract from the videotape. This agency demands hefty fees, but they do an excellent job. Most of the time, these "friends" of mine never follow up and contact that other guy and his son.

After lunch, I sat staring down at my legal pad, contemplating my next Elvis move. Helen came in about 3 o'clock and presented me her polished flaming red nails and new springy tight hairdo.

"I spent the 40 bucks I won in the lottery and another 100 bucks that I took from Harvey's savings account. What do you think?" she asked, patting her hair in pride.

She wore a tight, blue woolen dress, with a wide black belt and a high collar. She was also standing in 2-inch heels.

"Do you have a date tonight, Helen?"

"Hell yes. I'm taking myself and a girlfriend to Peter Luger's. Harvey said he was pissed off at me. I said, it's better to be pissed off than pissed on."

"Helen...as an old British girlfriend of mine used to say, you look smashing."

That night, Darcy found a Broadway show that was open. It was lively, entertaining and lacked profundity, which was exactly what we were looking for.

Afterwards, we cabbed home, all hands, lips and heat. We romped in the bed until midnight or so and then ordered a large pizza, eating like starved animals while watching an old Bette Davis movie. Before the movie ended, Darcy fell asleep on the couch, head resting on my lap. I gently brushed her cheek and stroked her hair. She was hypnotically beautiful, and an amazing lover. She had the rare gift of satisfying a man so generously and completely, that addiction and possessiveness just opened the door of the heart and took up residence. I'd hoped I'd done as much for her.

I remember that night, distinctly. After I helped her to bed, I watched her sleep—a dark figure enclosed like a mummy in sheet and blanket, hair scattered about the pillow. Suddenly, I began to sense danger. It was as if dark angry storm clouds rolled in, covering a shiny deep blue sky. My vision seemed to clear. My brain's sputtering engine caught, then growled to life.

I got up and paced, sipping a well-built glass of Jim Beam. I felt unstable and a bit confused. I should have never let Darcy come to New York. What the hell kind of pretend game was I playing? The woman was getting to me.

CHAPTER 9

On Tuesday morning, I stood gazing out of my office window at spotted white clouds, swimming a blue canvas sky. My sister, Ellen, would paint this sky, I thought. Watercolor. She was the artist of the family. She was the gentle saint of the family, married to a nice guy. They have two kids, Jimmy and Danny. Ellen and Darcy would probably hit it off.

Eighth Avenue was awake and moving. A bleating car alarm turned nobody's head as the ambitious and weary filed along the streets, looking resigned to a life sentence of toil and a little fun.

I'd left a sleepy Darcy in my warm, soft bed. She'd offered a willing cheek, placed my hand on her naked breast and tried to coax me back to paradise, but I, like a fool and the son of Mr. Cooper the worker bee extraordinaire, felt the relentless pull of responsibility. I was, after all, the servant of Abner Lipps. I owed him another week, and I wanted to find Elvis and close this case as soon as possible. I wanted Elvis out of the picture and off my mind.

I also wanted Darcy, although, I wasn't quite sure exactly what that meant. I'd spent part of the night fantasizing about the two of us strolling quiet beaches in the

Caribbean, sipping wine in some bamboo hut, under quiet palms, with the rasp of the sea in our ears. The nights were cool, the bed ready, the love-making a never-too-much tangle of play and pleasure. I'd spent the other part of the night wanting Darcy out of my apartment and out of my life.

Dane, Oh Dane-O Boy…no romantic, you! No heart-on-the-sleeve guy are you. No pining for a woman who can drive a stake through your heart when she's been unfaithful, or when she dies, or when she just walks away because the party ended when the real world made its inevitable appearance.

On the subway that went thundering down to 50th Street, I realized I'd fallen into that *Burnin' Love* that the "King", the real Elvis Presley, had sung about so expertly.

"A hunk a hunk a' burnin' love. Ooh…hoo…hoo, I feel my temperature risin'."

I could even see Elvis singing it, in his white rhinestone suit sparkling under the lights; his black raven hair careless over his forehead; his face damp with perspiration; his body writhing and twisting as he manipulated the microphone.

Now, coincidentally, the radio was playing, *"Love Me Tender."* Elvis never sounded so good. I turned to it, puzzled and intrigued.

I sipped coffee, hoping it would help revitalize me. No wonder. After all, I was over 10 years older than Darcy. My body felt like it had gone through a long football practice.

"I'm going to some of the museums today," Darcy had said, just before I left. "I'll call you."

I eventually pulled myself from the window and sat behind my desk. I struggled to focus on the emails I'd thumbed through earlier on my phone, but hadn't focused on. But my mind was pulled toward Rod Faulkner, Darcy's ex-husband. I reached for my yellow legal pad and black marker and I jotted down some notes.

1. Darcy's ex—Rod Faulkner—paper trail, address. Visit?
2. Visit Victor T. Papania at his law firm. His home? He surely knows Mrs. Johnson.
3. Call the doorman at 98½ Riverside Drive.

The coffee was nearly cold. I finished it and decided to go ahead and do a records check on Mr. Faulkner. I launched the site and went to work.

I found the records, leaned forward and studied the monitor.

Ron's marriage application listed him as a physical education teacher. He was 28 years old. Since that was a little over two and a half years ago, that would make him a little over 30.

Court records indicated that Rod Faulkner had been previously married, for only a little over a year. In that marriage, his wife had filed for a restraining order to protect her from domestic violence. She received an injunction banning him from the home. He was also ordered to surrender all firearms and ammunition. In her statement, she said that he owned three guns. They were divorced two months later.

In the nearly 3-year marriage to Darcy, the police were dispatched to the Faulkner home in two separate domestic disputes, involving a husband and wife argument and possible domestic violence. In one instance, Rod threw a chair that had shattered the front picture window of the home. The wife's mouth, Darcy's mouth, was bleeding. She maintained that she'd fallen prior to the argument and hurt herself.

However, based on Rod's past history and current in-cident, Darcy had received a temporary restraining order, prohibiting him from the home until he completed a three month anger management course.

Divorce decree claimed he had a fair income. Prop-erty was split equally, including the home, worth $193,000. He had paid all attorneys' fees. There were no children. The reason for the divorce was listed as irrec-oncilable differences. There was no alimony award.

The recent restraining order, granted to Darcy, was filed by affidavit in November. She returned to court in December for a special hearing to convince the court that the order should continue in the form of a temporary injunction. It was granted.

Since I was in the neighborhood, I decided to check Rod's voter registration records. Since last year was a voting year, they indicated that Rod was now living at 2237 Elmwood Drive, Morrisville, Pennsylvania.

Helen entered the office at some point and told me about her Monday night dinner. She was dressed in loose brown pants and a brown blouse, with swirls of green flowers on it that looked like big claws. "Good steak but expensive," Helen said. "Can't wait to see Harvey's face when he sees his credit card bill."

I lifted my eyes from my laptop monitor. "Helen, have you noticed that the radio seems to be playing more Elvis Presley lately?"

"Of course they are. Don't you read the papers or surf the internet? They've just released a new CD with Elvis' greatest hits, with some new enhanced sound or something."

I nodded, gratefully. "Good. That makes me feel bet-ter."

"How was your weekend?" she asked.

"Uneventful," I said, ducking down behind the laptop.

"You look pale, Dane. Eyes a little swollen, there. Are you getting enough sleep?"

"Oh, sure."

"What's up with Elvis Lipps?"

"I'm going downtown to see a man. He might have some answers."

"That kid has fallen into some big trouble, Dane. You know what I'm sayin'? Good looks, spell good times, spell big trouble."

"Did you make that up, Helen?"

She lifted her bountiful chest in pride. "Yes. And it's based on my own personal experience."

"That's the only kind of experience to have, Helen."

I arrived at 61 Broadway at around 11:30am. The buildings were all tall down there and many Wall Street types and lawyers inhabited the offices. I entered a broad white marble lobby, with art deco features, stopped at the lobby desk and wrote my name down in the guest book. I told the security man I wanted to see Victor T. Papania. He asked for my name and I told him. Elvis Lipps. He called up.

A moment later, the security guard gave me a temporary pass, told me the 11th floor was what I wanted, and pointed me toward the rear bank of elevators.

It was a dashingly elegant elevator, with cherry wood panels and plenty of body room. It elicited confidence and success and probably could rent for six hundred bucks a month if the right real estate agent got ahold of it. Everyone inside seemed contented or bored, I couldn't really tell.

On the 11th floor, I strolled across thick burgundy carpet and found the glass door with the names Green, Wexler and Papania printed on it. I opened the door and made my entrance into the reception area. A thin African American woman of about 25, with short hair and dark eyes of suspicion, looked up at me from behind her circular desk. Before she could speak, a paunchy man with a flush of concern and a saggy round face whipped in from the hallway, adjusting his loose red tie and white shirt. His wary eyes sized me up.

"Can I help you?"

"Are you Mr. Papania?"

"...Yes. Who are you? How did you get up here?"

"I'm Dane Cooper, a private investigator. I'm trying to locate Elvis Lipps and I thought maybe you could help me."

Doubt fell into alarm. He scratched his thinning head. "Was that you who just called saying you were Elvis Lipps?"

"Yes. I was afraid you wouldn't know the name Dane Cooper. I knew you'd know the name Elvis Lipps. I believe he lived in your co-op apartment for about six months. The one on Riverside Drive. Isn't that right?"

"I don't know what you're talking about. You need to leave right now," he said, trying to make his 5'10" body taller. "And I mean, now!"

"Do you know where Elvis is, Mr. Papania?"

"I said you need to leave right now."

"Do you know a Mrs. Johnson?"

His eyes bulged. "Unless you leave this instant, I'm going to have Ruth call security and have you escorted out of the building."

"Mr. Papania, Elvis' parents are very worried about him. If you know where he is, they'd appreciate your telling me."

He turned to the receptionist. "Ruth! Call security!"

She went searching. "I don't know that number."

"Then call the front desk, dammit! Do it! Now!"

Ruth didn't like his bark. Her face registered a class "A" Attitude, with raised eyebrows, tight mouth and rebel eyes.

"Don't bother, Ruth. I'm leaving," I said. "Mr. Papania, please give my best regards to Mrs. Johnson."

He was huffing and puffing and wanted to blow me down. I left.

I stood outside the building with a new roll of Rolos, growing colder by the minute, watching the lunch crowd come and go. At 12:40, Ruth, the receptionist, appeared. I pocketed the remaining chocolate domes and started toward her. She saw me approach and casually buttoned her full-length brown down coat, ignoring me when I stepped up.

"Hi Ruth."

"Are you really a private detective?" she asked, slanting me a look.

"I am. How long have you been working for Green, Wexler and Papania?"

"About two months. I'm a temp, and he gets all official and shit and asks me to call security. What kind of bullshit is that? Like I'm his servant or something."

"Can I walk with you?"

"What do you want?" she asked, sharply, still peeved.

I indicated toward the sidewalk. "Lunch. Possibly some information. I'll pay for it."

"For lunch or for the information?"

"Lunch for sure, the information, if you can give me the right information."

Having a head for business, she jerked a nod and started down the steps. I followed.

The deli had tables and plastic chairs, and Ruth and I found one. It was swarming with the hungry and impatient. The Asian women behind the cash registers had quick hands, focused eyes and no smiles. Ruth bit into a ham and cheese and I, a pastrami on rye, with extra mustard. We both had sodas nearby and pickles.

"Do you eat pickles?" I asked.

"Don't even think about askin' me for my pickle," she said, snappily.

"Some people don't eat them."

"I do eat them!"

"Do you keep a database of names and addresses that you send correspondence to?" I asked.

"Sure. I had to address all of the Christmas cards. Hard copy Christmas cards, not electronic ones. It was a bitch! My hand got all cramped up and sore."

"Did you send a Christmas card to Mrs. Johnson?"

"No. How much money do I get if I give you the right information?"

"That depends on the information. So, you've never heard of a Mrs. Johnson?"

"I didn't say that. I just said I didn't send her a company Christmas card."

I liked her smart-aleck approach. "Have you ever sent her anything—tweets, cards, email, packages, flowers?"

Ruth chewed and nodded. She waited until she swallowed down the bite before she spoke. "He, that is Mr. Papania, sends her flowers. Once a week."

"Really?"

"Really."

"Do you have her full name, address and phone number?"

"Yep."

"How much?"

"What are you going to do with it?" Ruth ask, chewing slowly and avoiding my eyes.

"You messin' with me, Ruth?"

She sipped her soda through a straw. "I don't want to be responsible for somebody catchin' shit who doesn't deserve it."

"I like your ethics, Ruth. Have you ever spoken to Mrs. Johnson?"

"No. What's she to you?"

"My client is a father looking for his lost son. I believe she knows where the son is."

That did it. She licked her lips, and looked at her watch. "Three hundred bucks. That's how much. I'll email you the info."

"That's a lot of pickles, Ruth."

"A hundred to my church; two hundred to school."

"What are you studying?"

"Paralegal."

"I can do a hundred fifty."

"Then I can't do nothin'."

"Two hundred. Max."

"Three hundred!"

"Do you like legal work?"

"I like making money."

"Try accounting."

"Don't like counting numbers. Don't like those people. Don't trust those people. Three hundred or nothing."

I took a bite of my sandwich, knowing full well that I had little choice but to give her what she wanted. Ruth wore a confident face—the face of a victor, who was showing no mercy.

"...All right. One fifty now. I'll give you the rest when I get your email. Use your personal email account and not the company's."

"I want all of the money. Now!" she demanded.

"Nope. It's my way, or no church tax write-off and no scholarship fund," I said.

She snatched her pickle and snapped off the head. "Okay. Gimme the money."

And after lunch, I found an ATM close by and handed off the $150 to Ruth. She promised to email the information within an hour. Before entering the subway, I called Helen to give her a heads-up about the email and to check-in. She told me that Abner Lipps had called—he said it was urgent and that I should call him right away.

I did not want to call him on my cellphone. I found the nearest phone booth, pulled my credit card, that I used exclusively for these kinds of things because my accountant insisted, and punched in Abner's number.

"It's Dane Cooper, Mr. Lipps."

"I've got good news, Mr. Cooper," he said, his voice alive with enthusiasm.

"Has Elvis contacted you?"

"No. But Lucille, my wife, just returned from seeing her psychic. The one she's been going to for years. Now listen to this: Elvis is in Las Vegas, Mr. Cooper. In Las Vegas! He's working on a lounge act there. The reason we haven't been able to find him is because he's using a different name. A different damn name!"

I'd twisted away from the booth, allowing my eyes to lift to the gray sky in a rare but much-needed prayer. I pulled the receiver away from my mouth and mumbled, "Please, give me some personal salvation."

"Did you hear me, Mr. Cooper?! Isn't this good news?!"

"I'm very happy for you, Mr. Lipps. I'll close out your file and send you the bill."

"No, no, no, Mr. Cooper," he said, rapidly. "You misunderstand me! I want you to go to Las Vegas with me. The psychic said there'll be complications."

"Very astute psychic," I said.

"Now I don't know anything about your business, Mr. Cooper. I'll need your experience and expertise in tracking my boy way over there."

"The psychic wasn't able to give you an address or phone number?" I asked, sarcastically. I just couldn't help myself and didn't want to help myself.

I heard the breath of his sigh in the phone. "You don't believe this do you, Mr. Cooper? You don't believe in the occult?"

"Mr. Lipps, I respect your right to believe whatever you want to believe, but I believe you would be much better served finding another private investigator."

"I don't want another private investigator, Mr. Cooper. You're my man! I believe in you—you're trustworthy and honorable—I sense that about you."

"I'm going to be frank, Mr. Lipps. You need to find another investigator."

As I waited for his response, I pulled my handkerchief and wiped my cold nose. Wind rushed and the lowering sky darkened. Snow had been forecasted. Vegas actually sounded good. Absurdity, irrationality and insanity did not.

"Mr. Cooper," Abner said, in a quiet and deliberate voice, "I'll give you a bonus of $25,000 if you stay on this case. I'll go even further than that. If at the end of this week, Friday at 6 p.m., you decide that after all of your investigations, you feel it's fruitless to go on, I'll still pay you $25,000. Now, when you find Elvis, as I know you will, I'll give you another $30,000 bonus. Now how's something like that sound?"

I glanced skyward, then turned back toward the booth, naturally feeling more engaged in the conversation. I let my mind work on it for a moment. "Only on one condition, Mr. Lipps."

"You name any damn condition you want to, Mr. Cooper."

"Unless I learn, in the next day or so, that the leads point me in the direction of Las Vegas, I won't go. I do not believe in psychics and I do not conduct my business based on information coming from them. It would not be fair to the majority of my clients."

"So be it, Mr. Cooper. So damn be it. I'll go to Vegas myself and if I learn anything, I'll call you immediately. Do I need to sign a contract with regard to that bonus, Mr. Cooper?"

"Yes, sir. I'll have my secretary FedEx one to you this afternoon. Please sign it and FedEx it back, ASAP."

"We've got a deal then?"

"Yes, sir."

"I believe in you, Mr. Cooper. I know you'll find my son."

"I'll do my best for you, sir."

As I started down the subway stairs, I glanced at my phone and noticed that Ruth's email had arrived. I memorized it. Ruth had included all the pertinent information.

Her name was Sylvia Carla Johnson. She had a West 84th Street address between Amsterdam and Columbus. I knew that area pretty well: renovated brownstones, noted for style and sophistication.

I called Helen and asked her to draw up the two bonus contracts for Abner Lipps. Helen exploded with happiness. She wanted new kitchen cabinets—she was certain to be in Home Depot before dinner.

If experience was any judge, after I'd left the nervous Mr. Papania, he'd immediately put in a call to Mrs. Johnson, warning her of my imminent contact. Depending on what had happened to Elvis, they were either working on contingency plans and potential ways of handling me, or they were trying to locate Elvis themselves. I figured that Mrs. Johnson was either a wealthy widow, the wife of a wealthy man who seldom found his way home at night, or she was a former lady of the evening, now a high class pimp. Call me jaded, but I had been down this dirty, dusty road before.

Trying to arrange a meeting with Mrs. Johnson would probably be difficult, although worth the try. At the very least, a background record's check might reveal some interesting information about the woman. Surveillance was another possibility, although that would take a lot longer than a week. If I went that route, I could hire someone part-time, as long as Abner Lipps approved the budget.

On the uptown subway, I decided to take a chance and pay Sylvia Johnson a visit. What did I have to lose?

CHAPTER 10

I left the subway at 86th Street and Broadway and started for 84th. I checked my phone for messages, hoping that Darcy had called. She hadn't. I pushed her out of my mind and dialed Sylvia Johnson's phone number. A male voice answered. It was a smooth male voice, breathy and a touch effeminate.

"All About Evenings."

I hesitated, wondering if I'd dialed the correct number. Then it hit me and made perfect sense. "Sylvia Johnson please..."

"And may I ask who's calling?"

Call me a crapshooter, I thought. "Elvis Lipps."

Silence. Then the voice got businesslike. "Please hold..."

Lilting romantic music kept me entertained while I waited. Then it went silent and I was transferred to another line. Two rings.

"Who is this?" a calm, deeply authoritative woman's voice asked.

"Is this Mrs. Johnson?" I asked.

"Who are you and what do you want?"

"My name's Dane Cooper. I'm a private investigator looking for Elvis Lipps. I know that you met him in

126

Knoxville, that he stayed for about six months at Victor T. Papania's apartment on Riverside Drive, and I was wondering if I could speak to you about where he might be."

A long silence. "Are you in New York, Mr. Cooper?" she asked. "Or Tennessee?"

Perhaps Victor had not called her. Why? "I'm about a block away from your apartment, Mrs. Johnson. I presume you are Mrs. Johnson?"

"I can give you ten minutes and only ten minutes."

Mrs. Johnson's brownstone had a beautiful emerald green wrought-iron gate, Victorian style door lamps and an impressive polished oak door. I let myself in through the gate, climbed the stairs and pressed the doorbell. I noticed two moving security cameras. I pushed open the door when I heard the buzzer and entered into a narrow foyer.

A real big white guy, at least two inches taller than my 6'2" frame, stood looking back at me with cool gray eyes. The black hair was short and stiff, the chest, built for defense and battle. The head, neck and shoulders, the assets of an intimidator. The dark suit fit perfectly, the charcoal blue silk shirt was impressive, the black tie shiny. I wondered if he dressed down on Friday.

We stood in a powder-blue-colored foyer that was garnished with plants, flowers and white statues of gods and goddesses. There were paintings of cherubs and daisies and clouds. I could imagine little nymphs and ferries dancing through the adjoining rooms in diaphanous white gowns, while singing some damn song about spring. Golden light from a chandelier made us look nearly angelic or, at least, possible candidates to be touched by an angel.

An impressive mahogany staircase led to the rooms above. Romantic piano music came from there, as if it were calling us to the upper regions of amour.

"I'm here to see Sylvia Johnson," I said.

Without speaking, he came to me.

"You carrying?" His voice was deep and flat.

"No."

He patted me down anyway, from shoulders to shoes. Then he turned and started for the staircase, motioning for me to join him. I did. On the second floor, he led me across deeply rich royal blue carpet to an awaiting white closed door. He knocked lightly.

"Mrs. Johnson... Dane Cooper to see you."

"Let him enter."

The big guy opened the door and I stepped onto a snow white carpet, deep and lush. The walls were rose, white trim baseboards. Above, a chandelier glittered, glowed and looked damn expensive. A Victorian style pleated burgundy couch, with matching love seat and chair, skirted the windows. Rich burgundy draperies matched the couch perfectly. The drapes were drawn. A comfortable fire burned in the rich cherry wood fireplace, enclosed behind little glass doors that were framed in antique brass. Very cozy.

A woman of perhaps 55 or 60 looked me over coolly from behind a glass desk, the one piece of furniture that seemed out of place. On her lap was a white curly pooch, who panted and stared, his little pink tongue darting in and out of his smug pug mouth. She stroked him, absently.

Mrs. Johnson's hair was a muted red, styled lavishly in waves and curls, similar to the styles of those Southern belles down on the Plantation in the old South. Her face was round, white and heavy with makeup. Shocking red lipstick covered thin tight lips.

She wore a deep blue dress, with pleats and flourishes and broad shoulders, taut at her thick waste, conservative at the neck. An impressive diamond choker hid the neck, which surely revealed the sag and rippled flesh of age.

This woman was the once, now older, heroine on the cover of a romance novel. She wasn't unattractive, but the sharp determined eyes and ice queen disposition contradicted the costume of a breathless, demure woman waiting for the bare-chested pirate about to crash through the door, cutlass sword a swingin', pirate ship awaitin'.

The door closed behind me. Powder and perfume nearly smothered. I coughed it away, pleasantly. The pooch stared. Mrs. Johnson stared. I blinked about the room at the paintings. All were oils of last century men, dressed smartly in dark suits or blue or red military uniforms, their gazes distant or aggressive. The antique clock on the mantel ticked away. There were tchotchkes, a miniature crystal unicorn, a collection of amethyst crystals and several ornate Victorian vases. The fire hissed and popped. The oil painting above the fireplace was of the pooch, no tongue out, no heavy panting. I removed my overcoat and took the liberty of draping it over the arm of the heavy oak chair before her desk.

"Who hired you?" she asked.

"Elvis' parents."

"Oh yes," she said, with a knowing nod and stingy smile.

"Do you know them?" I asked.

"Elvis spoke of them."

"Is he around?"

She lowered her eyes. "I wouldn't know."

"Would you know of anyone who might know?"

"You found me through Victor, didn't you?"

"It wasn't difficult, Mrs. Johnson. Elvis' parents gave me the Riverside address."

"You probably frightened poor Victor."

"Is that why the co-op board terminated his contract?" I asked.

"That's his business."

"Why should he be frightened?" I asked.

"He had to go to prison once over some silly stock trading thing a few years ago. He's never been the same."

"You've known him for awhile?"

"We've been friends for a time, yes. We're still friends, sometimes when I say so."

I motioned toward the chair. "Do you mind if I sit?"

She stared, stonily. "There's no need. We've just about concluded our business."

"Nice dog," I said, not really thinking so, but doing my PR thing. The dog actually reminded me of an Assistant D.A. I once had fighting words with. "What's his name?"

She looked at him tenderly. "Alistair."

"Sounds like he got a degree from Oxford."

Then in a whiny baby voice she said, "...Yes, he's so smart and cute. His only job is to keep his lover-girl happy."

I felt a stab of nausea. "Mrs. Johnson... was Elvis working for you?"

"Of course."

"Was he in some kind of trouble?"

Neither she nor the pooch had moved—except for that tongue—it was still in motion. It was distracting.

"The only reason I let you come up here is that I want Elvis back. I invested a lot of time and energy in him. When you find him—if you find him—I want him. I'll pay you, of course, very well. In cash."

"I see…"

"You don't see. He insulted and walked out on a client—one of my best clients—one of my best paying clients. That account alone is worth at least $100,000 a year. I have other clients begging for him. He's costing me thousands. It's unforgivable. He owes me!"

"So you're in the escort business, Mrs. Johnson?"

"You seem like a smart man, Mr. Cooper. I'm sure you've already figured that out."

"It seemed plausible."

"Yes, I'm in the escort business: male escorts, private dancers, models and massage practitioners—all male. I try to stay away from hiring women—they're much too much trouble. But, every once in awhile I get a boy like Elvis. So charming, so likeable, *SOooh* handsome and Oh, *so* much trouble."

"What were the circumstances of Elvis walking out on this client?"

Her voice dropped into reproach. "That's none of your business."

"Where did you meet him?"

"He was playing in some little bar in Knoxville, doing a very mediocre Elvis impersonation act. He had lied to the manager about his age; had said he was 21 years old and had a fake ID. He looked like Elvis, moved somewhat like Elvis, but he didn't have that raw truth and honesty that Elvis had. But he did have the sexual energy that women love and older women will pay handsomely for. I saw that right away. I pulled him off to the side and told him he was just wasting his time. I told him I could help him get into real show business."

I eased down into the chair. She didn't seem to notice. Her words "Some little bar" echoed. I could not picture this woman going to some little bar in Knoxville, Tennessee. She lived and breathed First Class Air, albeit polluted.

"Are you originally from Knoxville?" I asked.

"I grew up in Oak Ridge, not far away."

"Had you been to this bar before?"

I saw a wary flicker in her eyes. "You ask too many questions."

"When you told him what his duties would be, how did he respond?"

Mrs. Johnson stroked Alistair more aggressively. He didn't seem to mind. "Elvis wanted money and connections. I have both, in a variety of businesses. I know many powerful people in the movie and music business. I told him that once he proved himself to me, I would arrange for him to meet the right people."

"So, he came to New York with you?"

"He jumped at my offer. He wanted to get away from his parents and from that hick town. I immediately began working on transforming him into a man. He was very much a boy then. Exciting in a way, but no sophistication in his dress or speech or in the bedroom. Kids today have no class whatsoever. They're mostly vulgar, ignorant and dull. I put him up in the apartment on Riverside Drive, paid for his acting lessons and dance lessons and worked with him on the finer points of love-making. It wasn't easy... he's impatient. Two months later, I sent him out on his first appointment. The woman went mad over him. She was ready to drain her bank account. She raved about him. She wanted him exclusively. I told her that was quite impossible, of course. Every woman I sent him to was crazy for him."

"So he proved himself to you?"

She smiled, darkly. "Oh, yes..."

"Do you personally work with all of your new employees, Mrs. Johnson?"

"Only when I'm moved to do so. I was so moved."

I worked to frame the next question carefully. "Why would he jeopardize such a promising future by insulting a client and disappearing?"

She tilted her head back, smiled briefly, knowingly, her eyes showing an old worldly wisdom. "What else... a girl. A young girl. Sweet 15. "

I let the silence lengthen as I processed this. "You know who she is?"

"Yes. Like I said, Mr. Cooper, I have many connections."

"But you don't know where they are?"

"No..."

"Even with all your connections?"

She eyed me darkly. "No."

"Where did they meet?"

"Las Vegas."

"Las Vegas?" I asked. I thought of Abner and that damn psychic. "When?"

"I don't know for sure. Probably between November the 23rd and November 26th."

"Do you think Elvis is still there?"

"No... But Gina's father is."

"And Gina is the 15 year-old and her father is...?"

"... Is Paul Callo, the Assistant Manager of The Golden Sunset Hotel and Casino. As you may know, Mr. Cooper, the age of consent in Las Vegas is 16. I had some experience with 15-year-old girls and lawyers when I was working in Vegas. You can get prosecuted even if no rape occurred. If convicted, you might get prison time and pay a big fine. They can also put you on lifelong sex offender status. But Paul doesn't care about any of that.

Paul is a very angry, vindictive man. He just wants to take Elvis out because he 'soiled' his little girl."

"Do you know Paul?" I asked.

"Yes. And I've met his daughter, when she was 13 or so. Now she's 15, smart, sexy, ruthlessly rude and rebellious and, unfortunately, the love of her father's life."

I stood. She anticipated my next question.

"Yes, Mr. Cooper. He has hired someone to find them."

"When?"

"A few days after Thanksgiving."

I loosened my tie. "That's a long time ago. Well over a month."

"Paul has built up a lot of rage. Lost a lot of face. He wants Elvis killed. I, for one, don't want that to happen."

"Have you spoken with Mr. Callo?"

"Yes, I did. Years ago, I worked in Vegas. I knew Paul's father, in the biblical sense. Unfortunately, Gina is Paul's only daughter from a very rocky marriage. The divorce was ugly and the wife soaked him. She made his life a living hell. Gina's mother gladly gave her daughter about $30,000 cash to run off with Elvis. The wife hated Paul and, according to Paul, had little affection for Gina."

"Is the ex still alive?"

"Smart boy. Oddly enough, she was the victim of a hit-and-run two weeks later. She's dead. They never found the car or the driver. What a surprise."

"So you pled Elvis' case, but Paul wasn't interested."

She nodded. "When you called, I thought you might be Paul's man. He's been here, before, once, about three weeks ago. A charming man really, if you like killers. Big, broad and brawny, maybe 5'8", 190 pounds, short gray hair, blank, cold blue eyes. Says little. I've seen his type: born predators with eyes like a snake."

"The kids are living on cash?" I asked. "No credit cards, no cellphones, laptops, nothing traceable."

"I can only speculate, but it would seem so. Elvis probably had $10,000 or so that I gave him. I'm sure Gina's mother instructed her daughter on the finer points of hiding and surviving. From what I've been able to learn, Gina's mother was the daughter of a cop."

"Has the father cop investigated this hit-and-run?"

"I heard he's snooping around. But Vegas is... well.. Vegas is full of big boys and big connections and big, big money."

"Do you think the kids left the country?" I asked.

"Maybe… Probably. Maybe not."

"What was Gina's mother's name and where was she from?"

"Sophia. I don't know her last name. She was from Long Island somewhere. Hicksville maybe."

I thought about this. "Those kids are going to need a lot more cash, probably soon. You think Elvis will come to you?"

"Paul seems to think so. They've also been watching and following Elvis' father. You must know, they've also been following you."

I looked sideways and sighed. "Of course," I said, softly, trying to think it all through. I took a few steps forward. "I've never known a kid who inspired so much passion and hate," I said.

"Have you ever met Elvis?"

"No…"

"You might say that Elvis has a genius for attracting the opposite sex, and causing his own sex to want to kill him." She grinned. It was a wicked grin. "He's simply overwhelmingly irresistible."

Mrs. Johnson finally released Alistair from her lap. He hit the floor, waddled over to the fireplace and hunkered down on the blue-tiled hearth.

She stood. She was tall, with a commanding presence. On the desk was a gold cigarette case, undoubtedly antique. She opened it slowly, reached for a cigarette and placed it between her lips. With the gold cigarette lighter nearby, she lit it, blowing the smoke evenly through her lips.

She stared with frosty eyes. "I do want him back, Mr. Cooper. Alive. I like him and I think he's grown rather comfortable with me. I also have big plans for him. I think you should go talk to Paul, see if you can reason with him."

"If you couldn't reason with him, what makes you think I can?"

She reached for a crystal pitcher filled with water. She poured only one glass full. I was thirsty, but she didn't offer. My mother raised me not to ask if not offered. As she drank, she kept her eyes on me.

"He thinks of me as an old silly whore." She shrugged. "You, after all, are a man. Rather large and impressive, although not threateningly so. You're hard around the edges, like a seasoned cop, but I suspect, a little too soft inside at times. You're soft because you took this case. A ridiculous case that no cop in his right mind would have taken."

I tried not to sound defensive. "The money's not bad, and I didn't know about Paul Callo, Gina and the guy with eyes like a snake when I took this case. I also didn't know about you."

She gave me a chilly grin. "I'll pay you well to call me first when you find Elvis."

"You find Elvis that attractive?" I asked, wiping my damp forehead with the back of my hand.

"Let's just say, I want him back, for those cold lonely nights...and for other reasons."

Mrs. Johnson disturbed me. Her presence, expressions, the way she smoked, the slow flutter of her long eyelashes, all suggested the practiced art of selfishness and indulgence. She was a kind of honey-dipped debauched doll in her own honey-dipped debauched dollhouse.

"I already have a client," I said.

She dismissed the suggestion with the flicker of her hand. "That buffoon of a father. That weak, silly mother, who sexually molested him. Give me a break. I can make him a great movie star. Bigger than the real Elvis ever was."

"He'll make you a fortune," I said.

"You bet he will! And I deserve it, because I discovered him."

"When did you last see him?"

"Friday, November 23rd. He left for Las Vegas with the client I told you about. They were supposed to return on Monday evening of the 26th. When my client went to the casinos to gamble, she'd left Elvis in the room, because he was underage. She had a bit of luck and stayed at the blackjack table for six hours. When she returned to the room, Elvis had left. She figured he'd return soon. She waited until morning, then called me. He emailed me that night. He said he had fallen in love and was quitting. That was it. Of course, I immediately called the super where Elvis had the apartment on Riverside Drive and I was told he'd already moved out."

"What day was that?"

"Tuesday, November 27th. He'd flown back on the 25th, gathered his things and moved out."

"What does Gina look like?"

"She was a blond the last time I saw her. She's thin, cheaply sexy. No great beauty. Why he's throwing his life away on that nothing of a bitch is beyond me."

"Do you know a man named Buddy Blue?"

"Yes. He's been with me for four years."

"He's an escort?"

"Yes..."

She seemed on the verge of adding something else. She smoked quietly for a moment. "Buddy Blue used to be my favorite..."

I stared coolly. Mrs. Johnson didn't have to say anything else. "...Until Elvis came on the scene. He's jealous?"

"Insanely. He tried to run Elvis over once."

I watched the smoke from her cigarette rise and curl toward the ceiling. "Where is Buddy, now?"

"In Martinique, with a client. He'll be back tonight."

"I'll need his address and phone number."

"No."

"He may know where Elvis is."

"He would have told me. I've told him to leave Elvis alone."

"Do you think he'll listen?"

She hesitated, patting at her curls, going for a coquette look of 18. She failed. "Well, he is quite attached to me. I can't seem to control his obsession."

She took a piece of paper from the desk, and with a gold and ivory pen, scratched down the information. When she handed it to me, I saw an easy vanity in her eyes. They seemed to say, "It's such a burden to be the object of such an unmanageable desire, but I'll have to bear it somehow."

"Is Elvis friends with any other of your escorts, someone he might have confided in?"

"No… I keep them apart, for just this reason. Buddy happened to find out because… well, because Buddy and I are close."

"What about clients? Would he go to them for money?"

From her expression, I could see that the thought had occurred to her.

She began twisting her hands. "No…no, he wouldn't do that," she said, trying to convince yourself.

"I'd like to contact them. Just to make sure."

"Absolutely not! That's a stupid thing to ask. Many are married. If I betrayed their trust and secrecy I'd be out of business in a week. The media would finish me. Surely you have the brains to realize that."

I sunk my hands into my pockets. "Would they call you if he contacted them directly?"

Sylvia Johnson's face twisted into irritation. She turned from me and crushed out her cigarette. "Of course!"

"If I was Elvis, that's what I would do."

She whirled to face me, jaw rigid, eyes burning. "He won't do that, I tell you! Now just shut up about it! Whatever Elvis' father is paying you, I'll increase it by $10,000. Just make sure you call me first."

"Like I said, Mrs. Johnson, I already have a client."

"Then you're incredibly stupid, Mr. Cooper. If you manage to find Elvis before Paul's man does, my men will be all over you."

The silence was charged and threatening. This was an idle threat. She was a small time whore, puffed in self-importance. She was not the player she thought she was.

I leveled my eyes on her. "Yes, ma'am. I may point out that if your men are anywhere around when Paul's man finds Elvis... well, it might look as if you're meddling where you shouldn't be meddling. I suspect Paul wouldn't like it. And if you find Elvis first, how are you going to hide him or explain it to Paul? I suspect he wouldn't be happy about that either."

She glowered at me. "That's why I'm counting on you to change Paul's mind."

I grinned a little sideways grin and I added an arch of my right eyebrow. "Didn't you just say that this was a ridiculous case that no cop in his right mind would have taken? Are you changing your opinion of me, Mrs. Johnson?"

"I'm finding you tiresome, Mr. Cooper."

"Do you have Paul Callo's contact information?" I asked.

She scribbled it down and handed it to me.

I went for my coat. After I slid into it, I started for the door. I turned. "If Elvis contacts you, will you contact me, Mrs. Johnson?"

She barked out a mirthless laugh. "Paul has a great advantage over you, Mr. Cooper. He knows Gina's background, friends and places she might hide."

"All true... Your point being?"

"You'd better hurry. You'd better go see Paul right away."

"The kids need cash, Mrs. Johnson. Who will they go to, to get it? That's the question."

She crossed her arms, as her eyes slid away from me.

I opened the door and left.

Outside, flurries fell, drifting and blowing, with no ac-cumulation. I walked down Broadway, and pulled an uneasy breath. I looked about to see if anyone was lingering in a doorway, near a tree, behind a car. Nothing obvious.

So now it was a different kind of case: find Elvis, then keep him alive. I didn't like it. Paul's man was a professional killer. I wouldn't have given this case a second thought if I'd known all the facts. But then, isn't every case like this? You never know what the hell's around the next corner; where the ghosts are lurking; who the real bad guys are?

I'd have to call Abner and let him know. But first, I'd have to decide if I was going to drop the whole thing. The chances of me finding Elvis alive had diminished considerably. Even if I found him, the chances of me keeping him alive were slim, unless I could convince Paul Callo to drop the hit, or somehow pay him off.

I pulled my phone and checked messages. Nothing from Darcy and it was nearly four o'clock! My stomach turned sour. I tossed a Rolo in my mouth.

CHAPTER 11

Back at the office, I called Darcy every 15 minutes. She didn't answer. I texted her. I left messages. Oh, how the restless mind loves to spin out stories of intrigue, betrayal and tragedy, when jealousy titillates. It becomes an enemy of the body, a wicked little image-maker projecting lurid, grainy previews upon the screen of the mind. I wrestled them away, but they skittered back on rat's feet.

Maybe Darcy's mind had snapped and she was wandering the streets of New York, lost and bewildered. Maybe the cops had found her, examined her wallet and cellphone, found her Tennessee address, called and didn't receive an answer. They'd call every person in her contact list—surely I was listed. Surely?

But maybe she hadn't snapped at all. Maybe she'd had Elvis' cell number all along, written on her favorite pink paper, neatly folded and tucked away in some hidden pocket in her purse, and she'd called him.

Yes! There they are, Elvis and Darcy in the thick of the night, stealing down a dark alley, arm in arm, passing a seedy bar where a blue neon babe, with curves, shimmies. As they move on toward a dark hotel, their guilty faces are caught in the harsh glare of a streetlight, and they turn to make sure they're not being followed. They're trapped in that world where people smile and deceive, where bleak, tarnished souls struggle to survive their own worst traits and motivations, knowing full well that they'll fail and fall from grace. So, they dart inside for a quick shot of whiskey and some desperate moments of quivering passion.

Perhaps they were meeting at his very moment, having splendid sex, not in a seedy hotel, but in a first class hotel, where champagne and a fruit basket were delivered by a surly little bell hop with a lusty eye.

Darcy and Elvis. Teacher and former student. A talented and creative teacher, who inspires prolonged and frequent lovemaking. Elvis Lipps, who seems more like the reincarnation of Don Juan than Elvis Presley.

Thankfully, Helen stuck her head into my office and shut down the endless stream of stampeding images. "You okay?" she asked, narrowing her eyes. "Your eyes look funny—like two gun barrels about to fire bullets."

"Have you ever been jealous, Helen?"

She scratched her head and thought about it. "Yes... twice. Once, right after I was married, Harvey and me ran into his old high school sweetheart. I saw the hotness in his eyes while they talked. As soon as we got home, I jumped him."

"You jumped Harvey?" I asked.

"Yeah, you know..." she said, winking, "let him know he was all mine. Worked him over real good. Then, about ten years later, he had a fling with some bimbo where he worked."

"You knew about it?"

"Of course. He worked the press for awhile and then she worked on him, in quality-control. It got back to me."

I leaned forward and folded my hands on the desk. "What did you do?"

"I went to see her. Told her if she didn't leave him alone, I'd kick her little fat ass. About a week later, she was fired for stealing. It almost ruined our marriage, but I didn't let it."

"Did you ever talk to Harvey about it?"

"Never... but he knew that I knew, and he never messed around again..." She looked around suspiciously. "At least, as far as I know."

"Did you need to see me about something?" I asked.

"Kitchen cabinets: What do you think? Red Oak, Maple or Hickory?"

"Not a clue. Not my specialty. What's Harvey say?"

"Red Oak."

"So?"

"So I don't like Red Oak. Harvey's always had bad taste—except for me, of course."

"Go with the Maple. You can't go wrong with Maple. Maple leaves... Maple Syrup. The word has nice word associations."

Helen shook her head and walked away.

I doodled on my legal pad, while I considered the possibilities. I was greatly surprised that Elvis and Gina had lasted this long. Over a month! How did they get out of Vegas without leaving some trace? Did Gina know of her mother's death? Surely Paul and the killer had been at the funeral, just in case she'd shown up. Did Gina know how dangerous her father was? Most certainly. Who had helped them or was helping them? An old friend of her mother's?

I pondered another possibility: that Rod Faulkner had been tailing Elvis for some time. He lived close by, in Pennsylvania—probably no more than a 45-minute train ride into the city. It was conceivable that if anyone knew where Elvis was, Rod Faulkner did. That's assuming, of course, that he really meant what he said when he told both Darcy and Elvis that he would kill them.

I had to consider another possibility that I had already considered: that they were both dead, by accident or design. So far, the last contact anyone had with Elvis was Darcy, on December 12th. No word, no trace since then. Nothing at Christmas, New Year's, his birthday and his mother's birthday. The contract on him was unsuccessful, which meant that Gina had not been in touch with any of her friends or family. No credit listings, no calls, no sightings. I had to at least entertain the possibility that Rod Faulkner had found Elvis and carried out his threat. Had he killed Gina too?

As to Vegas, Paul and the contract on Elvis, the more I considered it, the more I saw the near impossibility of trying to convince Paul to cancel it. He'd already killed his ex-wife. He was pissed off, probably had never gotten in touch with his inner teddy bear, and didn't sound like the type who was particularly interested in doing so. He only wanted revenge. He wouldn't care about money, so the only card I could play was why he shouldn't kill Elvis: "Your daughter will hate you for it." He probably had enough skill to trump it with the card, "She's 15. She'll get over it."

I pulled Abner's file, reached for my cellphone and called him. It was time to drop this case. After the third ring, I hung up and leaned back in my chair. What about Darcy? If I left the case, what would she do? Had I gotten personally involved?

On second thought, maybe a trip to Vegas wouldn't hurt. There was an off-chance that I could convince Paul to drop the hit. I might even learn something that would tip the game in my favor.

After I left Sylvia Johnson, she'd probably reached for the phone and called every female client she had and, in her own charming and clandestine way, was frantically trying to learn whether Elvis had been in touch with any of them. If he had, she had big problems, business and personal. Either way, I'd know nothing about it. She'd use her own people. But, if she located Elvis, the challenge would be finding a creative and practical hideout for him. That could prove deadly for her. Paul would probably kill her if he learned the truth and, of course, he would learn the truth, since she wanted to make Elvis a movie star. I didn't believe she was so attached to Elvis that she would risk her life for him. And again, I didn't believe she had people out looking for him. But, then, I didn't want to underestimate the power of Elvis over women or an old whore's desperate vanity. And maybe Sylvia had another trick up her very pleated, doll-baby dress.

Buddy Blue? Who knows? I'd find out tomorrow morning.

I'd call Abner in the morning.

It was 6:35 when I arrived back at my apartment. I'm not really sure what I expected when I opened the door: a dark, empty apartment, for sure; a note from Darcy saying she'd left for home or for Europe was a possibility. I wouldn't have been surprised to find a note that said she'd contacted Elvis and had run off to meet him.

Reality was different. Those demonic little pictures produced and directed by my corrupt mind could never have captured what I saw standing before me in the middle of my living room. Darcy, grinning, glowing, gorgeous and grand. There were probably better words to describe her, but right then I didn't care about trying to find them. I just wanted to take her in. She wore a short golden dress, with skinny shoulder straps and a plunging neckline. It exalted her legs, promoted her splendid figure. The thin gold necklace dazzled, and the 3-inch emerald green satin heels gave her the startling sexy stature of a "Bond Girl." Her hair was stylishly teased and it glittered under the light. I hardly noticed that she was surrounded by shopping bags.

Her grin was wonderfully wicked. "What do you think, Mr. Private Detective?"

"I think I should be hitting the museums more often."

She giggled. "I didn't make it to a single museum. I tried the Met, but it was packed with crowds and tourists, so I wound up shopping all-day. I got so possessed that... Oh, I finally got your messages."

"Why didn't you call?" I asked, trying not to sound irritated.

"Oh, I forgot to take my phone. I'm so disoriented. I was lost without it, but then I thought, no, I'm not going back. It's good that I forgot it. I'm glad I don't have the damn thing. I felt free and released. I just wanted to have fun and forget everything—and I did."

I managed a tight smile. I still didn't trust her. Hell, I didn't trust myself. I fought off a barrage of frustration. I wanted to dump this idiotic case and get back to my normal, insane life. At least I'd know where I was, who I was and what the hell was going on. I felt twisted and dulled by doubt, jealousy and disorder.

Darcy gently kicked the shopping bags aside, sashayed over and wrapped her arms around my neck.

"So, where are you taking me tonight?"

"How about to the bedroom?"

She kissed my nose "That's a given. But I'm hungry."

"I know a great diner."

"I love New York diners!"

"That was a joke. The Greek waiters would kick me out the back door, feed you baklava and wine and make you dance the Kalymniko."

"The what?"

"They dance it at weddings on Kalymnos. The bride dances it."

"How do you know that?"

"You learn a lot as a homicide detective in the NYPD. One of the detectives was Greek. We went to his wedding and he made us dance and memorize the name of the dance. He said it would impress the pretty Greek girls."

She gave me a reproachful look. "And did it impress the pretty Greek girls?"

"Well, let me put it this way. I ate a lot of Greek salads for a while."

She moved in close and we kissed long and deep.

I took her to the Arte Café on 73rd between Amsterdam in Columbus. It's drenched in Italian atmosphere, with salmon colored walls, visible stylish wine racks, a fireplace and a lively neighborhood clientele. I did my best to make sure the Italian hostess gave us a table where Darcy would be as visible as possible. Call me ostentatious Cooper. Heads turned when I helped her out of her coat. At the table, I held her chair and she sat with a girlish elegance. A waiter spotted her, and like a bird dog after a duck, he scampered over with happy eyes and an eager manner. He leaned in close to Darcy's magnetic aura and declared the specialties, slowly and distinctly, as if each word to her was a declaration of his undying loyalty and love. One thing you can say about New York waiters: they all have their own distinctive style.

When the red wine was poured into those magnificent voluptuous wineglasses, Darcy proposed a toast to the Metropolitan Museum of Art. I allowed my eyes to roam her dress and all that was inside, then nodded firmly. We joined glasses and took a long delicious drink.

During dinner, our conversation was on shopping, eccentric family members and what it was like for me growing up in Brooklyn.

After dinner, we nibbled on fresh biscotti and lingered over coffee. After she drained her coffee and laid the cup aside, Darcy grew quiet and reflective.

"You want to know how the investigation is going, don't you?"

She shook her head. "No... yes. Of course. I'm curious."

"I'm not going to talk about it."

I turned toward the fireplace. It glowed and comforted. The restaurant had emptied some and was only about half full. The conversations fell into murmurs. Waiters moved at an easy pace.

"I guess I'll go back home tomorrow," she said, quietly.

"Why?"

"I said I'd only stay a couple of days."

"Do you want to go?" I asked.

She stared into my eyes. "No...I feel safe with you. I can trust you." She paused. Her eyes widened in emphasis. "I *can* trust you, can't I?"

"You can. If you're honest with me."

"I'll have to go eventually," she said.

"And start your new life?"

She turned thoughtful. "Something like that."

"And what does that life look like?" I asked.

"Oh, I don't know. What about you? What does your life look like?"

"We were talking about you."

Darcy gave me a cagey glance and a demure smile. "Maybe we should talk about us."

Once again, she'd surprised me. "When this is over, we'll talk about us, " I said. "We have no reality until this is finished. It's all been fast and it's all been make believe."

Her smile faded. "That means you're not interested or you don't trust me."

I leaned forward. "It means that you've been through a lot in the last few months. You need time to put yourself back together. It means, I'm not sure how this is all going to end and what will happen when it's all over."

"What does it mean, when it's all over? When you find Elvis? Will that really change anything? When I leave and return to Knoxville? Will it all be over then? When I pack all my things and leave for someplace out west. Is that when it will all be over?"

I eased back in the chair, nudging my coffee cup aside. "What do you want, Darcy?"

"I don't know what I want!" she said, sharply, looking away. Then, after a moment, she faced me. "I want a normal life again. I want to feel good about myself again. I want the past to go away."

"It never will go away. It's part of you. But you can give it a nod, look at it square in the face and say 'I'm a big girl. I can deal with it' and then move on. But you need more time."

"Is that what you did when your wife was killed in that car accident?"

That made me feel mean, but I held it in, remaining silent.

Darcy slumped deeply in her chair. She shut her eyes. "I'm sorry. I shouldn't have said that. I'm just not myself anymore."

When her eyes opened, I was taking a long, final swallow of coffee. I stared down into the cup's empty bottom. "It was a fair question, Darcy. I look it square in the face everyday. I curse fate and I've been known to feel very sorry for myself from time to time. Have I moved on?" I shrugged. "It's a work in progress."

She considered my answer, then stood and started for the entrance. I hailed the waiter and paid the check. I saw Darcy retrieve her coat, slip it on and leave the restaurant.

I joined her outside a few moments later. She was smoking.

"I haven't had a cigarette in almost two days. It's such a stupid, filthy habit."

"Relax. There are many worse habits. Let's walk."

We started west toward Amsterdam. The air was cold, but still. Streetlights glowed in a foggy haze, making bizarre shadows. I listened to our footsteps as they scratched along the sidewalk.

"I used to think I was a strong person, Dane. All of my friends thought I was as solid as a rock—not a saint or anything—but certainly not reckless or destructive."

"You've got to stop this beating up on yourself."

"I'm trying... I should call my parents and let them know where I am and how I am, but I just can't seem to get up the energy. They're going to ask me who I'm with and what I'm doing."

"So tell them who you're with and what you're doing."

"I don't know what I'm doing."

As I listened to Darcy, I sensed again that we were being followed; that odd little tickle of nerves in the pit of my stomach. Before we'd entered the restaurant, I'd noticed a man across the street gazing up at a brownstone, as if searching for an address. I'd taken a mental photograph. He wasn't a big man, maybe 5'7" to 5'9". He wore a baseball cap, pinched at the bill, and a long black woolen overcoat with the collar turned up. Maybe it was Paul's man. Maybe Mrs. Johnson's?

I purposely dropped a quarter on the ground. When I leaned to pick it up, I glanced right and saw the same man edging in and out of the shadows across the street, about 20 feet behind us. This guy wasn't a pro. He was a clown. Probably Johnson's clown.

At Amsterdam I lifted my hand. The taxi approached and stopped. We climbed in and shot away from the curb. I glimpsed a look over my shoulder. Clown emerged, hands on hips.

The love making that night was unpredictable. Darcy immediately took charge, barely giving me enough time to take off my coat. There was a seriousness and confidence about her, as she pulled me toward her, removing clothes, but not her dress.

Her touch was firmer, her kisses hard and wet. She mounted me and soon fell into that easy rhythm that I'd nearly grown addicted to. Her eyes examined me coolly, her mouth parted. She called to me in low, intimate whispers.

She refused to give way to her rising desire, though I could feel her body shivering, beginning to erupt. Felt my own surge. She fought it, as if trying to tame or control it, whipping her head about, breath coming fast. She persisted, twisting, ramping, grabbing. But passion finally won out. She burst into a delightful chaos, losing herself completely, wonderfully.

Later, she sank into my arms and buried her head into my chest. I covered her with a sheet, held her and she slept. I heard the distant sounds of the city and wondered if I could ever leave New York City and move to the west or live anywhere else.

I couldn't walk away from the case. Not now. Call it honor or call it stupidity. I wanted to control it. I wanted to pin it to the ground like a triumphant wrestler. I wanted it to be over. Maybe then, Darcy and I could decide if a long term relationship was possible.

CHAPTER 12

On Wednesday morning, the 20th, I left Darcy sleeping—a beautiful form of tangled hair, milky skin and pouty pink lips. Her new dress lay crumbled on the floor, like an exhausted thing. But the gold stirred up sizzling memories of a job well done the night before. My eyes wandered back to her. The early light seemed proud to rest with her—proud to define her body and touch her skin.

How the hell do you describe love? What is it? Where does it come from? Can you really trust it? Is it love or lust or both or neither and no one has yet found the right words to define it? You can't see it, touch it, take a picture of it. It defies logic. There's nothing to investigate because it is as invisible as the air. And yet, like the air, we humans need it to survive. Need it and go searching for it. Need it and find joy in it. Need it and will die for it. Need it and will kill themselves over it. Need it and will kill someone else for it. Is all that love?

I gave up trying to figure it out, even with Connie. It was just there, I accepted it. I lived with it and liked it. I could easily say and often did say, "I love you," but I was never comfortable with the fact that I could only touch her; that I could only make love to her, but I could never prove what that love was or locate the source of it.

One thing I knew for sure. Darcy-Lynn was seductive, sexy and beautiful. Men like those things in a woman. They get vulnerable and confused by them, but they like them. They get possessive and jealous when someone else moves in. They miss the experience of closeness, the trust, the delightful sex. They want to own. Men kill and destroy over such things. But then, so do women. Not politically correct, but a lot of men and women aren't political and very often, in the secret regions of the heart, not correct. I'm not. Is that love?

I left Darcy a note on the kitchen table to call me as soon as she woke up. I wanted to know what she planned on doing for the day.

I was at the office by 8:15, pounding through the emails and looking over some of the invoices that Helen had dropped off.

My eyes kept stealing toward Abner's file, toward the phone.

By the time I finished my sesame bagel with cream cheese and coffee, Helen came in bearing catalogs filled with photographs of kitchen cabinets. She forced me to choose at least three preferences, and circle them with a black magic marker, before she allowed me out the door to my first appointment: Buddy Blue.

Buddy had a West Village apartment on Waverly. It was an easy walk from the number 9 train, and since it was a day with abundant sunshine, I even caught myself whistling *The Unchained Melody* as I strolled along. I couldn't remember whether Elvis had ever recorded the song or not, but I knew The Righteous Brothers had, because my mother loved The Righteous Brothers and she loved the movie *Ghost.*

Buddy Blue's building was a quaint red brick, adjoining other quaint little red bricks that had heavy wrought-iron fences and gates. I found a white buzzer next to the name BLUE and pressed. As I waited, I turned left to see a man approach the building, plastic shopping bag dangling from his right hand, staring at me quizzically. His loosely cut hair was sandy-colored, his complexion, sandy, his jacket, kind of sandy colored. He reminded me of a sandy beach guy. When he stepped up, he took off his blue tinted sunglasses and I saw the Blue—in his eyes. He was about six feet, maybe 32 to 36, a tanned confident face, athletic body and a cool-dog suavity.

"You must be Buddy Blue," I said.

He squinted at me. "I might be."

"I'm Dane Cooper, a private investigator. I was hoping I could talk to you a few minutes about Elvis Lipps."

He didn't move. "You must be shittin' me."

I detected a slight southern accent, something he probably used for effect. "I'm not."

He shook his head. "His Daddy hire you?"

"Yep."

"You surely know Elvis is in deep shit."

"What can you tell me about it?" I asked, leaning back against the wrought-iron railing, trying for a relaxed pose.

"In Vegas he started banging some Mafioso's 15-year daughter, then ran off with her. The Papa's gonna find them and shoot Elvis. I say, go Papa."

"You don't like Elvis?"

"No… I don't."

"Why?"

"He thinks he owns the world and everything in it."

"I hear you tried to run him over once."

He laughed. "You must have talked to Mrs. Johnson."
"I did."
"Yeah, I tried to scare him. I did, too."
"Do you have any idea where Elvis might have gone?"
He thought for a minute. "I talked to that hit man, you know. He came to Mrs. Johnson's when I was there. That's what you call them isn't it? Hit man?"
"Among other things. Did he ask you the same question? Where Elvis might have gone?"
"Yeah."
"What did you tell him?"
"I told him he probably went home to Momma."
"But you don't believe that, do you?"
He paused, setting the plastic bag on the first step of three. "No. He may have contacted his old teacher."
I pushed away from the railing, alert. "Old teacher?"
"Well, she's not old—she's in her 20's. Elvis used to always talk about this music teacher he had back in Tennessee. He was really gone on her. Said she was the sexiest woman he ever knew. She came up to see him some weekend back in November, I think. They shacked up for like two days or something. After she left, he was sick about it. Wandered around like some puppy. He said she was the only woman he really wanted. He said he could trust her. Said she'd do anything for him and he'd do anything for her. So, what I figure, is that if you find this teacher, she's gonna know where Elvis is."
I tried for a blank expression, but inside, I felt an inferno of jealousy. It was hell. It was hot. I suddenly hated everybody. "Did you tell all this to the hit man?" I asked.
"No. I didn't like the way he'd scared Mrs. Johnson. He's a cold looking son of a bitch. But, I guess that's pretty much what you'd expect from somebody like that."

I nodded. "When Elvis was working, did he have a favorite client that he may have told you about?"

He watched me, carefully. I noticed that the morning haze was beginning to thicken.

"I think you're asking me if Elvis is stupid enough to go directly to a client and not tell Mrs. Johnson about it. Yes. He's stupid because of his arrogance. It's nothing new. It's happened before, you know. One guy who did that wound up in the hospital for a week."

"Who would Elvis go to?"

Buddy smiled, sliding his sunglasses up on top of his head, into the thick sandy hair. They glinted in the sunlight.

"If I knew that, I'd tell Mrs. Johnson. Let me tell you where I think he is. Makin' porn flicks."

"And you know that because…"

"I introduced him to a guy back in November. He was going to pay Elvis good money, but Elvis said no way, he'd never do it."

I shifted my weight to my right foot. "But now you think he is making porn flicks. What do you think changed his mind?"

"Obviously, Elvis needs cash. I don't really think he's stupid enough to go to one of his old clients. He knows he'd get nailed. I think he'd do the flicks first."

"Have you spoken to your old buddy about it?"

"Yeah. I called him twice, about two weeks ago and left a message. He never called me back though. Then I left for Toronto and Martinique."

"Where does this guy make the films?"

"In and around New York. He moves around a lot."

"Have you told Mrs. Johnson about your thoughts?"

"No, I didn't know for sure. And why upset her?"

"And you didn't tell the hit man?"

Buddy put his hands in his jacket pocket and watched as a shiny red Corvette crept by and turned the corner. "No. I spoke to that guy over three weeks ago. I hadn't thought about it until about two weeks ago."

"You hate Elvis that much?"

"Let me put it this way. I don't like what he's done to Mrs. Johnson."

"And that is?"

He turned angry, yanking his hands from his jacket pockets. The words exploded from his mouth. "She's all fucked up over him, okay!? I was number one! Number one! I've waited on her and kissed her ass. I've taken every silly little client—even those slobbering, drunk old bitches who whine and strip and want you to kiss their wrinkled, fat asses while you tell them how beautiful they are! I'm 35 years old and I'm sick of that shit!" He caught himself, regained his composure and lowered his voice.

"She promised me a partnership. She was going to pull back and let me take over some of the business. She promised me... until Elvis showed up. Now she says, she's thinking about it. Bullshit! She's thinking about Elvis and only Elvis! She'll give it to him! I over-heard her say so."

He adjusted the collar on his coat. "If I could kill him and get away with it, I would. But I don't have to. That's the hit man's job, right? You don't have a chance finding him alive."

He snatched the plastic bag, brushed by me and started for the front door, key poised and ready for a lock.

I said, "Since I don't have a chance, can you give me the number of your guy who does the porn flicks?"

Buddy faced me. He smiled, but I saw the rancid malice in his eyes. "Hey, why not? It makes it more interesting."

He dictated and I wrote it all down. His name was Donovan Lassiter. His studio was on 11th Avenue and 32nd Street.

About a block from the Christopher Street subway, my phone rang. It was Darcy's sleepy voice. She was definitely going to the museums today, she said. No more shopping.

My voice must have sounded remote, when I told her my day was going well enough.

"Is anything wrong?" she asked.

"No... I may have to go to Vegas tonight or tomorrow. I'll let you know by this afternoon."

"... Is it because of Elvis?"

"No, unrelated. Different case."

"How long?"

"Not sure."

"You sound funny. You sure nothing's wrong?" she asked.

"You should come with me, if I go, that is."

Her voice sounded awkwardly happy. "...I'm ...glad you asked... I'm already packed, since I haven't unpacked."

"You'll bring the golden dress?"

"I'm afraid it got ripped. I'll buy another."

I said I'd see her around seven o'clock and hung up.

Before getting on the subway, I called Donovan Lassiter, the name Buddy Blue had given me. His phone had been disconnected. There was no forwarding number. Buddy didn't have Donovan's address. I called

Helen and asked her to run his name through records. I asked her to run Paul Callo's name as well. I needed some leverage with Paul Callo. I needed to know his past, who he worked for and where he came from. I needed something I could use that might loosen his grip on Elvis.

I left the subway at 50th Street and Broadway and walked West to 49th Street to the car rental. Thirty minutes later, I was driving my silver Skylark to Morrisville, Pennsylvania under a partly cloudy sky. If I'd read the map correctly it would take me about an hour and 15 minutes, depending on traffic.

On I-95 South, moving through a steady flow of cars, tour busses and thundering trucks, I stared at the moving pavement, entranced by the blurring white lines, marking time, place and speed. I allowed myself the luxury of remembering last night's frolic, complete with the shared bottle of Beck's Beer and the bag of stale pretzels. Darcy and I had finally tumbled off to bed at five o'clock in the morning.

Relationships, marriages and close friendships are based on such events. Bare feet on the cold kitchen floor, desperately searching the cupboards for snacks; munching the snacks with beer or wine and listening to music and to the intimate quiet of early morning. And you are so very content in that quiet, wishing it would last forever, seeing the same wish in the other's eyes. Then strawberry dawn spreads across the sky and awakens you like an alarm. You take your lover to bed, to love, to sleep and all seems rosy and right with the world. And as you drift off to sleep, you ponder how you can hold on to the magic and keep it contained and pure in that delicate champagne bubble, keenly aware that the moment is exceptional, and in its own way, holy.

I stubbornly pushed those thoughts aside and wondered if Rod Faulkner still had such thoughts and memories about his ex-wife. About Darcy. I was curious to know what he would say about her, and, of course, what he would say about Elvis. Would the jealous fire still be there, burning away in his eyes? Would the wounds of betrayal still show on his face, and in the gnarled constriction of his body language? Would he stand before me—jealousy and anger incarnate?

I found a cozy little restaurant just inside Morrisville. I ordered a Swiss cheese on rye with lettuce and tomato, a chocolate milkshake and extra coleslaw. The waitress told me the local high school got out at three o'clock. By the time I finished my lunch, it was after two. I decided to bypass the high school and drive straight to Rod's house.

I found the house easily, in the middle of a quiet tree-lined street, where modest 2-3 story homes had been aluminum tiled white, light blue or gray. The lawns were little plots that sloped down from porches to uneven front sidewalks.

Rod's was the light blue, with an empty narrow driveway and comfortable porch, complete with a porch swing. I saw a two-car garage in the rear.

I parked across the street, settled down in the seat and took in the area. All was quiet. Parents at work, children in daycare or school. It was 2:30. All of that would change in a half hour or so.

I studied Rod's house. I decided to go in.

CHAPTER 13

I climbed out of the car and glanced about casually. Amazingly, no one was about. Not a dog, cat or squirrel. It must have been siesta time for the entire animal/human neighborhood. I was happy about that. The sun was covered by a fat gray cloud and there was a bite to the wind. I crossed the street, with an easy deliberate stride, using the driveway to get to the back of the house.

I climbed the five back cement stairs to the screen door, then did another quick neighborhood check to make sure no one was calling 911 or peeping from some window, binoculars in hand, or worse, framing me in the cross hairs of a rifle. Dramatic, yes, but you think about such things in this day and age when you're breaking and entering and when everything is so unnaturally quiet.

Then a dog barked, but it was coming from across the narrow canal, where little houses lay nestled behind bare branched trees. I quickly slipped on some latex gloves.

I pulled my black leather case that held my key picks and opened the screen door. I quickly studied the silver lock, midway up the white wooden door. I used a technique known as scrubbing. I'd learned it from an old private investigator, also a former NYPD cop, who'd had an office up in the Bronx for 20 years.

I inserted the pick, hoping I wouldn't have to concentrate on individual pins. I focused on two pins during the first stroke of the pick. I tried again. It took several strokes until I found the correct torque and pressure. I felt the release. I was in!

I entered into the kitchen and gently closed the door behind me, passing one last backward glance to make sure I wasn't being watched.

I recognized the kitchen of a bachelor. A microwave, coffeemaker, dirty dishes in the sink, but not piled high. No curtains over the windows. I saw specks of dust spinning lazily in the dull afternoon light. The walls were white; linoleum light brown with a subtle blue pattern, slightly worn near the sink and stove. The countertops were clean.

I left the kitchen and entered the dining room. The light blue walls were bare—no paintings, no mirrors. The dining room table and matching chairs were oak, but looked as though they hadn't been used for some time. A thin layer of dust covered everything. In the living room, I stepped across deep brown carpet and noticed a masonry fireplace, the golden couch with matching easy chair and a 32-inch television set. There was only one framed photograph on the entire first floor. It rested on the mantel above the fireplace. I went over and examined it without picking it up. It was a gold frame, holding a 5 X 7 color photograph of Darcy and Rod during happier times. They were at the beach on a bright summer day, the ocean shimmering in the background. She was dressed in a two-piece blue bikini that was skimpy and sexy. Her smile was timid, posture awkward, eyes focused away from Rod, who had wrapped a meaty arm around her shoulder, pulling her into his bare, broad and hairy chest. I examined him closely. As Darcy had said, he was a big man, robust, with a slight paunch. He had the eager eyes of an extravert, but the frosty smile of a man who is brusque and businesslike. His face was broad, brown hair thinning and short. I sensed the kind of energy that liked to win—the body language and rigid posture of a man who was used to backing up his beliefs and threats.

What was most revealing was a vertical crack in the glass, which ran right through Darcy's body. I'm not superstitious, but I didn't like that. I turned away.

I climbed the stairs to the second floor and wandered into the bedroom. It was militaristically clean. Nothing out of place. The double bed was covered by a blue quilt; the chest of drawers barren of any objects. On the night table next to the bed, I spotted a gun. I crept over. It was a Ruger LCR .38 Special, five-shot pocket revolver. Without touching it, I looked it over. I'd fired this same revolver at a shooting range a couple of months back. It's a small frame revolver with a smooth, easy-to-control trigger and manageable recoil. The cylinder frame is made of aluminum; the grip frame from a high-tech polymer. I wondered if Rod had a permit for it.

I left the bedroom and wandered into what looked like a little study, except that there were few books. Just a white computer desk, a laptop, printer, some CDs and a mug filled with pens and pencils. I stepped to the desk. There were two drawers. I slid open the top drawer. Neatness. Yellow Post-Its stacked perfectly, paperclips in a little clear holder, a black stapler ready and handy.

The bottom drawer held letters. Two ordered stacks, fastened by red rubber bands. I reached for the first stack and read the address. The handwriting was clear and precise. It was addressed to Rod, at his current address. They were from Darcy, from her Knoxville address. I looked at the stamped date. The top letter was only three weeks old!

I carefully released the rubber bands, set them on the desk and extracted the folded letter from the envelope. I opened it and read.

Rod:

You're not supposed to be writing me. We're not supposed to have any contact whatsoever, according to the restraining order, so this is my last letter to you. I have told you time and time again how sorry I am, and that if there was anything I could do to change what has happened, I would. But I can't. You say you want us to get back together—to try again—but you're the one who always brings up the past and demands to know why I betrayed you. You demand the truth. You demand an explanation. How many times does it take for me to tell you? Why do you keep torturing yourself and me?

You're the one who had the affair two years ago with that 18-year old and then told me it didn't mean anything. You're the one who had the fling with Mrs. Thompson and then denied it, even after she finally confessed it to me in a near state of hysteria. Then, you said that didn't mean anything to you either. I was the only woman you loved, you said.

It's too late, Rod. I'm in love now, and it does mean something to me. I'm going to do everything I can to make it work. What I did was inexcusable, but I did it out of love. I love Elvis Lipps, no matter how foolish and adolescent that might sound to you and to many others. But it's the truth and I'm not going to deny it anymore. He loves me, too, and he needs me. He's had a terrible life and he's mixed up and confused. I can help him. I need somebody who needs me. You don't need me.

In your last letter, you said you'd never let anyone else have me, especially Elvis. You'd kill him first and me. I have placed your last letter in a safe place, addressed to my attorney, and, in the event that anything happens to Elvis or me, he will receive that letter.

It's too late, Rod. Elvis, and only Elvis, has me now. We love each other. Rod, our marriage, our relationship is over. It's time to move on now.

I will not write again. Get on with your life, as I am getting on with mine.

Darcy-Lynn

I read parts of the letter twice, then folded it and slipped it back into the envelope. I stared at the wall for a long time, feeling a stinging anger. Feeling a bad and perfect fool. As I gently re-wrapped the stack with the rubber bands, and placed it in its exact previous location in the bottom drawer, I heard a car engine.

I glanced at my watch. It was only a little after 3 o'clock! I shut the bottom drawer and stepped to the naked window that looked out on the street below. I saw an emerald green 1999 Accord pull into Rod's driveway.

I edged away from the window, keeping my gaze on the car. It rolled a quarter way up the drive and stopped. A big man got out and chunked the door shut. It was Rod, dressed in brown pleated pants, brown leather jacket and blue baseball cap. He started for the front door, moving out of my line of vision. I heard him climb the wooden stairs to the porch. I stepped back, glanced about the room searching for concealment, saw a closet on the opposite side of the room and hurried over. I opened the closet door and peered in. It was filled with unpacked cardboard boxes. I just managed to squeeze in and pull the door closed, when I heard the front door close downstairs. His heavy footsteps were like little tremors as he moved beneath me.

Unfortunately, the boxes were dusty—not that I'm allergic to dust—but for some reason, just the awareness that a sneeze would be tantamount to setting off a hand grenade in the quiet house, it planted the frightening suggestion in my head, and I felt the threat of a tickle in my nose. I suppressed it, peeking out through the one-inch sliver of the opened door. I was in big trouble if Rod was in for the night. I was already agonizingly uncomfortable. I suddenly remembered my cellphone. I tugged it from my overcoat pocket and turned it off. I strained my ears listening for any sounds below.

I heard the rattle of pipes, the swish of water. Rod had probably just taken a leak and flushed. A few moments later, I heard footsteps on the stairs, rising to the second floor.

All was suddenly quiet. Then I heard footsteps enter the room I occupied, and Rod passed across the sliver of my limited vision. I kept thinking of that .38 caliber Ruger in the other room. I receded deeper into the dim closet.

He picked up the phone and dialed.

"Paula...? Yeah... I'm here, at the house. Come on over. I left school early so we could meet," his big voice said, in a southern accent.

"Oh, come on! You said that the last time...You said you were coming," he said, irritated. "Look, you've got three hours before he gets home. That's plenty of time for us to ..."

His voice took on an edge. "Okay, just forget it! But don't expect me to wait around for you... You keep backing out..."

"Meet? Where? ... Blackouts? Okay, all right. That's on Atkins, isn't it? All right, then we'll come back here.

Yes, it will be dark and nobody will see you. Okay, I'm leaving right now. Ten minutes."

As Rod started down the stairs, I heard him mumble something under his breath. The front door slammed shut, but I didn't leave the closet until I heard the car engine roar to life. I pushed the closet door open and stepped to the window, in time to see Rod's car back out of the drive, bounce into the street and shoot away, leaving a trail of oil smoke in the air.

I released the trapped air from my lungs, and thanked the good fate gods for all nervous adulterers, who wanted the cover of night to hide in shadows and flee in shadows, after the shadow play of desire, disgust and fear.

I descended the stairs and started for the back door. I opened it, gave a quick scan of the area, exited, and closed the door securely behind me.

When I hit the sidewalk, a next-door neighbor emerged, an elderly man of perhaps 80. He waved and said, "Hello! How's it going at the school?" He was leaning on a silver cane.

I waved as I crossed the street, moving quickly to my car. "Fantastic! Couldn't be better," I said.

I opened the door and slid behind the wheel. I waved at the gentleman as I shot away from the curb. He waved back with his cane, enthusiastically.

Two blocks up, I found a service station and asked the cashier for directions to Blackouts. It was only four blocks away and he said I couldn't miss it because it had a big golden sign and a faded green awning.

I found it easily. When I turned sharply into the bloated parking lot, I saw Rod's Accord near the front entrance, just under the golden sign. It was a low, dark shingled building that lacked any attractive qualities whatsoever, except for the crooked neon beer signs that blinked and glared in the two tinted windows. I managed to find a parking place in the rear, near a dumpster. There was a rear entrance to the place, so I took it.

Blackouts was square, murky and dismal. I was immediately slapped by a stifling heat and the stale smell of beer and body odor. The L-shaped bar, dark wooden booths and yellow hanging lamps, seemed lost in a smoky fog. A disquieting melancholy hovered like a bad hangover.

Some bars are fun, with a kind of electric energy and a feeling of spontaneous celebration. Some are simple watering holes for folks who need a break from the daily slog, and then there are the bars for those who have been spirit-killed. Blackouts was one of those.

A slouching slack-faced man, with a sad mustache, stood behind the bar. He poured booze lazily, as if in slow motion, for another man who looked like he was the recent recipient of the Sad-Sack Award.

An old drunk-slurred woman, in a drab dress and a tired wrinkled face, grasped a bottle of beer and babbled something to the bartender, who had long since turned off the sound in those big arching ears.

The booths were half-filled. Two squawky women hovered over flat beers; a fat man drank alone, and from his expression and bowed shoulders, he was well-practiced in the art of misery and bleakness.

Across from him sat a younger man, well-dressed in a suit and tie, who was throwing back shots and nodding. Perhaps a salesman, dampened by dead-end prospects.

Rod Faulkner was stuffed in a booth, alone, under a yellow lamp that illumined his white Polo dress shirt. He nursed a lite beer and an expression of resentment and aggravation.

The booth across from him was empty, so I approached it. I took off my overcoat and slid in, tossing my coat to the opposite side. I carefully reached for my wallet, lifted out a 10 dollar bill and palmed it. After replacing my wallet, I let my arm drop casually down and away from the booth. I opened my hand. The $10 dropped to the gritty floor and Alexander Hamilton gazed up at me as if to ask, "Why, Dane? Why?"

Rod was still in his own world, looking anxiously at his watch and throwing dart glances toward the front door, obviously anticipating a rendezvous.

I glanced over. "Excuse me..."

He turned, annoyed. "What?"

I pointed to the 10 dollar bill on the floor. "Did you drop that?"

He looked at it. "No... I don't think so."

"Well, I just got here and I know I didn't drop it. It must be yours. I mean, there's no one else around."

He softened. "You sure it's not yours?"

"I'm positive. I just recently got divorced, and I know where every dollar and dime is. I've got to know or I'm out of money by the end of the month. I mean, the wife got nearly everything and she was the one who was playing around on the side, if you know what I mean?"

Rod looked at me for the first time, sizing me up. "Yeah, well they're all pretty much bitches, aren't they," he said, staring down at the money.

I reached over, scooped it up and handed it to him. He took it and slapped it down on the table next to his beer.

"You've got a Southern accent," I said. "You from the South?"

"Tennessee, originally."

"My wife's southern. Ex-wife, I mean. She's from Alabama. Well, what the hell are you going to do?" I continued. "It's the old live with them live without them thing, isn't it? I mean, what I really wanted to do was catch them together, you know what I'm saying?"

His face darkened. "Yeah..."

"I mean, he messed up my life, didn't he?"

"Yeah, it's tough," Rod said, hunching forward. "But that's the way it goes."

"You married?" I asked.

"Was... divorced."

"You think it's never going to happen to you. You think you've got the most loyal and loving wife in the world...then it happens. And you can't believe it! You can't! You know what I really want to do? I'd really like to get the guy who was nailing her, you know what I'm saying? I never found out." I pounded the table. "Never! She wouldn't tell me. And it just pisses me off!"

Rod's lips tightened. He blinked fast.

A slow, chubby waitress appeared. She chewed gum and gave me a flash of horsey upper gums when she asked me what I wanted. I ordered whiskey on the rocks. She shuffled away, lost in a desolate timelessness.

I turned back to Rod. He had drained his glass and poured the remaining beer from the bottle into it. I watched as it foamed and he seethed.

I lowered my voice and leaned my head a little closer toward his booth, like a petty thief about to announce a petty idea. "You know what I was thinking, and maybe you'll think I'm a little crazy here, but I've been thinking I'd like to hire somebody to take that little prick out. You know what I'm saying?"

Rod turned slowly, his face steeped in bad thoughts. "You have the right to kill the fucker."

"I've been thinking about it—dreaming about it."

"Don't dream about it! Find a way," Rod said. "Do it!"

It was time to pull away, to see if I could reel him in. I shrugged and turned away from him, silent, head down, staring into the icy depths of the grainy scared table.

"Did you hear me?" he persisted.

I shrugged again.

He grabbed his beer and came over. He pushed my coat aside and sat opposite me, elbows anchored, leaning forward. "Who are you?" he asked.

I got shy and a little with-holding. "Name's Bill Austin. I was an account exec. at a printing company in Philadelphia. I lost my job."

The waitress brought my whiskey. She gave us both dirty looks before she shambled away, as if we were intruding on her own personal hell, where her misery didn't want company.

Rod said, "If you don't do something, you're going to have to live with it for the rest of your life. It's going to eat away at you, day and night."

I took a sip of the whiskey and eyed him carefully. "You sound like somebody who's thought about this... maybe been through this."

His half-hooded eyes took me in conspiratorially. "I'll tell you this much: I have plans and when the time is right, and the time is almost right, I'm going to execute those plans. No one will ever know."

I laughed, nervously. "You serious?"

Rod was insulted. "Of course I'm serious!"

I looked around, then back to him, nibbling on my lower lip.

He glowered. "You're all talk! You ain't gonna do shit, are you?"

"Well what's your plan? Maybe I can learn something from it—you know figure out my own from yours."

He laughed, deep in his throat. "Bullshit! I'm not telling you anything. You know who you're like? Like those teenagers I teach. Like the boys who play football, but don't want to take the time to build themselves up slowly. They want the six-pack abs and granite pecs, just like those bozos on Wrestlemania. They want to add strength or speed. So they get "on the juice." They use steroids. Injectable steroids. Very powerful. Kids 10 years old are doing it. Nobody wants to plan and practice and build carefully anymore."

He drained his beer and continued, reveling in his own philosophy. "You've got to have brains and drive to come up with your own plan. You've got to work it, play by play, like a football game. You've got to be bold and inventive, and you've got to be patient."

I'd twisted uncomfortably and made my voice sound meek. "Well, I'll think about it."

He sat back, shaking his head. "You're just a big mouth! A candy ass big mouth! You won't do shit!"

I shrank away, stammering. "I...I... I don't know, I mean... I've got to think about it, don't I?"

Rod looked at me as if I was an ugly fungus specimen. "You fucking candy ass!"

He grabbed his beer, slid out of the booth and went back to his own. He looked over one last time with dark disgust. "Enjoy your chicken shit life!"

I didn't leave right away. I huddled over my glass of whiskey and waited until Rod's date arrived.

She entered wearing a kerchief, sunglasses, tight jeans and a medium length coat. It was the thin body of an athlete—perhaps a runner—probably in her middle 20s. With head down, she crossed the floor and joined Rod, sitting opposite him, all fidgety and apology. She didn't remove her coat, but adjusted it often. They weren't going to stay long. Rod was already reaching for his coat. She lifted her head to him and smiled wryly. I sense a woman infatuated by the forbidden and yet conscience-choked. She was looking to Rod to nudge her into perdition.

Their conversation fell in private whispers.

When I stood and eased into my coat, Rod gave me a final toxic glance. I went to the bar and paid my bill. As I was making my way toward the rear entrance I threw one last glance over my shoulder toward Rod's booth. The woman was standing outside the booth. He stood and reached for her. He kissed her boldly. She wrenched away, trembling.

Rod seized her arm and yanked her into him.

I left.

It was time to call Abner and make a decision.

CHAPTER 14

Despite heavy traffic, I was back in New York by 6:30. I dropped the car off at the rental agency and called Darcy to tell her I was going to be late. Her cellphone rang and then it dropped me into her voicemail. I left a message.

As I strolled up a busy Eighth Avenue on my way to the office, I called home and heard my old voice greeting. I didn't leave a message.

Inside the office, I flipped on the light, passed through reception and went to my desk. I switched on my halogen lamp and sat. My eyes fell to a stapled piece of paper that Helen had written, READ THIS, in bold red letters.

I flipped the page and read.

Dane:

Donovan Lassiter is dead. His body was found in his studio on 11th Avenue and 32nd Street, about two weeks ago, by a girlfriend. The side of his head was bashed in. Police have no suspects but believe the motive was either drug-related or had something to do with his pornography business. The girlfriend had been out of town. She is not a suspect. If you need more information, let me know and I'll follow-up tomorrow morning.

—Helen

I called Darcy again. No answer.

I found Abner's cell number and dialed. After three rings, I heard his exuberant southern draw.

"Hello! This Is Abner Lipps speaking and I see that you are Dane Cooper."

"Yes, Mr. Lipps."

"I am so damn glad to hear from you. How the hell are you?"

"Are you in Vegas?" I asked.

"I'm standing right outside the Monte Carlo on Las Vegas Boulevard. What a wonderful place this is. Just a damn wonder! It has these spectacular fountains and swimming pools and I believe, Mr. Cooper, the best, the sexiest and the friendliest girls I've seen since I left Tennessee. It's 66 degrees, the sun is shining full and bright and everybody around me is in a damn good mood. Now, how are things in New York and I hope you have brought me good news about my son, Elvis."

I eased back in my chair. "I take it you haven't learned anything about him there?"

"Not yet, Mr. Cooper, but I've been showing his picture around to a lot of places and I'm just prayin' to the good Lord in Heaven that it won't be long before someone can point, with an enthusiastic finger, in the direction where Elvis is either performing or residing."

I sighed. "Mr. Lipps, the case has taken a rather dramatic change."

"Oh?"

"I would have preferred to talk to you about this in person. It's involved."

"Hell, you got me all stirred up here, Mr. Cooper. You've got me nervous. Out with it!"

"There's no easy way to say this, Mr. Lipps. Elvis' life is in danger. There's been a contract put out on him."

"A contract? You mean like a mob contract? Like a hit man who's supposed to hunt him down and shoot him dead!?"

"Yes sir, that's what I mean."

Abner's voice took on urgency. "No... no, no, nooo... Dammit! I can't believe this! I can't! Are you sure you know what you're talking about, Mr. Cooper!?"

"Yes sir, I'm afraid I do. Elvis ran off with a 15-year-old girl from Vegas. The father's in Vegas and... well let's say he's connected and angry. He wants revenge."

The life in Abner's voice fell into a raspy despair. "My Lord God, Mr. Cooper. My Lord God... Who is this man? I'll talk to him. I'll reason with him!"

"That would only make matters worse for you and your wife."

"Well, we've got to do something!"

"I can try talking with him, although, in all honesty, I don't think it will do much good. And it could cost a lot of money. I'd try to pay him off. Try to convince him to drop the hit."

"I don't care about the damn money! Come to Vegas. Talk to him! Dammit, talk to the man and save my son, Mr. Cooper!"

I stood and began massaging my tired eyes. "How much can I offer him, Mr. Lipps?"

"I don't know anything about this kind of thing, Mr. Cooper. I'm a wealthy man, but I have my limits and my businesses aren't doing as well as they were a couple of years ago. I mean, the damn economy has punched me hard in the gut, Mr. Cooper."

"I'll start with $500,000 and see where it goes. My guess is, if he's interested at all, he'll want at least a million."

Silence.

"Mr. Lipps?"

His voice was a low whisper. "Yes... yes, go ahead, make the offer."

"He may ask for more. What's your limit?"

"...I suppose I could raise another couple million, but not much more than that," Abner said, his voice cracking with emotion. "A lot of my money is tied up, Mr. Cooper. I'm not all that liquid these days."

"I'll see what I can do. Ideally, our best shot would be for me to find Elvis and the girl first. Then I could take her back to her father and see if that'll be enough." I knew it wouldn't be, but I wanted Mr. Lipps to have some hope. "Anyway, I need more time. I have made some progress. Elvis will need protection in any event."

"And that means you want more money, Mr. Cooper?"

"The case has changed from a simple missing persons investigation. Finding your son will continue to be a challenge, but protecting him after I do, will be a greater one. I'm not overly fond of getting shot at. We may have to hire professionals to do this kind of thing."

"How much!" Abner said, pointedly. "Lord, God, how much!?

"Let's not worry about that now. We'll hire the protection later, if we need it. I have to find Elvis first."

"Should we go to the police about all this, Mr. Cooper? Will it help us?"

"That's your decision, Mr. Lipps. It's a cold trail for a missing person's case. From my experience, the police wouldn't be able to put many resources on it, if any. There's no proof of the hit and time is running out."

"Talk to this father, Mr. Cooper. Reason with him. Appeal to him as one hurting father to another, and convince him to release this contract on my boy. I'm counting on you."

"I'll do my best, Mr. Lipps. I don't want to make promises I can't keep. It won't be easy."

"What hotel will you be staying at in Vegas?" Abner asked. "I'll meet you."

"I don't think that's a good idea, Mr. Lipps. Until I've spoken with this man, I'd prefer that you and I not meet."

"Well... you're the professional. If that's what you think."

"There's one last thing, Mr. Lipps. All of what I'm about to tell you will be in the written report, but, since I have you on the line I might as well tell you now. I have found Mrs. Johnson and Buddy Blue."

"Well that's damn good news, Mr. Cooper. Have they been able to shed any light on Elvis' whereabouts?"

"Possibly. There are some things I'm going to be following up on. Mrs. Johnson runs an escort service and Buddy Blue works for her. Elvis worked for her too."

"Escort service!" His voice was strained. "What the hell kind of escort service?"

"Mostly an escort service for well-to-do older women."

"I see..." his voice almost fell into a whisper. "Yes, I see." Then, his tone changed. It took on an edge. "Well, I'm sure there's some mistake here, sir. I'm damn sure you're wrong about this. My boy, Elvis, would never get involved in this kind of sick and disgusting thing. We raised him up good, Mr. Cooper. We raised him up good and God-fearing and I know, without a doubt—any doubt—that my boy, Elvis, is not, and never has been, or ever will be, involved in this kind of awful and disgusting thing."

I let silence be my response.

"Are you there, Mr. Cooper?"

"Mr. Lipps...you hired me to do a job and to give reports. That is what I'm doing. These are the facts as I have found them. If you want me to stop reporting on the investigation, I will. If you want to stop the investigation, I will, but if I'm going to work with you, you've got to trust me. If you can't do that, I'll walk away and you will be free to hire someone else."

His voice was small and melancholy. "Mr. Cooper... I am a man in a great deal of emotional pain. I hurt like hell over my lost boy. You must know that. You must have some understanding of that. If you were a parent you'd know how a father has such high hopes and dignified aspirations for his son. It just hurts, Mr. Cooper. It just hurts me like hell."

I softened my tone. "I will help you to find your son, Mr. Lipps. I'll do everything I can to find Elvis."

"Mr. Cooper, you are making progress. Please contact me as soon as you have spoken with that man here in Vegas." His voice faded into sorrow. "All right, Mr. Cooper. All right then. I'm in room 2203, if you need to see me or talk to me."

After I hung up, I opened my lower desk door and took out a bottle of Jim Beam. I poured a stingy cup full and switched off the light. I sipped it in darkness, listening to muffled Eighth Avenue sounds of evening: car horns, tires thudding into shallow pot holes, the murmur of theatre crowds passing below on their way to restaurants.

I needed a minute to regroup. I'd decided not to tell Abner about my conversation with Rod Faulkner and about "his plan." He'd sounded defeated enough. I'm not sure he could've taken it—two people plotting to kill his son. Frankly, and yet once again, I wanted to walk away from the whole thing. But Abner's broken, quivering voice got to me a little, and there was the thing about the money. The money was good. And then there was Darcy.

After reading Darcy's final letter to Rod, where she had boldly declared her love for Elvis, I'd concluded that she was obviously a little out of her mind. She had to be aware of what Rod's response would be. It wasn't the letter of someone who was trying to appease. She was angry, and bravely or foolishly, taunting him or challenging him. Perhaps she'd just had enough and was ready for a gunfight at high noon. Did she really intend to find Elvis and marry him?

I had stupidly let myself get involved with Darcy, and it was apparent that she was using me, and our relationship, as "a bridge over troubled water," a song Elvis Presley sang very well. She must have considered me intelligent enough to realize that, and my reward, in turn, was the delightful pleasures of her lovemaking. Okay, it was a fair trade.

The case had become a ticking time bomb, as they say in those old movies, and I wasn't entirely sure if I was capable of defusing it. I could find help. But I'd tried that once—hiring another PI—and all it did was add another layer of complexity. PI's are PI's because most are lone wolves. They have their own styles, habits and work hours. They are competitive.

On the other hand, maybe I'm the problem. Maybe I'm the lone wolf. Maybe I prefer my own style and habits. Maybe I'm competitive. Maybe that's why I haven't hired another PI or joined an agency, where you all work together. Maybe I like doing it all myself, win or fail.

I needed to follow-up on the murder of Donovan Lassiter. There could be a connection. I'd call Pat Shanahan and see if he knew anything.

After finishing my drink, I switched on the light and called Darcy again. Again, I got her voicemail. Frustrated, I called home and got my voicemail. It was 7:20.

I called Shanahan. Fortunately, he was just finishing dinner. Jean never let him speak to anyone during family dinner. It was a hard and fast rule.

"Jean's got me on another diet," Pat said.

"Is it working?" I asked.

"Oddly enough, it is. I've lost a pound."

"So what's the diet?"

"Maybe a spinach omelet for breakfast, a yogurt smoothie for lunch and a turkey burger on a whole-grain bun for dinner. We just had the turkey burger."

"And...?"

He whispered. "Is being overweight so bad, Dane-O?"

"You on the back porch?" I asked, whispering too, although I had no reason to.

"Yep... sneaking a smoke while Jean's talking to her mother."

"So have a cheese Danish in the morning with extra cream and sugar in your coffee like you always do. We're not going to live forever anyway. Die fat and happy."

"Jean's been on the warpath with me and the kids. Everybody's too fat. Frankly, I think she's too thin."

"Hey, buddy, she's the daughter of an ex-Army Major. It's in her DNA."

"Okay, Dane-O, you didn't call me to learn about power foods. What's up?"

"Donavan Lassiter. The porn flick maker who was murdered. Have you heard anything about it?"

"Not really. I think that case went to Midtown South Central."

"Didn't Bob Rickson come from there?"

"Yeah, he was there for awhile. I'll ask him about it. Make up some damn thing. You know how naturally suspicious he is of everybody. So, tell me, Dane-O, what's the latest on the missing boy?"

I filled Pat in on most of the details, leaving out a few choice bits.

"I wouldn't trust this Rod guy's ex," he said. "What's her name?"

"Let's just call her Missy."

"Okay. Watch Missy. She sounds unstable."

"She is."

"Somebody must be hiding the kids."

"You think so?"

"Mob hits don't mess around. You know that. They'd have found them by now. These aren't pros, you know, they're just kids. Maybe they're already dead."

"I thought that, too. On the other hand, maybe these kids are smarter than we think. Kids are sharper today than in my day. They're tech savvy, world savvy and sex savvy. Something else has been bugging me. Maybe the hit is waiting. Maybe he has instructions to wait."

"You got me, Dane-O. Don't know what you're going for."

"What if the guy who hired the hit is being watched by somebody above? Maybe his superiors don't care one way or the other about his 15-year-old daughter who ran off with some low life?"

"Maybe. A lot of maybes, Dane."

"Yes, and Rod still has his plan in the works. He must know something I don't."

"Ain't that always the way it is, Dane-O? I'll get back with you."

Before I left the office, I called Paul Callo's office in Las Vegas and spoke with his secretary. I wanted to be sure that he was going to be in the office tomorrow afternoon. I told her I was an old friend passing through town and wanted to drop by and see him. She assured me he'd be there and then asked for my name and phone number. I declined, saying that it was to be a surprise.

I then called Romina, my travel agent, and booked two first class round-trip tickets to Las Vegas on the morning flight. I wouldn't charge Abner for the tickets. I would business expense it, hand it off to Helen, who'd pass me a disapproving glare, before passing it off to my accountant. He would call and demand I justify it.

Romina also booked us a room at the Golden Sunset Hotel and Casino for one night. While I massaged the back of my neck, Romina related that the hotel is about a twenty minute drive from the strip, has three fine dining restaurants, a 12-screen cinema movie theater, but no spa, health club or wedding chapel. "But the hotel does have a beautiful golf course," she concluded.

"I won't be golfing," I said. "I sold my clubs three years ago after I snapped the nine iron over my knee on the 16th hole."

"But listen to this, Dane," Romina continued, "I can get you a beautiful suite, complete with bar, Jacuzzi, stocked refrigerator, complete entertainment center and king-sized bed for only $220. And, the casino is 80,000 square feet."

"Well, we'll have plenty of room. Would you like to come along?"

"You already have a woman going with you," Romina said.

"She won't mind."

"My husband will."

"Bring him along."

She blew a sigh into the phone. "Now you've taken all the romance out of it."

I left the office and hailed a cab. As we were passing Columbus Circle, my phone rang. It was Darcy.

"Why haven't you called?" I asked, sternly.

"You sound angry. Don't be. I just got a little carried away, that's all. You know, the museums... and I went shopping again. I couldn't help myself."

Her voice sounded strange, forced into an artificially bright tone.

"Where are you?" I asked.

"I'm in a cab crossing Central Park on my way to the West Side. How was your day? Any news?"

"We're leaving for Las Vegas in the morning, on an 8 o'clock flight."

"Oh..." she said, flatly.

"You've changed your mind?"

"No... I mean... Well, when are we coming back?"

"First thing Friday morning. What's happened, Darcy? You don't sound like yourself."

"I'm fine, really. Just a little tired, that's all."

I paused. "I'll see you back at the apartment."

"Okay...I'll see you."

We stayed in on Wednesday night, ordered Chinese and watched television. Darcy was absorbed and distant. She kept saying she was just tired and still recuperating from the past months of sleeplessness and worry. She didn't say much about the museums, just that she enjoyed the Met. When I asked for specifics, she mentioned that she liked the Egyptian Wing and the Greek sculpture.

I was in bed before her, with the bedroom lamp on low. She lingered in the bathroom longer than usual. When she drifted in, naked and perfumed with musk, I lifted to my elbows. She slid under the sheets and rolled toward me, her body warm, her eyes probing. She reached for me, touched and stroked. Then gently, she brushed me with her breasts, beginning her stirring, warm kisses.

Her ardor was strong that night. There was no evidence of fatigue in her lovemaking. She slept fitfully, and called out several times for someone, but I couldn't understand the name. It definitely didn't sound like Dane.

I got up once, went into the kitchen and had a couple of shots of whiskey. I paced the apartment for a time, then went back into the bedroom and studied Darcy's gray sleeping body. Something had shifted. What little trust I'd had in her, had vanished. Now, she seemed like an enemy.

CHAPTER 15

The plane was full, but it didn't matter. Darcy and I were in first class, with all the other high rollers. I tried to appear smug and aloof; nose a little higher than normal, eyes alert for any service infraction or lapse of personal attention. Our seats were wide, roomy and comfortable. I had seldom flown first class, mainly because it was too damn pricy and because I'd never considered myself to be a first class kind of guy. My father would have flown in the baggage compartment, for a discount, and my mother scoffed at such extravagance as "sinful" and "a ridiculous waste of money." They'd flown to Hawaii, stuffed into those coach seats so compactly that I imagined it took two German frau broad-shouldered stewardesses, with a big shoehorn, to pry them out. Dad had put on some heft in the last few years and Mom—well let's just say that she has the appetite of a wolf, God love her.

But I wanted private conversation with Darcy and I wanted leg room. At 6'2" my legs get stuck under seats and my bum leg has the unfortunate tendency to fall asleep, refusing to awaken, even with slaps and hand chops.

We were 30,000 feet above the Earth, cutting a silver path through the sea blue sky. Curling white clouds were far below, with occasional breaks, where green and brown appeared and then slid away under the quilted white comforter.

Darcy had the window seat and she stared out blankly, seemingly lost in her thoughts. She had spoken little all morning and I didn't push. I didn't have much to say either. I was waiting for the right moment. After an hour or so, I turned to her.

She was drinking a Diet Coke, I a coffee.

"Did you love your husband?" I asked.

She turned her attention to me. The blue silk blouse she was wearing brought out the blue in her inquiring eyes. "Why?"

"You married him. You said you liked being married."

She nodded. "Yes, I loved him, at first. He was attentive, thoughtful and supportive. We were both in education and felt we were making a difference. But I soon learned that Rod had two sides to him. He was also jealous, possessive, violent and unfaithful."

"That's more like four sides. And were you faithful?"

Her eyes slid away. "Until Elvis, yes."

"So he had no reason to be jealous?"

"No."

"You must have done something to make him jealous."

She looked at me again, not pleasantly. "Why?"

"What made him jealous?"

"What are you trying to get at, Dane? What are you trying to do?"

"Had you ever flirted with any other of your students?"

She was insulted. "No! No, of course not."

"With any of the other teachers?"

"Why are you doing this?"

189

"When did you decide you didn't love Rod anymore?"

"That's none of your business!"

"Was it six months, a year, two years?"

Darcy drew herself up in defiance. "The last two years of our marriage he accused me of sleeping around. He was the one who was sleeping around. It was his guilt. Then he'd come home and beat me. Accuse me!"

Darcy took an angry sip of her soda and turned back to the window. "I thought I could trust you."

"Then be honest with me."

"I have been."

"No, you haven't."

She faced me again. "What's the matter with you?"

"Where did you go yesterday? And don't tell me you went to the museum."

"I did!"

"Where else?"

She hesitated, avoiding my eyes.

"Darcy... did you meet Elvis yesterday?"

Her head dropped, averting my eyes. "No..."

"I don't believe you. You're lying."

She looked up, eyes pleading. "No..."

"He got in touch with you and you met him. Darcy, his life is in danger. Your life is in danger. You have got to tell me!"

She drank and swallowed, her entire body tense, trembling. She tried to gather herself, but lost the battle, closing her eyes and massaging her temple. "I called home to Knoxville yesterday afternoon to get my messages. Elvis had called...at 7 o'clock in the morning. He left a number where I could reach him, but he said he'd only be there for a few minutes. By the time I called, I got the wrong number or something. I kept calling and kept getting the same wrong number. I checked it... I don't know."

"Did he say where he was or if he'd call back?"

"No. He just said that he needed my help and to call him."

"Why doesn't he call your cell number?"

"Because I changed numbers and I didn't give it to him."

"But you kept your same home number?"

"Well I moved...Okay, I gave him my home number. I told him only to call me if it was an emergency."

"Why didn't you tell me this before?"

She shook her head. "I don't know."

"Yes, you do, Darcy. Why?"

Her eyes opened suddenly. "Stop pushing me!"

"Then tell me the truth!"

"Then tell me what you know! What you've learned. Why are we going to Las Vegas?"

"I can't tell you why."

"Can't or won't?"

"Doesn't matter."

She turned away. "It's time I went home. I'm going to catch the first plane back."

"Back to what? To Elvis?"

"No!" she said, fuming. "I'm going to finish packing and leave. Leave for Arizona or San Diego like I should've done weeks ago."

"And when Elvis calls you again. Then what?"

She was silent.

I took the edge off my voice. "Look at you, Darcy. You know you can't walk away from this thing. You can't ignore it. You've got to finish it. We both know you came to New York with me because you thought I'd find Elvis. Okay, fine. We both know I let you come because I thought you might lead me to Elvis. Okay, fine again. Now what?"

She started to speak, but the words didn't come.

"Darcy... Help me. Give me a couple more days."

Her face reddened. "I don't want to see him, don't you understand! Don't you see how humiliated I feel! I don't ever want to see Elvis again!"

To our right, I watched a leggy stewardess offer a portly middle-aged couple a glass of champagne.

"Darcy, stop lying to yourself. You want to see Elvis again and, since we're on our way to Vegas, I'll lay odds 5 to 1 that you will see him again."

She fumed.

"Just tell me the truth, Darcy. All of it."

She looked at me with bold accusing eyes. "The truth? The truth is I love him. Is that what you want to hear!? I love him! I would do anything for him. Anything! Is that what you want to hear?!"

I sat staring...staring past her. Staring at nothing. "No, Darcy. I didn't want to hear that."

We landed at McCarran International Airport at 11:30am Las Vegas time and took our carry-ons to the car rental agency. We were silent as we picked up our reserved maroon Buick Regal, walking through the dry desert air and abundant sunshine. Darcy lifted her face toward the sun, like a flower in need of nourishment.

We left the terminal, turning onto East Russell Road, beginning our ten-minute journey to the Golden Sunset Hotel. I kept recalling Darcy's expression when she'd told me she loved Elvis. It was the expression of someone who had just discovered a violence she had no idea was inside her. Her eyes were raw with astonishment, disgust and a twinkle of satisfaction.

All I wanted to do now was to finish the case as quickly as possible and remove these broken people from my life. From here to the end, I'd shut down every other thought and feeling and just concentrate on the case.

Darcy rolled her window down halfway and lit a cigarette.

"It used to be only elevators and buses," I said, breaking the silence.

She looked over, waiting for my explanation.

"Those were the only two places in Nevada where smoking was banned. Now many of the casinos have non-smoking sections. They even have non-smoking poker rooms. Pat Shanahan, my old NYPD partner, comes here twice a year. He smokes. That's how I know."

Darcy didn't respond.

The flat desert landscape was easy on the eyes and the cool wind puffing in from the window was refreshing.

"Have you been here before?" I asked.

"Once. I didn't like it much. Not my thing."

"Do you gamble?"

"I've played the slots, some blackjack."

"Blackjack is unique among casino games," I said. "Past performance can affect future results."

"Just like life itself," Darcy said, sarcastically.

"That's right. Unlike craps or roulette, where the dice or ball doesn't have a memory, the casino's mathematical advantage in blackjack fluctuates during the course of play. A smart player can benefit by betting big when the house's edge is reduced."

Darcy looked at me coldly. "Don't bet big on me."

"I'm talking about blackjack, Darcy."

"Sure you are."

Her phone rang. I glanced over, sharply attentive, as she checked the number. "Oh god, it's Carol again."

"Your old high school friend, Carol Hemmings?" I asked.

"Yeah…She's driving me crazy. She just keeps calling and calling. She keeps going on and on about how Rod and I should get back together."

"Tell her not to call you."

"I can't. She's a good friend. She's concerned about me."

The Golden Sunset Hotel and Casino had a Mediterranean flair, with golden spires, domes and arches. There were shimmering pools and spacious fountains with high arching water that soared within colored lights.

In the lobby, I passed giggling buxom blonds, dressed-down chubby tourists and children playing combat with agitated parents. Everywhere I looked I saw the energy of magnificent possibility on the faces of those who streamed to and from the casino, as if this gleaming royal wonderland really could offer the possibility of living happily ever after.

Our check-in was flawlessly efficient. The dome-glass elevator shot us up to the 12th floor and we stepped out onto a plush golden carpet, where the hallways were clean, broad and quiet.

We stepped into our spacious suite, radiantly golden and red and filled with temptation: a golden king sized bed, a wide HD TV, a sunken Jacuzzi and champagne, iced and perched in a crystal cooler. On the dining table, fresh fruit and flowers filled the air with sweet smells and sexy possibilities for those who swung that way. In blue color dishes, little square chocolates beckoned. The bathrooms were huge, with large granite sink counters, opulent red towels and a deep tub big enough for a fat gambler and all his imagined money.

With the golden pleated drapes parted, we looked out on a cloudless blue sky and a spectacular view of the simmering distant desert.

Darcy stood, gazing out the window. "Are you angry with me?" she asked.

"What for?"

"Don't be obtuse."

I began unpacking. I hung my light gray suit in the closet. "That's a big school teacher word."

"You're not stupid, Dane, even though you let people think you are sometimes."

I looked at her. "I'm going to find Elvis, Darcy. When I do find him, you can make your own decisions. You're a big girl. But stay close to me. There are bad guys out there who would probably like to have some words with you."

"That's it?" she asked. "You have nothing else to say to me?"

I should have opted for silence. "That's it."

A few minutes later, Darcy turned from the window. "I suppose you want me to call home to see if Elvis has called?"

"Yes. I'd also like the number he left you."

Her voice was hesitant and small. "Okay... if that's what you want."

Darcy stared at me for a long moment, walked to the bed and grabbed her purse. She opened it and took out a white sheet of paper. She gave me one final, icy glance before thrusting it at me. "Take it!"

I took it. I looked at it. "Thank you." From the area code I was certain the owner lived in Long Island, New York.

Doug K. Pennington

"And now?" she asked, in a challenge.

"Now, I have an appointment with a man who has a daughter who is a wild card."

"And what am I?" Darcy asked.

I was silent. Sometimes silence provokes. Sometimes it answers all questions. Sometimes it gets one into deep trouble. I was throwing the dice.

She took her phone and dialed. I waited. She turned away from me, listening for messages. Suddenly, she reached for a pen that was conveniently next to the bed, and quickly scribbled down a phone number on creamy hotel stationery. She turned and pushed that one at me. It was a different number from the previous one. This number had a different area code. The phone was almost certainly owned by someone who lived in New York City. The numbers would be easy to trace over the internet: owner's name and address, household members and more.

Darcy hung up. She glanced at her watch. I could see that she was trying to fortify herself with courage. "He just left a message on my machine. He's at this number now. He said he's desperate."

I looked at the number. "Call him," I said. "Tell him I have to talk to him."

Darcy hesitated. I didn't push, but I wanted to. Finally, she snatched the paper from me and dialed. She slowly raked her fingers through her hair and adjusted her posture, rigidly, so that her breasts became sharp and alluring. I saw a slow blush come to her cheeks, a dreamy hunger in her eyes. It was as if her lover—her real lover—was near, approaching her with a ready passion and she could feel the heat of him. I could feel hers. Yes, I was jealous.

196

When she spoke, her voice was weak. It trembled. "...El..vis...?"

I inched closer, taking in her perfume and hearing the tiny muffled voice coming through the phone. Darcy stepped away from me.

"Where are you? Yes, it *is* important. Tell me... Okay..., yes, I can help you but first... Elvis, listen to me. There's someone here I want you to talk to... you don't know him... Elvis, you've got to trust me. I said I can help you, but I want to... Elvis, calm down. Yes, I can give you $10,000, but I want you to talk..."

I yanked the phone from her hand. "Elvis?"

"Who's this?" Elvis asked, in an alarmed southern baritone voice.

"My name's Dane Cooper. I'm a private investigator."

"I've got nothing to say to you. Put Darcy back on!"

"Elvis, I need you to tell me where you are."

"I'm not telling you anything. Put Darcy back on or I'm hanging up."

"Elvis, you're in a lot of danger."

"No shit! I need a private detective to tell me that? Don't you think I know that?"

Darcy was looking at me intensely. I wanted to mention Gina Callo, but I didn't want Darcy to hear the name.

"Are you alone?" I asked.

"That's none of your business."

"You and I both know why you're in this mess."

"Have you told Darcy?" Elvis asked, his voice sounding strained.

"No. It's time you let it go."

"You mean, let go of Gina?"

"Yes. Let go."

"No way... I'm not letting Gina go back to her father! She's scared of him. She hates him. The guy's a maniac! Anyway, he'd kill us both. He said he was going to kill me."

"Elvis, they're going to find you unless you let it go."

Darcy nudged in, concerned. "Let what go?" she whispered.

I waved her off.

Elvis said, "I love her and she loves me. All we need is another $10,000 and we can leave the country."

I turned away from Darcy and walked toward the windows. "You won't make it."

"We've made it so far."

"You've been extremely lucky. Your luck won't last. It's just a matter of time and your time is running out. Fast."

"My father hired you, didn't he?"

"Look, Elvis, I can help you, but you've got to let me know where you are."

"I've got nothing else to say to you. Put Darcy back on!"

I had to think of something to keep him on the phone. "Elvis, your father's had a heart attack. He's dying."

Darcy's eyes narrowed on me, suspiciously.

Elvis got quiet. "I don't believe you!"

"It's true. The strain finally got to him."

"When?"

"Two days ago. He's been asking for you."

"Dammit!"

"We can meet someplace. I can take you to him."

Now he sounded frightened. "No... no I've got to think about this. Dammit! I've got to think."

"Can I reach you at this number?" I asked, quickly.

"No... no. No way!"

He hung up.

"Elvis? Elvis?"

I immediately called back. It rang five times, then I heard the click of a cut-off and a dial tone. I felt my shoulders drop. I slowly eased down onto the bed. I closed my eyes and put a fist to my forehead, massaging it.

Darcy stared. "Is his father dying?"

I ignored her. Elvis would probably call his father and learn the truth: that I was lying. But at least he would have made contact and his parents would know he was alive.

I opened my eyes and caught hers, studying me. I quickly dialed Elvis' number again. Again, I got a hang up and dial tone.

I put both numbers in my phone's contacts list. I stood. "I have an appointment," I said.

"Dane... what did you mean when you said, let it go?"

I ignored the question. "Will you be here when I get back?" I asked.

Her eyes revealed little. "I don't know. I can't trust you anymore."

"I think it's more a matter of you not trusting yourself."

She retreated to the bathroom and shut the door.

While Darcy showered, I changed out of my jeans and olive cotton shirt, into my suit and light blue tie. I called the office for any messages and Helen said there was nothing urgent, but she had received a call from Pat Shanahan about Donavan Lassiter. He said detectives had questioned a 20s something girl and a guy named Buddy Blue. That's all the information he had. He said he'd get in touch when he learned more.

I left before Darcy emerged from the bathroom. I wondered if she'd flee. I couldn't stop her. I had to focus on saving Elvis' life another way, without her. She was just a distraction now and, in truth, she had always been. I heard the old "wish we could have met at a better time" banter in my head as I left the room, closing the door.

I hoped Paul Callo would respond to something resembling reason and take Abner Lipps' money. If he did, then all I had to worry about was Rod Faulkner.

The elevator doors opened and I stepped in, while I reached into my pocket for a Rolo. I pressed L for LOBBY and dropped the chocolate dome into my mouth.

As I stepped out into the lobby, striding across the red carpet toward the management offices, I had the sinking feeling I was on a fool's errand.

CHAPTER 16

Security stopped me at the steel gray door entrance to the administrative offices. I had anticipated it, and had my password ready. I told them who I was, who I wanted to see and mentioned that it concerned Elvis Lipps, the infamous name that always opens doors, wins and loses friends and definitely influences people. No-nonsense security called Paul's secretary.

A few minutes later, a hulking elephant security guard was escorting me through the magic door, down a long hallway. We arrived at a little waiting room, with red carpet and black leather chairs. Security then proceeded to frisk me to see if I was carrying. I wasn't. I'd left my .38-caliber Smith & Wesson Model 10 at home.

After he was satisfied, he asked me to take a seat and he stood by the doorway watching me with the blank face of the departed, as I thumbed through magazines. Catchy songs played from an overhead speaker and reminded me of bouncy animation from Disney. I checked my phone for messages and thumbed through old ones.

About 15 minutes later, a woman appeared—a tall brunette in her late 20s, who was of Latino descent. She looked like she was ready for her *Vogue* close-up. Her sleeveless red dress won points for meeting all the re-

quirements of satisfying my eyes and the eyes of the
hulking elephant. His dead features came to life. We
tried to pull our eyes away, without much effort and
without any success.

I stood.

"Mr. Cooper?" she asked.

"Yes, ma'am."

"I'm Margaret Sanchez, Mr. Callo's secretary. Mr.
Callo will see you now. Please follow me."

We traveled across more red carpet, soon arriving at
an impressive space of lavish vases filled with exotic
flowers and more comfortable looking black leather
chairs. On the stucco-style walls were oil paintings of
mountains and deserts and a cityscape of Las Vegas
blazing in the night. Ceiling-to-wall windows looked out
to towering lazy palms and a distant gleaming golf course.

Ms. Sanchez led me past her broad mahogany desk
with a 17" flat screen monitor, to a closed door that had a
polished brass panel announcing:

Paul Callo
Assistant Manager

Ms. Sanchez opened the door and indicated inside
with an elegant arm. I followed and entered into the
generous office space, standing on more red carpet. The
door closed.

Paul Callo sat behind an L shaped mahogany desk,
hands folded on it, brooding eyes fixed on me. His
Armani suit was dark blue, shirt burgundy, tie dark. I saw
a conference table, black leather couch, a large-screen TV
and a portable bar. My eyes lingered on the portable bar
for a moment.

"So you're the private dick?" he said, coarsely, in a
voice I associated with some actor from the *Sopranos*.

"I am."

"Sylvia Johnson said I might hear from you. She's an old whore, but she still has some connections here."

Paul didn't look like an ugly, smirking villain. In fact, he reminded me of a middle-aged Dean Martin. I half expected him to break out into *Everybody Loves Somebody Sometime.*

He stood and flashed me a charismatic smile. "If I wasn't so pissed off, I'd laugh my ass off at this whole fuckin' mess. But I'm not laughing. What the hell's your first name?"

"Dane."

"Dane? What the hell kind of name is that?"

"English, I guess."

"Cooper is the last name?" Paul asked.

"Yes. It's Scottish, I'm told."

"I'm into genealogy. It's a little hobby of mine, not that I have any fucking time for it, but I dabble. I've traced my family back to the 1700's to Naples. Our real last name was Calasso, but my father changed it years ago. He thought Callo sounded more simpatico. Not so ethnic, if you know what I mean. Calasso is from the pre-Latin word, "cala" which means steep side of the mountain. Well, anyway, you want a drink or something?"

"Whiskey on the rocks. Jim Beam if you have it. Any, if you don't."

Paul went to the bar. "I've got Makers and Blantons."

"Blantons works," I said.

He made the drinks and handed me mine.

"My office should be high up in the fuckin' clouds with all the other managers, but I don't like heights. Makes me dizzy. So I stay down here, close to the peasants and close to golf."

I took a drink. It soothed my dry throat. It had a long, smooth finish. I held up the glass. "Nice."

"You always worked out of New York?" Paul asked.

"Yeah."

"You work alone?"

"A secretary."

"Who works alone anymore in your business? Most agencies have at least three or four helpers."

"I like alone. I trust myself. I can get help when I need it."

He eyes flashed anger. "You fuckin' need help on this one, Cooper!"

"Maybe... But it cuts down on the profits. And I don't argue much with myself."

I saw just the hint of a grin. "You should move out here. There's lots of opportunities for a guy in your field—if he's smart."

"I'd miss the seasons and the diners."

"Why did you leave the NYPD and go private?"

"I didn't get along with my superiors. I got restless. I wanted a change for some personal reasons."

Paul scratched his nose and slanted me a look. "What are you sellin', Dane?"

I shrugged. "Goodwill among fathers?"

Paul coughed a laugh. "Do I look like I have any goodwill?"

"Well, my mother used to say that we all have potential."

"You don't look like the type who always listened to your mother. Look at the fuckin' business you're in."

"She still thinks there's hope for me."

He looked at me doubtfully. "Fuckin' kids. They drive you crazy. You got any?"

"No. I had the chance once. Didn't work out."

"You're better off." Paul chewed on a piece of ice. "Do you know where Elvis is?"

"Your hired gun must have told you that I don't."

"You ever met Elvis?"

"No. He sounds like a mixed up kid. Like most kids. I was a mixed up kid. Hell, I'm still mixed up."

His face hardened. "That kid's a smart-ass teenage prick who's fuckin' my 15-year-old daughter. Fifteen! She's my only kid! Just an innocent little girl!"

"Elvis' father isn't happy about it either."

"Elvis Lipps! What a fuckin' pretentious bullshit name to give a kid. The father must be a fuckin' idiot! Anyway this Elvis kid called me once about five weeks ago and threatened me! He said I didn't deserve Gina! Do you believe this fuckin' guy!? He said I should never try to contact her again. My own daughter! My own daughter who doesn't even have a mother now and this guy has the nerve to tell me to never contact my daughter again!"

He turned away sharply, then spun back to face me. The memory brought a mounting rage, and angry words boiled out of him. "That fuckin' Elvis kid is dead! Okay, Dane! He's fuckin' dead!"

"If I could bring her back to you would you..."

He cut me off. "*I'm* going to bring her back! *I'm* going to find them, blow his brains out, and bring her back! Okay!"

"Your daughter may not think much of your plan."

He thrust an angry finger into my face. "Don't bullshit me! I don't give a damn what she thinks! She's not even old enough to think! You know what her problem is? You know what all these fuckin' teenagers' problem is? They're all spoiled on junk food, sex shows on TV, soda and that shit music they listen to. Then there's all that tech shit they're wired into, and the fuckin' media telling them what to wear so they can get high or laid! The whole society is sick, Cooper. Fuckin' corrupt, greedy and sick! You know what I'm talking about, being in the shit business you're in!"

I tried for sympathy and understanding. "Mr. Callo, they're just kids. Kids make mistakes. We all make mistakes."

He didn't hear me. "When I get her back here, I'm going to beat the shit out of her and lock her up in her fuckin' room for a month!"

I eased away, and strolled over to the window that presented a good view of the golf course. Heat shimmered off the electric green grass. Golfers strolled. I kept my back to him. "Mr. Callo, I can offer you a million dollars to cancel the contract."

He laughed darkly. "Are you fuckin' with me, Cooper?"

I turned. "No, I'm not."

"And if I take the money, then what? Then his father gives his asshole son a tongue lashing? Meanwhile, I've been insulted and my little girl's been abused by this jerkoff and he just walks away, because you know some fuckin' lawyer will jerk me around on the statutory rape case. Like I want to go through all that shit. No fuckin' way! I'm not made that way. I'm not the forgiving type, Cooper. And I bet you're not either. Would you forgive that fuckin' loser if it was your daughter?"

Our gazes locked.

"I can go to two million."

Paul approached me, fuming. "How much is Elvis' father worth?"

"I don't know." I suspected Paul had a ballpark knowledge of what Abner Lipps was worth.

"I want everything. I want it all—all his money, his houses, boats, cars, what ever he owns, that's what I want. I want him to hurt. I want him and his wife to bleed! I want him to be beaten and sorry that he ever brought that little prick into the world! I want him to be as sick to his stomach as I am! That's my price. That's my fuckin' price, okay? If he won't agree to that, then his little Elvis impersonator bastard is dead! You got that!? And if you or anybody else gets in the way, they're dead too. Okay!?"

I finished my drink. I stared down into the empty glass. I swirled the ice around, listening to its ice music. I nodded. "Yeah... Okay. I'll pass along the message."

I let the silence stretch out. I felt his burning speculating eyes on me.

I'd have to go down another road. A dark road. "Mr. Callo...You work for a very respectable and prosperous company: Aliton Enterprises. They own hotels and casinos here in Las Vegas, in South America and in Europe. They own a string of fast food restaurants that stick out in those sprawling malls all across this great land of ours. They own real estate and marinas and investment firms. The board of directors are respected and some are well-known CEOs and financial consultants. I noticed that at least one has advised Presidents Bush and Obama during the financial crisis of 2008. I also noted that the big boss has given millions in campaign contributions to a certain political party. All that is big news. There are a lot of big eyes watching all that big news."

Paul nearly growled at me. "What the fuck are you getting at, Cooper?"

"Mr. Callo, your guy hasn't found the kids. Why?"

"He'll find them. He'll fuckin' find them!"

I rolled my shoulders and inhaled a breath, indicating the expansive room with a sweep of my hand. "You're an ambitious man, Mr. Callo. And you're smart. You have an MBA from Michigan State. Your father is Anthony Callo. He has been a very successful and careful business man. He owns restaurants and hotels. He has controlling interests in some tech companies and media companies, whose names many people would easily recognize. Mr. Callo...you are a very savvy and wise man. You are methodical, according to the background history I received from my low-paid, but very efficient, secretary."

Callo started toward me, his face twisted up in a threat. "You better be very careful with me, Cooper. Very fuckin' careful."

I set my glass down on the bar. "Mr. Callo. If things go wrong, and in my experience in this business, things always go wrong—your—let's say, superiors would not be happy with you. There are just too many what ifs to throw the dice and hope for the best. What if Elvis is killed by your man? Elvis' father does have money and some influence to make some noise. He knows the governor of Tennessee. His brother is a lawyer and prosperous businessman. Yes, Mr. Abner Lipps could make noise. Media noise. I suspect you know that your wife's father is an ex-cop. He's probably waiting for you to make a mistake. You know this man better than I, since I've never met him but... Well, like I said, there are a number of what ifs."

Paul glared at me.

"Mr. Callo, maybe you recall some recent news. Some NYPD detectives and a state prosecutor have sifted through many hours of cellphone logs, videotape and even some cigarette butts. As a result, there are some guys back in the city who are facing federal murder charges."

Callo said, sharply. "Is this your 'let's scare the dumb-shit', Cooper?"

I kept going. "I imagine your Assistant title would just go away, and I don't mean in the way of a promotion. You might wind up working for your father, Mr. Callo. And my understanding is, neither of you particularly cares a lot for the other. You have worked very hard to separate yourself from your father and to make your own way in the world. And, you have succeeded. These are interesting times, Mr. Callo. More careful and sensitive times. Today, the smart guys who get ahead, fly under the radar. They don't let themselves stand out too much. The Big guys don't like it. And the Big guys watch everything these days. At least, that's been my experience."

Many things passed across Paul's face: rage, fear, calculation and a slow, struggling recognition. He stepped over to the window and locked his hands behind his back. He turned slowly, watching me. "Mr. Cooper, you fuckin' surprise me."

I counted 10 beats. "Mr. Callo, I can make all this bad business go away. I can make it all end nice for you and me and everybody else. You'll get your daughter back and you'll make a lot of money to boot. Three million dollars will hurt Abner Lipps. It may bankrupt him. Surely, you've had some of your people crunch his numbers. The economy is killing him. Cars aren't selling. His restaurants are struggling and his carpet outlets down in Georgia are all in the red. He's straining to keep all of his ducks in a row. You know that. Three million will hurt him real bad. It might break him into a lot of painful little pieces. Elvis will not stay with his parents under any circumstances. That will break the father and the mother.

That will most likely destroy Mr. Abner Lipps. Elvis will eventually—sooner than later—self destruct. He's not the type to make friends easily. Enemies yes. Good friends. No."

Callo nodded, absently, mind churning. A dark smile cracked his lips.

I was almost finished. "Hell, Mr. Callo, I'll even scare Elvis with hit man stories and then knock him around a little bit. He's caused me a lot of trouble too." I narrowed my eyes on Callo's. He was blinking fast. "Your superiors, Mr. Callo, must be aware of what happened to your wife. They, as you and I both know, are watching you with great interest. They must be thinking something like this: Promotion? Or no promotion? That is the question. Is Callo smart or is he a little bit too emotional over trivial things for us to trust him with bigger and better things? Is he smart or is he an emotional stupid? Is his interest of and for the group, or is it of the selfish kind? Me first, the hell with the company."

Callo paced, hands flexing. I could almost hear his mind working. He stopped, giving me a long, icy stare. "Are you threatening me, Cooper?"

"No, sir. I don't need to. You're threatening yourself and you and I both know it."

I'd taken it as far as I dared. I turned and started for the door. Paul's voice stopped me. "Where are you staying, Cooper?"

I faced him. "Here. It's a nice place. Well managed. Congratulations."

He considered me, I thought, with an eye of cold calculation. "The room...everything is on the house."

"Thank you," I said.

"Now let me give you some advice, Cooper. You're smart. But don't be too smart. Too smart is dumb.

Whatever the old man's paying you, it's not worth it. You should get out of this. Like you said, Cooper, something always goes wrong. Do you really want to be there when that something goes wrong?"

"Well, my father wanted me to go into the construction business with him. I think about it sometimes."

Callo coughed out another mirthless laugh. "Fathers… that's another whole fucked up thing isn't it, Cooper?"

"I'm a big boy, Mr. Callo."

"But not stupid, I hope."

"Only in love, Mr. Callo. In love, I'm a complete fool."

He grinned, a big broad grin that showed perfect white teeth. "Aren't we all, Mr. Cooper? When it comes to love, aren't we all fuckin' fools?"

We were both nodding, when his phone rang. I left.

I found a lounge that was relatively quiet and dark. A guitar player strummed tunes from the '60s and '70s, as I sat in a dark booth and had another Blantons. I re-ran the conversation with Paul in my head. What would he do? I didn't have a clue.

My phone rang. I grabbed it quickly, rose from the table and started for the lobby.

"Dane Cooper! It's Abner Lipps!" His voice was high with enthusiasm. "We just heard from Elvis. He's alive! He is well! He called his mother. He said you had talked to him and told him that I'd had a damn heart attack!"

Abner laughed wildly. "Well Lucille nearly had one when he called her and told her that! So then Lucille calls me, all in a state of hysteria, and then after I get her calmed down, I get a call from Elvis! Well, I nearly did have that damn heart attack, Mr. Cooper! You found him! You son of a bitch, you found him and he is alive!"

CHAPTER 17

I walked along The Desert Passage shopping center that wrapped around the Aladdin. I was on my way to meet Abner at a restaurant called Cheeseburger At The Oasis, at 2:30. I passed shops selling Hawaiian items, but the store wasn't particularly busy. I was still walking at my usual New York move-out-of-the-way pace, but no one else was in any hurry, so I slowed down as well.

The sun had disappeared behind a bank of rolling white clouds, and there was a kind of softness to the air. I took a couple of deep breaths to help still my racing thoughts. I spotted the restaurant, near a fountain, and loosened my tie before entering.

Inside, I noticed that the waitresses wore grass skirts. The place had potential! The flowers at the entrance were long, slender and exotic; the walls a jungle green; the accompanying colors, exotic yellows and reds. It brought thoughts of big girly drinks with fruit and little colored umbrellas that were awesome and expensive. This was the land of Cheeseburgers, Mai-Tais, and Rock N' Roll! Ah, how wonderfully American! But somehow it made me long for the gentle sliding twang of an Hawaiian guitar, the peaceful rasp of the sea lapping at the shore and a warm Polynesian smile.

Abner saw me and waved me over to his table. We said our hellos and I sat.

Abner was still in a good mood. He wore khaki pants, a yellow polo shirt and a brown ball cap. Reading glasses were perched on his nose.

"This is some place, huh, Dane? Exotic as hell. Reminds me of the trip to Hawaii, Elvis, Lucille and I took about two years ago. We went to this bar, where Elvis sang *All Shook up*, *Teddy Bear* and *Love Me Tender*. He brought the damn house down. They loved him! Absolutely loved him! People came up to him telling him how talented he was, how much he reminded them of Elvis Presley and how he would surely be a big star some day."

"How did you leave it with Elvis when you spoke with him?" I said, bluntly, shattering his good memory.

He looked over the menu, ignoring me. "I am so fond of cheeseburgers. I think I'm going to get that five-napkin cheeseburger with mushrooms, guacamole and green chilies. What about you?"

"I'm not hungry," I said, setting the menu aside.

"How about a damn Mai-Tai?" Abner asked, eagerly.

"No thanks. Maybe a beer."

"You got to think exotic, Mr. Cooper."

I looked away, playing back some of my conversation with Paul Callo. I could have said more and I could have said less.

"Mr. Cooper, I'm thinking that Lucille and me should go on a long trip when this is all over. Maybe to Paris or Rome. I recall a good friend of mine telling me to be careful of pickpockets over there. He said he was robbed in a train station. Now you're a detective—how can I protect myself?"

It took effort to focus on his question. It annoyed me. "Carry your wallet in your front pocket and don't wear loose-fitting pants. And wrap a thick rubberband around your wallet. The rubber makes it harder for pickpockets to slide the wallet out smoothly. The best thing is to buy a belt-loop wallet. It attaches to the belt and tucks inside the pants behind the front pocket."

Abner looked at me in grateful admiration. "Now I'll just do that, Mr. Cooper. Thank you. That's dammed good advice."

"When you spoke with Elvis, did he tell you where he was?" I asked.

Abner took off his reading glasses and tossed them on the table. "Why don't you let me enjoy the fact that I've just learned that my son is alive? It's the first time in weeks that I have been able to pull a comfortable breath. Why don't you, Mr. Cooper?"

"Because we're running out of time."

Abner drummed his fingers on the table and closed his eyes. "I take it that your little meeting didn't go so well?"

"I don't know. Time will tell and we don't have much of that."

"How much did you offer him?" Mr. Lipps asked, averting my eyes.

"He wanted more than just the money. He wanted everything you've got."

Abner opened his hot, bulging eyes and reached for the glass of ice water. He swallowed half of it down. "That son of a bitch! Tell me who he is. I'll kick his ass all over Las Vegas!"

"Mr. Lipps..."

"Tell me!" He demanded.

"No! Now listen to me!"

The waitress appeared. She had the young innocent face of an angel. I wondered if she was. She must have seen the conflict in our faces. She became meek and retiring. Abner barked his order at her. I presented one of my most practiced pleasant faces, but she looked at me strangely as she retreated, so it probably needed more work. I hadn't ordered anything.

Abner became inward and agitated. "Elvis wouldn't tell me where he was. He was pissed off because I didn't have a heart attack. He blamed everything on me. No matter what I said he turned everything against me. I told him I'd help him do whatever he wanted. I told him I would stay out of his way, if that's what he wanted. I begged him to tell me where he was so I could come and see him, but he just hung up on me."

"You tried again?"

"Sure. I'd hear him pick up, then hang up. I called him two more times, but he just picked up, then hanged up."

"You called him immediately after you spoke with him? I mean, as soon as he hung up, you called him right back?"

"Yes."

I leaned forward. "Have you called that number since then?"

"Yes, but it was a wrong number or something. The kid I spoke with said he didn't know Elvis. I told him this was the number Elvis called me from. The kid just hung up on me. I don't understand nothing anymore. Nothing! Everything is just all messed up."

"Give me that number," I said.

Abner did. I added it to my phone's contact list. I noticed the number was a different number from the one Elvis had given to Darcy. It was a 646 area code which meant the phone was owned by someone in New York City, the Bronx or Brooklyn.

Abner looked up, alertly. "What now?"

"I'm not going to get into specifics, Mr. Lipps, but I believe I'll be able to find Elvis soon."

Abner lifted his hands, helplessly. "How? When?"

"I'm not ready to discuss it right now."

Abner regarded me with irritation.

I continued. "I'm going to fly back to New York tonight. I'll be back by early morning."

"I'll go with you."

"No. You should go home and be with your wife. I'll call you as soon as I know something."

Abner surged forward and seized my arm. "You're gonna protect my boy, Cooper, right? No matter what, you'll take care of my boy?"

I looked into his anguished wide eyes. "Mr. Lipps...I'll do everything I can."

His eyes dropped, then came back up on me. He relaxed his grip and his arm fell to the table. "I'm not so hungry anymore, Mr. Cooper."

I looked away, contemplating my next move. I needed some air, so I said my goodbyes and walked away feeling low and troubled, as if something inside had been punched loose and was banging around in my gut. What the hell was it? Pride? Frustration? Jealousy? Fear?

I called Darcy. I heard persistent ringing and then the fall into voicemail.

"Hello, this is Darcy-Lynn, please leave me a message."

"Darcy. Dane. Call me."

Then I texted her the same message.

I marched toward the hotel. Some years ago when I was still with the NYPD, Shanahan had fallen for a sexy young bartender who worked at a reputable hotel on the upper East side. He had it bad and he was married and had a baby. He agonized about it.

"I love her, Dane. I can't help it, I just love her."

We stood outside an 8th Avenue Deli, sharing a bag of chips and gulping down sodas. It was lightly raining and it was night. I'd never seen him so haggard and defeated. He hadn't slept, he chained smoked and he couldn't focus on the job.

"What the hell do I do, Dane-O?" he asked. "I don't know... what the hell to do?"

"What do you mean what do you do? You've got a wife. You've got a beautiful baby at home. What the hell's the matter with you? There's no question here."

Shanahan didn't seem to hear or see anything. He stared off into the cold rain, his trench coat open and flapping in the autumn wind. A couple drew up to us. They were 30 something and they were huddled under a broad red umbrella, cozy and laughing. Obviously tourists, they asked us for directions. Shanahan didn't even see them. That's how troubled he was. I gave them directions and they giggled away.

I turned to Pat. "When something's obvious, partner, you don't have to ask any questions. Who the hell is this bartender? Some girl you met two months ago? How long have you been married? It doesn't make sense."

Shanahan faced me, eyes burning. "Yeah, that's right. So what? Huh? You know what, Dane, this girl comes from a good family. She's good. She works hard. She's going to Hunter College. She likes me. Respects what I do. She's majoring in history or premed or..., I don't know, some damn thing. I should know that. Why don't I remember that?"

I shook my head. "So what? You have a wife, Pat. I don't care if this girl is like a saint. So what? Listen to me. You have a wife and kid. That's it. End of story here."

Shanahan glared at me. "Is everything really that simple for you, Cooper? Is everything so fucking simple? Don't you understand how things just happen sometimes? Things that you can't control. Things that make you think about how different your life could have been or still could be? Maybe you find the happiness you didn't think was ever coming your way. You ever think about that, Cooper? Well, I do. I just can't control this."

"Or maybe you just don't want to control it," I said.

Shanahan drained his soda. "So it *is* that simple for you, isn't it, Cooper?"

I shrugged. "Yeah. It's that simple. This is simple."

"You are full of shit, you know that. Full of self-righteous shit!"

He left me there. I watched him brace against the wind, his big shoulders hunched, head down and he shambled off into the foggy night.

Why did I think it was simple? Why?

I entered the hotel, crossed the wide lobby filled with chatty conference people wearing name tags, and found the bank of elevators. I pressed the silver round button and waited, folding my arms.

I had been in love only once. I married Connie because I was in love and I knew I was in love. It was simple. I think I even told Shanahan that. I'm sure I told him it was just so simple and maybe that's why he'd latched on to the phrase. I loved Connie and there was never any doubt about it.

A few weeks later, Pat stopped seeing the bartender. He was in a dark funk for weeks. He brooded, drank heavily and sent his wife, Jean, off on a vacation to the Caribbean with a girlfriend. The baby got dropped off with her parents.

Finally, one night as Pat and I sat over a beer after work, Pat opened up a bit.

He told me that he and the bartender had broken it off. "I told her I was married and had a kid. I told her I couldn't go on because I felt like a sack of shit all the time. She said love was all fucked up. I knew what she meant. I knew just what she meant. Hell, I didn't understand anything about it and I was sick of thinking about it. You know what she said, Dane-O? She said she loved me. She said it over and over till I couldn't stand it anymore. So, I told her to stop it. Just stop it!"

Pat gripped the base of his beer glass, staring at it like it was some kind of dead thing, then he lowered his head in humiliation. "I did the most stupid thing, Dane. I mean, the most stupid fucking thing. I gave her money. It was, I don't know, like a thousand bucks or something. You know what she did? She kept it. She said, I'm keeping this. I said, fine, keep it. I want you to have it. Then she reached up, pulled my head down to hers and she kissed me. Kissed me long and hard. And she was crying. Big tears. Jesus, Cooper, leaving her was the toughest thing. Really, a hurtful tough thing to do. It was like a stab in the chest."

That was the last time Pat ever spoke about it. But I noticed that from then on, something in Pat had shifted; he was different. He was a little more distant, and he was harder, like he'd thrown up a big concrete wall over his big chest and nothing was going to knock that wall down and nobody was ever going to scale it.

When I swiped the room key, pushed the door open and entered, I looked about. I shut the door quietly, and gradually worked my way over to the blond coffee table that held magazines and a white sheet of hotel note paper. I picked it up. I read the following:

Dearest Dane:

I'm leaving. I'm not sure where I'm going yet, but I'm leaving. Thank you for all you did for me. I'm at least able to stand and breathe and feel like I can go on now. Thank you for that. I don't know how this whole thing will end, but I don't want to be around when it does end. It would kill me. I wish things were easier. But nothing in life is simple is it? Good luck, dear Dane. Take care of yourself and please forgive me for all of my many shortcomings.

Love,

Darcy

As I lay on the bed, my arm resting over my eyes, I thought about Elvis' phone calls. Earlier, I'd used my phone and the internet to find the location of the cell-phone numbers I'd received from Darcy and Abner: 2 numbers were from New York. One, Long Island. What was Elvis doing? How was he communicating? He was keeping it simple. Smart boy. He was keeping it very simple.

It was an incident that had occurred a few months back, while I stood in a morning coffee line at the Star Struck Deli in Manhattan. I felt a tap on my shoulder. I turned. She smiled, a young girl showing perfect white teeth, short blond hair and a diamond stud on the right side of her little up-turned nose.

"Can I use your phone for a minute to call my boy-friend?" she asked. "I dropped my phone and it's dead."

My flight was at 11:45pm. I'd be back in New York about 7:30am. I got up. I had three hours before I had to be at the airport. I ordered a pot of coffee and the club sandwich. As I chewed, I strained to collect my thoughts so I could catalog them and arrange them into some logical order. Every image that flashed through my head had a fuzzy edge around it. No two images matched and I couldn't connect the dots from one fragment of thought to another. My eyes burned from lack of sleep. I had a headache.

Finally, I called Darcy. Voicemail. I didn't leave a message. I thumbed through email messages: nothing important. I sat and made a steeple with my fingers and placed it at the tip of my nose. I stared at my phone. It seemed to speak to me. "Dane," it said. "Make the calls."

My mind slowly cleared and I shut my eyes to focus. I lowered my steeple hands and grabbed my phone. I scrolled through my contact list until I found the three phone numbers: the two Darcy had given me and the number Abner gave me. I touched the first number: Elvis' first call to Darcy. It rang three times.

"This is Neil," the deep male voice said.

I said, "Neil... you don't know me. I'm Dane Cooper."

"Yeah, I don't know you. Whassup?"

"I'm trying to reach a friend we both may know. Elvis Lipps?"

"Don't know him. You must have the wrong number, buddy."

"No, wait! Maybe you let someone use your phone...maybe yesterday? Wednesday?"

"My phone... no I don't... oh wait a minute. Yesterday?"

"Yes. Yesterday?"

"Oh, yeah. I let some dude use it for a phone call. He gave me twenty bucks. We were in a diner."

"Was he a good looking guy? Maybe 20 years old?"

"Yeah. Black hair. Good lookin' dude, yeah."

I took a quick, anxious breath. "Where was this, Neil?"

"In a diner. In Montauk."

"Montauk, New York?"

"Yeah. My girlfriend and I drove out yesterday morning. We went to the lighthouse. I asked her to marry me out there."

"Oh, well… Congratulations, Neil. Look. Was he with anyone?"

"Look, man, I'm at work. We've got to cut this short."

"Okay. Okay. Did you notice if he was with anyone?"

"A girl. Kind of trashy lookin' young thing. Lots of tattoos on her forearms. Flowers and like a Buddha or something like that. Lots of red lipstick. Lots of bleached blond hair with dark roots."

"Did the guy talk to you?"

"No. Just said he needed to use the phone and gave me the money. He went outside. That made me kind of nervous, but I watched him. He brought it back. Nice dude."

"Were they eating there?"

"Yeah, look I've got to go, man."

"Did they say they were staying in Montauk?"

"No… I don't know. I'm goin' man. Cheers."

He hung up.

I shot up, snatched my legal pad and wrote down everything as I remembered it. I retrieved my phone and tapped on the next number. This was the second number. The number that Darcy had given me from our morning talk with Elvis. The phone rang 8 times and dropped into voicemail. It was a young, girlish, playful voice. "Hey, Marilyn here. But I'm not here. Message me."

I didn't leave a message. I called every fifteen minutes for an hour. Finally my phone rang. It was Marilyn's number. I answered. "Dane Cooper."

I heard Marilyn's cautious voice. "Who is this?"

"Dane Cooper...I was..."

She cut me off. "Why do you keep calling me?"

"Marilyn, I'm trying to reach a friend and I think you may have lent him your phone to make a call this morning."

"What friend? What's his name?"

"Elvis Lipps."

"What the hell kind of a name is that?"

"You don't know him?" I asked.

"No way. You have the wrong number. Stop calling me, man. You're like freaking me out."

"Marilyn, wait a minute. Did some guy borrow your phone this morning? Maybe he gave you some money to use it?"

A long silence. "Yeah...a real good lookin' guy. Sweet. Good smile. Real hot lookin' guy. He gave me 20 bucks. Is that your friend?"

"Yes, that's him. Where were you when you gave him the phone?"

Marilyn's voice softened and grew with interest. "I was in a diner in Montauk. Some girlfriends and I went out for the day. We just got back. We were eating breakfast at a place there. Anthony's."

I worked on relaxing my voice. "Did you talk to the guy?"

"Yeah, some. He said he was staying out there for awhile. Said he had family out there, but he left his phone at the house. So he asked to use mine."

"Did he say where the house was?"

"Why are you asking so many questions? Why don't you call him?"

"Because he's not answering his phone. I'm getting worried about him."

"Oh...well, he seemed okay. He didn't say where he was staying. Hey, why don't you give me his number? I'll keep calling and see if I can reach him? I gave him my number just in case. When you reach him, tell him to call me."

I thought, Elvis should be captured by the CIA, trained and used as a secret weapon. His powers over women should not be wasted on old whores, school teachers and 15-year-old kids. His infinite magnetism needed a global exposure—skillfully applied to toppling evil regimes by intrepid liaisons with the wives of dictators, Russian premiers, evil presidents and a corrupt Senator or two. I had to keep this kid alive if only for purely selfish reasons: I wanted to experience this kid's powers first hand.

"Thanks, Marilyn, but Elvis must have lost his phone."

"My name is Marilyn Siegal. I'm on Facebook and..."

I interrupted. "Was he with anybody?"

"No, he was sitting alone at the counter.

"Did he say anything else to you?"

"Not really. He was outside on the phone for ten or fifteen minutes. Then he came back in, thanked me and left. I asked him if he wanted to join us but he said he had to go."

"Thanks, Marilyn. If you think of anything else, please call me."

"Yeah, sure."

I scribbled down everything on the legal pad and stood. I pinched the bridge of my nose and blew out a sigh. Yep, I should have realized what Elvis was up to this morning! It was obvious—red flashing light—train coming-down-the-track-right-at-you obvious! Okay, so I'm not as tech-brain savvy as I should be. But sometimes the most obvious things are blocked by twenty other things that are standing right in front of you shouting at you for attention. Too many thoughts! Too many emotions! Too many possibilities! Too many people! It can make you stupid and that's what had happened. I had been Big Time Stupid!

Love is blind and love makes one stupid—Me stupid! Callo's man would not be so stupid. He knew Darcy was the prime contact and that sooner or later Elvis would contact her, and she would undoubtedly run to him. Rod Faulkner surely knew the same thing. But Darcy would never run to Elvis as long as she was with me. So, my choice was to either wait and follow her, or stay and plead my case to Paul Callo. I'd chosen Callo.

Dane Cooper, maybe you're just not as smart, good lookin' or skilled as you think you are! Maybe you could use a partner to bounce ideas off of. Someone not so entangled, so caught up and so damn stupid!

I packed and left the hotel.

CHAPTER 18

I sat in first class luxury, sipping bourbon, staring out into a mass of stars. In the right front seat, a man watched an old black and white movie on his portable DVD player that starred Robert Mitchum. Mitchum was a private detective, and as I recall, an angry one. I silently toasted him, wishing all detectives—real and imagined—big pay, easy assignments and gorgeous buxom babes. I wished them a big suitcase full of cash, with a free ticket to some South American town where the emerald sea dazzled, the exotic drinks kept a comin' and "where never is heard a discouraging word and the sky is not cloudy all day."

The truth was, I missed Connie. Didn't I always miss her when I was bone tired and feeling sorry for myself? I closed my eyes and imagined her there in that quaint South American town. She's wearing a two-piece red bikini, a white fedora perched stylishly on her head, staring out at a calm, turquoise sea. She calls to me and I lope across the sand toward her, splashing through foaming surf, feeling the warm sun bake my shoulders and back. We meet and I say something like, "Did you know you were married to a hopeless romantic?"

And she says, in her low throaty voice that used to drive me crazy with love, "You, Dane Cooper, are about as romantic as a bull charging a matador."

I say, "Sounds romantic to me."

She says, "Shut up and charge me. I'll drop my cape."

Who knows, after Connie died, maybe she went to that South American town. She loved the sea. She loved exotic drinks and I think she even liked cowboy songs. Most certainly she listened to Country and Western music.

This was one of those nights when I ached for her. I finished the bourbon, felt the welcomed waves of darkness wash over me and I drifted off to sleep in that little town. Sentimental? Only when I watch Robert Mitchum movies in a first class seat, 35,000 feet above the Earth.

After we touched down at LaGuardia and taxied to the gate, I checked messages and emails. Nothing from Darcy. I had a text from Shanahan. It concerned Donavan Lassiter's murder.

"Murder weapon—wine bottle. Cabernet! Detectives r lookin' for ur boy Elvis."

I texted him back. *"Tell them to stand in line."*

In the taxi on the Long Island Expressway, we swerved and weaved through early morning traffic, racing along as if this Olympian yellow cab driver was going for the Gold. I didn't say anything, even though a light snow was shooting past us in hectic patterns. This driver was from some Middle Eastern country and was surely proud that he had mastered the New York art of crazy haste, anytime day or night. He'd also mastered the distant glare and matter-of-fact attitude of you like it? Good. You don't like it? I don't care. I admired him. I gave him a good tip and he nodded at me, smiling broadly, showing some gapped teeth. It was a nice face. A tired face. The face of good man. He told me he worked 12 hours a day and was barely making a living. No wonder he was going for the Gold. He didn't have much choice.

Inside my apartment, I parked my carry-on near the bed, shed my clothes and stepped into the shower. The thin spray of water warmed and soothed my sore leg. Flying, even in first class, always brought a stiff, aching leg. I closed my eyes, presenting my face to the spray.

I needed a quick nap. But I wouldn't get one. I stared at the bed and smelled Darcy's perfumed pillow. Where had Darcy-Lynn gone? Back to Knoxville? Back to Elvis in Montauk? Darcy intended to give Elvis the $10,000. She said so. I believed her. She would have to meet him. She would demand a meeting, anyway. I knew Darcy that well. What would happen? Would she ask him to go away with her? Would Elvis tell her about his 15-year-old lover, who he intended to escape to Europe with? Did Darcy call Rod and tell her about the potential meeting?

Where was Paul Callo's man? Had Elvis contacted Mrs. Johnson?

I glanced over at the ember digital clock: 8:50am.

At 9:45am, I had picked up my rental car, a silver gray Corolla, and was traveling to Montauk, New York. I had texted and called Darcy repeatedly, but there was no response.

I texted Helen. *"Off to Montauk. Call if you need to talk to me."*

I had been to Montauk only once, when I was around 12 years old. My parents took us there to see the light-house and to eat seafood at Gosman's Dock Restaurant that overlooked Long Island Sound. Montauk is located

on the far eastern tip of Long Island. You see bumper
stickers that say **Montauk The End** or **The Last Resort**
or **The Living End**.

Montauk is known for its fishing, for its lighthouse
(the first lighthouse built in New York, in 1796) and for
its history. In the 1920's Carl Fisher, the celebrated real
estate magnate who helped develop the Miami Beach
resort, traveled to Montauk and was struck by its rugged
beauty: the sprawling broad beaches, craggy cliffs and
wide expanse of sea. It reminded him of England and
Scotland. He purchased thousands of acres of land, with
the intention of developing Montauk much as he'd done
Miami Beach. Unfortunately, after Mr. Fisher put up the
massive Tudor-style Montauk Inn, a yacht club, golf
course and surf club, the depression slammed in, sucking
the life out of him and his money supply. He died a few
years later and Montauk was reclaimed by sand, sea and
fishermen.

Many "Montaukians" are grateful for his misfortune,
believing Montauk blessed to be the drowsy, unspoiled
town that they have known and loved for many years.
Though it swells with tourist population in summer, it
remains raw, rough and remote in winter, with a vast
heaving sea that explodes against jagged cliffs and sprawls
across broad deserted beaches. Montauk is still a destina-
tion for fishermen and fisherwomen worldwide, and it
remains a small town with no stoplights, one chain store
and no billboards shouting out things we all buy and talk
about or wear and toss into dumps, or things we eat and
drink and shit and forget.

I left Amagansett at 12:45pm. Montauk was only minutes away. The overcast sky was gray and rolling north-
east in a hurry. Noisy gusts shuddered the car and mad
snowflakes circled and crashed and fled into trees and

undulating sand dunes. I replayed Abner Lipps' words in my head.

"If at the end of this week, Friday at 6pm, you decide that after all of your investigations, you feel it's fruitless to go on, I'll still pay you $25,000."

I had used the three hours traveling time in hard labor thought, swinging pick and shovel, heaving bits of shattered conversation, memory and emotional rock, struggling to unearth some understanding of what the hell I hoped to accomplish in Montauk and how I'd gotten myself into this chain gang mess to begin with.

Well, it had started with money. I needed money. Abner gave me money. Lots of money. It was a simple missing persons case. I believed I'd find the kid. I believed it would be easy, given the information Abner had related. Kids are easy to track today. There are technology trails everywhere to track them. Kids love to communicate and share every silly bit of minutia about every silly minute of their silly day. Take the money, Cooper. Take two weeks and find the kid. Okay, well it has been two weeks.

But it was a ridiculous case to begin with. A kid named Elvis who looked like Elvis, who was the reincarnation of Elvis, whose weird controlling parents wanted to keep controlling Elvis because the mother was nuts and the father was well, an Elvis fruitcake fan. Okay, fine, Cooper, you took the money because it was a job and that's what investigators do. They take the money when it comes and they investigate. Okay, I can't really fault you for that. The rent must be paid and Helen must have new kitchen cabinets.

But then, what the hell were you thinking about when you frolicked and play-pinned Darcy-Lynn Roberts? Simple? Her ex-husband wants to kill her. She probably wants to kill him. Paul Callo wants to kill Elvis and so does Darcy's husband. Who knows, maybe the old whore who would be Queen, wants Elvis dead too, to keep him away from her pink and puffed and well-buffed ladies.

So did I have a plan? Could I protect Elvis from Paul Callo's hit? Could I send Elvis back home to Momma? Would Elvis leave Gina, the tattooed kid from the desert land of Vegas? What would Darcy do when she learned that Elvis was jetting off to Europe with her ten thousand bucks, but not jetting off with her? Was she fragile enough to break down and go crazy?

This case was not what I had imagined when I left the NYPD to go private. What had I imagined? Not this.

Old Montauk highway unraveled in two lanes, rising with a clear view of the wide gray sea and then settling comfortably down into a quiet trail, past motels, a seaside restaurant and modest private homes. All seemed locked down and in a deep, tranquil sleep. Except the sea. It was turgid and restless. Huge gray slabs of it pounded the beach.

As I approached the town of Montauk and felt the expanse and freedom of big sea and sky, it occurred to me that life is not realistic. It's a dream, a nightmare and a series of abrupt encounters, mad collisions and emotional tangles. And then the game changes and the faces change and the rules change. Then that game ends and another begins. At least baseball has rules.

Where are the rules for life? They seemed written and true and agreed upon until a death, a natural disaster, a terrorist attack or a relationship goes sour. Then the rules change. Then the acid anger of revenge takes over—and then the exalted and beautifully written words and phrases that were scribed and repeated at weddings and at monuments are replaced by hate, a gun, a bomb or threats. New words and phrases stabilize and preserve the present insanity for a time, until the next insult, death or attack. And then for a while, we settle back into our uneasy chair while "sanity" awaits the next charge of the insane person or event.

Well, it was a three hour drive and I couldn't find a static-free radio station, I had no CDs and I'd never been a good whistler. Call me fast food philosopher Cooper. I'm cheap, quick and full of salt.

Anthony's Restaurant was on Main Street and the street was quiet. I easily found a parking space, parked and killed the engine. My Smith and Wesson .38-caliber was under my seat, packed in the leather holster. I considered strapping it on my hip and then hesitated. Who'd need a gun in a diner in the sleepy town of Montauk? I didn't strap it on. By rights, I should have visited the local sheriff to tell him I was in town, but I didn't. I wanted to come and step quietly. I'd hoped the encounters I was about to have would be unobtrusive.

I reached for my cashmere topcoat and the manila envelope that held Elvis' head shot and left the car. I shouldered into the coat and made my way along a peaceful street to Anthony's. I passed a pizza parlor and corner drugstore. I noticed that directly across the street was another diner name John's. Maybe Anthony and John had once been family? One was known for its pancakes. The other for being there first?

I pulled the glass door open and entered. The welcomed warmth felt good. There were two rooms, the front room being the main dining room. It had the diner style Formica table tops and green padded chairs. A counter with 10 stools was left. The second room was roped off, probably only used during the summer season.

As I strolled to the counter, two locals wearing baseball caps and flannel shirts lifted their eyes and followed me with mild interest. I slid out of my coat, laid it on the stool and sat on a revolving stool. I felt right at home. It was after one o'clock and I noticed a sign on the door that said they close at 2pm.

Another sign on the wall said the place had been there since 1952. It still had the look and feel of the 1950s. There were vintage Coca Cola signs, an antique sturdy steel cash register and some slightly faded black and white photos of fishermen on a marina posing with proud squinting grins, their catches held high.

I had a moment to pull my phone and check messages. There was nothing from Darcy, or Helen. Obviously, they'd all forgotten me. Perhaps it was all for the best. Darcy had me worried, though. Very worried. She'd not answered one of my several texts or phone messages.

A sturdy built woman of middle age approached with a coffee pot. She had the hint of a smile and an all business expression that suggested lunch was the most important meal of the day for her.

"Coffee?"

"Yes. Thanks."

She turned the white cup over and poured. I watched the coffee curl, rise and steam. I cupped my cold hands around its warmth.

"Know what you want?" she asked.

"Can I still get breakfast?"

"Yep."

"Two scrambled, ham, rye toast, please."

She nodded. Business done. She was gone.

When she brought the plate of ready food, I slid Elvis' photo toward her. She glanced at it as she slid the plate before me. As I'd anticipated, her face expanded and colored and opened to a youthful grin and joyful acknowledgment.

"I know him. He comes in here!"

"Yes... so I've heard."

"He's so nice. Real handsome boy. More handsome in person than in that picture. Looks a little like Elvis Presley. He said he's an actor. Are you his agent or something?" she asked, flushed now.

I wanted to slap the counter with the flat of my hand and say "Okay, dammit, enough already! I have had it up to here with this Elvis guy. Give me a break. Nobody is that good looking!"

But I didn't. I seized on her idea. "Yes, I'm his agent and he's sort of run away. He won't take my calls and I'm trying to get in touch with him because I've got a TV role for him and a contract for him to sign. Do you happen to know where he is?"

"What TV show is it?"

I drew a blank. "It's one of those Law and Order things."

Her face lit up anew. "Really? What role?"

I drew another blank. "...A detective."

She stared at me, doubtfully. "He seems too young for that."

"Well, yeah... but he's a young detective."

She thought about that and I spoke up before she thought too much. "Do you know where he is?"

"Oh yeah. He's staying right down the street at the Memory Motel. Just go out and turn left. I told them there were better places than that but he said he liked it there. He said he knew the Rolling Stones' song about the Memory Motel. That's why he stayed there. He said he knew all the words to the song and sang it sometimes. He said he'd sing it for me."

"That's nice."

"Yeah, the Stones stayed in Montauk back in the 1970s."

"I didn't know that. Is he alone?"

She frowned a little. "He has a girl with him. She seems a little young and she's all tattooed up. I just can't get used to all those tattoos…but my last boyfriend had a couple on both of his arms."

I marveled about how Elvis opened all doors and all mouths. "Well, thank you, Ms.?"

"Millie. Just call me Millie."

"Thanks, Millie."

She left reluctantly. I scooped the eggs, ate and pondered my next step. A few minutes later my phone rang. I looked down. It was Abner Lipps.

I turned away and cupped my hand over the phone. "Yes, Mr. Lipps."

"Have you found my boy, Mr. Cooper?"

"I'm close. Very close now."

"Fantastic! I know you'll get to him before that other guy gets him, Mr. Cooper. I have prayed about it and I feel it in my heart. Now, everything is working out just right and perfect, Mr. Cooper. And just like you said in the very beginning, you have got this thing all locked up, and you did it in only two weeks."

"I didn't really say I'd…"

He cut me off. "Look, Mr. Cooper, when you find Elvis, tell him I've got a Hollywood agent just waiting to take him on. His name is Jack August. He's big, Dane. He has Tom Cruise, Owen Wilson and a lot of boys like that. Elvis will be so thrilled, Mr. Cooper. I just know he'll be so damn thrilled when you tell him that. I know he'll want to get in touch with me as soon as you tell him that!"

I tried to break in "... Mr. Lipps, I don't know..."

He trampled on my words again. "Now listen to this, Mr. Cooper. Just listen to this!"

I wondered if he'd been drinking. He sounded over-heated. Forced.

"I showed Jack August some of Elvis' videos, you know, from Elvis' website, when he was singing in some clubs, and when he did those two local commercials, and I'm telling you Dane, Jack August said, and I'm quoting him here, 'Bring Elvis to see me as soon as you can. I think I can put him in touch with some people who are putting together a new movie about Elvis.' That's what he said, Mr. Cooper! Can you imagine?"

I tried to speak again. "Mr. Lipps, we first need to..."

"It's a movie about Elvis' young life—you know, just before he hit the big time. I'm just so damn excited, Mr. Cooper. Find my boy now and tell him that. I just know he's gonna be thrilled and come running home. I just know it!"

I surrendered. "Okay, Mr. Lipps. When I find him, I'll tell him."

I drained my coffee, gathered myself, waved to Millie and started off to the Memory Motel. Maybe Abner Lipps was right. Maybe Elvis would be thrilled. Maybe he'd jump at the chance to be a big Hollywood star. Something in my gut told me otherwise. Something in my gut told me that Elvis had already moved well beyond the dreams his father and mother had for him.

CHAPTER 19

Outside, there was blast of ocean wind that stung my face. I adjusted the collar of my coat and hunched up my shoulders, hearing the distant hiss of the sea. There was a magnificent bleakness to the day and to the town, all gray and misty. As I strolled toward the motel, I felt abandoned and isolated, as if I was in an old Twilight Zone episode, where I was one of the last men alive, after some yet-to-be discovered tragic event. As I pondered this, I also thought what a great hideaway Montauk was. These kids weren't stupid.

I saw a man approach, from the direction of The Memory Motel. He was a big man, about my height, but heavier. He wore a royal blue parka, brown Timberland boots and a blue ski cap, which he peeled off as he drew near. His black hair was tousled. He smoothed it with his broad ungloved hand.

I recognized him and I stopped abruptly. It was Rod Faulkner! He came within a few feet and planted his feet firmly before me. I noticed one hand was tucked into a deep pocket.

"Lost any 10 dollar bills lately?" he said, in a low, deep sinister voice.

I stared at him. I needed a minute to think—to re-cover from the shock. Had he been to the motel? Was Elvis dead? What had he done with Gina? How did he get here? Who could have tipped him off? Darcy? Was she here? My mind was a stunned, muddled mess. "I hope you spent it wisely," I said. "These are hard times."

He shook his head, not amused. "I was in the diner across the street when I saw you enter that other diner. It took me a minute to recognize you. Okay, who the hell are you?"

For some reason, I thought of Millie. Was she watch-ing us from the window? She had infinite breakfast and lunch experience tuning-in to customers' body language, facial expressions and low murmurs of conversation. Maybe her antenna was up. Would she sense danger and call for help? But I realized we were out of her line of vision, even if she was peering out the window.

"So who are you?" Rod repeated, forcefully.

"What are your intentions?" I said, sizing Rod up again. He was a bigger man than I'd remembered. He probably had ten to fifteen pounds on me. I saw no humor in his hard black, carnivorous eyes. I saw no fear there either. I saw firm purpose and determination in his broad 30s something face. I saw a man looking for challenge—for confrontation.

When he spoke, his voice was low and threatening. "Look, asshole. If you were following me back in Penn-sylvania, it must have something to do with Darcy-Lynn."

His macho manner provoked me. I should have con-trolled myself, but I didn't. "How do I know you're not following me?"

His eyes narrowed and shot hatred at me. "Are you trying to be an asshole?"

I stared back. "Yes... I am. I'm told I'm very good at it."

He blinked fast, telegraphing impatience. "Okay, fine. Have it your way." With his head he indicated right, down an asphalt road that led to the beach. "Let's go, down to the beach."

"It's cold out here. Why don't we go for another cup of coffee and discuss this."

His hand bulged forward in his right pocket. "Look, jerkoff, I'm only going to ask you one more time! Move!"

I remembered his house. I remembered seeing the .38 caliber Ruger. I remembered the two-inch barrel. I remembered my Smith & Wesson lying under my car seat. So close and oh so out of reach. I moved, turned left and walked a few steps ahead of him.

"A real smart ass..." Rod said, at a grumbling whisper.

I thought, "Okay, smart ass Cooper, now what?"

Naturally, since we all think of our own survival first, no matter how noble we are, how brave we are or how much money we've been paid to protect another, I wondered if Rod Faulkner was going to shoot me in the head down on the beach. If he'd already killed Elvis and Gina and maybe Darcy, wherever the hell she was, he had nothing else to lose. And, there was no friendliness about him. He did not seem in the mood to listen to any reason, not that I had any good reason to offer except for maybe a clumsy lie or two about something I had not been able to come up with yet.

A royal blue SUV crawled toward us. I noticed that its color exactly matched Rod Faulkner's Parka. It passed, the gray-haired female driver giving us no acknowledgement.

We strolled on, hearing the thunder of the sea; hearing the cries of seagulls and watching their drifting, balanced flight. The frigid wind punched away at us. I rubbed my ears while Rod ski-capped his head. Why did I never even think about wearing a hat? No hat, no gun and no options. What were my options? Make a break for it? If he had a gun, he'd drop me easily. My left limping leg would help see to it.

"Why are you limping?" Rod asked, as we approached a dune path.

"An old wound."

"Where, in Iraq?"

"No…" I calculated how much information to impart. "I had a kind of confrontation."

We started up the path, my wing tip shoes slipping in sand and taking on sand. Rod seemed to climb the path easily in his well-prepared-for-hikes outdoor apparel. We crested the dune hill and worked down to the beach, calculating slide, drift and balance. I swept the wide beach with hopeful eyes but saw no one. Waves curled, rolled and broke hard on the hard packed beach.

Rod surveyed the area and, when all was clear, he faced me with an expression of arrogant conquest. He snaked the gun from his pocket. It was the Ruger LCR.

"Nice gun," I said, feeling my saliva thicken.

"Now, tell me who you are and why you were following me?"

I had one plan. Tell him the truth. Make it sound businesslike and mercenary and try not to provoke. "My name is Dane Cooper. I'm a private detective. I was hired by Abner Lipps to find his missing son, Elvis."

Rod took a long time to consider this. I couldn't read anything on his face. "And have you found him?"

I had to speak loudly. The ocean was close to high tide. This was the question I had anticipated. "Not yet… but I will. Have you found him?"

Again, his face was a white piece of blank paper. No expression. His eyes were steady and I could almost feel them listening. "I know Elvis is here in town somewhere. I know Darcy-Lynn is on her way to meet him. I'll find them, together. That's what I'm waiting for and that's why I'm here, waiting for the right time. When I find them, I'll kill them. So I'm waiting. And then, while I'm waiting, what do you think happened? I find you. So, why were you following me?"

I had to be careful. "Routine. Your name came up when my secretary was researching Elvis' history," I said.

"How did it come up?"

I shrugged. "Your wife came up. Elvis and your wife. Anybody could find out about your married life through public records. Everything's public these days."

I saw a flash of anger in his eyes. "Why were you following me then? What the hell do I have to do with anything?"

"I was trying to find Elvis. I was following every lead. When I interviewed your ex-wife, she told me that you had threatened to kill Elvis. Naturally, I had to find out whether that was true or not."

"And what have you learned, Mr. Private Detective?"

My ears were stinging from the cold. I wiped my runny nose. "Well, since I haven't found Elvis, you would know more about that than I would."

Again, no expression.

"So where do you think Elvis is staying?" I asked.

He grinned, but it wasn't pleasant. "Yeah, where? How did you find out Elvis was here?"

I opened my hands. "I got an anonymous tip. But I think it's a dead end. Have you found him?"

"Maybe we got the same anonymous tip?"

"We can compare notes," I said, feeling my heart thump harder than normal. I did not like nor did I want that gun pointed at my gut. I have never particularly liked guns, except of course, when some nut case is trying to shoot me with one. Then I like my gun. Right now, I wished I had my gun.

"Did you sleep with my wife, Mr. Private Detective?"

I gave him a long, careful look. "So you're going to kill her?"

"Didn't answer the question, Mr. Private Detective."

"Maybe I didn't answer it because it's none of your business. You are legally divorced. If your ex-wife chose to sleep with me, and I will keep that to myself, it was her choice and my choice."

He took a step closer. His bare hand had pinkened from the cold, but he didn't seem to feel it. "Once you told me your name, I recognized it. I know all about you and Darcy-Lynn." His Tennessee accent stressed Darcy-Lynn, as if he was saying All Mine. "You see, asshole, I have a friend—a real good friend. She just happens to be friends with both Darcy-Lynn and me. She and Darcy-Lynn are kind of like sisters. They've known each other since high school."

I felt the hair on the back of neck tingle. I felt sick. I knew who that was. It was Carol Hemmings. She had tipped Rod off.

Rod continued. While he spoke, the gun, his nose, his eyes and his malevolent intention all seemed pointed at me, ready to fire. "Darcy-Lynn tells her everything. You see, this good friend still believes that Darcy-Lynn and I should get back together. She's a real romantic. I'm sure I know more about you, Mr. Private Detective, than you'll ever know about me."

I knew then what his intention was. I saw it in his flat dark eyes. He was going to drop me. He would toss my body down some sandy hole or in some deep water eddy off Long island Sound. Hell, maybe he'd just leave me where I fell on the beach. They don't call Montauk The End, for nothing.

I have experienced terror a few times in my life. In the NYPD as a uniformed cop, I was once trapped in a burning apartment on the Lower East Side of Manhattan. The fire had been set by a drug-pushing sociopath. It was a run-down, rat trap of a place with boarded up windows and only one door. I had been an idiot. I was young, inexperienced and oh so gung-ho to prove myself. I was locked inside the room, the blistering fire was spreading, and waiting outside in the hallway, was a welcoming shotgun. I heard the screaming fire trucks approach. I had few options.

Fortunately, my partner showed up and wasted the guy. I was saved. It took days for that terror to dissolve from my eyes and from my dreams. That fire had been close and hot. I was on my knees, coughing up a lung, waving away black, acrid smoke.

In the movies, the hero escapes with his life into the arms of a pretty girl. But in real life, you shake a lot, you drink a lot of Jim Beam and you wake up with night sweats. You yell at your best friend and your family over trivial things like, "This damn pizza's not hot enough! Your kids are too loud! Don't treat me like I'm 10 years old! Just leave me alone!" Sometimes you jerk awake in the middle of the night, terrified, and you want to shoot at sounds and shadows.

So here was Rod Faulkner pointing that damn gun at me. It was cold, the wind was sharp and I was hot with nerves and beginning to perspire. I was scared. What the hell were my options? Run? No. He'd just shoot me in the back. Beg for mercy? No. I could charge him—die like an honorable soldier who refused to stand flatfooted and be shot.

Rod sneered at me. "I suspect, Mr. Private Detective, that you are a low life piece of shit and the world would be a whole lot better off without you."

I began digging my heels into the sand, preparing myself for a good launch at him. "I can tell you're a school teacher. You're very articulate."

That angered him. That both pleased me and displeased me. He inched closer. "Look, asshole. I know all about Darcy-Lynn shacking up with you in your apartment in New York. I know details, because Darcy-Lynn gave our friend intimate details. Darcy-Lynn is a lot more kinky than you think, Mr. Private Detective. Or maybe you know that too. Did she talk dirty to you? Did she dance for you and try on all those wigs? Did she smoke dope with you, Mr. Private Detective? Did she threaten to shoot you with the handgun I bought her? I taught her how to shoot, Mr. Detective. She got real good at it. Believe it or not, she's a better shot than I am. She pulled it on me once. Then do you know what she did? She started stripping. Took off every little stitch of clothes, while she kept that gun pointed right at me."

He grinned, darkly. "I'll leave the rest for your imagination, Mr. Private Detective."

"I'd love to hear all about it," I said.

"I just bet you would, asshole."

I was ready to go. I might be able to hit him, deflect the gunshot and tackle him. It was the only chance I had and it was a slim one. I braced. My pulse was high and pounding.

"She's a real sexy bitch ain't she, Mr. Private Detective?"

I was about to attack when he did something that stopped me. He shoved the gun into his jacket pocket. He unzipped the parka, took it off and flung it away. It hit the sand. The gun anchored it against the wind. The parka flopped and writhed like something wounded.

My eyes shifted.

He glared, his face a mass of rage. "I'm gonna beat the shit out of you, Mr. Private Detective, and then I'm going to shoot you."

He wore a heavy black sweatshirt. His chest was thick. His arms, two heavy tree limbs with fists on the end.

He leapt at me. Amazingly, I stepped aside. He landed to my right, fists poised and ready for battle. "Come on, chicken shit! Come on."

I calculated distance and strategy. He ran at me, I backed off. He came again, head down and tucked, jabbing. This time, I cocked and fired a right. He knocked it away, swinging a swift right fist. He had swung through the target. He caught me in the ear. Pain stabbed. My ear rang. The ocean slammed the beach, sounding like exploding bombs. Off balance, I struggled to anchor my bum left leg, just as Rod came in with a low punch to my stomach and another to my right jaw. I went flying, falling, bouncing on the sand. I tasted blood. I felt out of touch. Reality? The world got all fuzzy. Rod had a right like a prize fighter. Didn't I read in his bio that he had boxed in college? Was that true or was my brain on the high swinging seat of a Ferris wheel, teetering, ready to drop?

He loomed large over me and I couldn't believe my eyes. He was actually dancing, jabbing into the air, inhaling, exhaling white vapor, waiting for me to get up.

When I took longer than I should have, he hitched up a sturdy leg and kicked me in the gut. I seemed to spill and roll and keep on rolling. For some weird reason, I remembered that on one of our first dates, Connie and I had gone bowling. I tasted sand. The sky was rolling. The sea was rolling and out of the corner of my eye I saw Rod edging toward me, dancing, shifting, shadowboxing. He gave whistling grunts of effort as he punched at the air.

My body felt punished. My head was spinning. "Get up, Dane!" I heard inside my pounding head. "Get up and fight!"

Pat Shanahan used to call it the Dane-O reserve. That reserve of strength and adrenalin that kicks in, when you feel like all the friendly energy and hope has fled your body and taken up residence in your opponent's, giving him all your well thought-out advantages.

I am not a fair fighter. I am not an honorable fighter or a good sport fighter. I fight to win, and I fight to survive.

I pushed to my knees as Rod came at me, his face rock-determined, his bulging, confident eyes leveling on me. I heaved a fist of sand into his face. Then another. He yelled in surprise, bicycling backwards, hands wiping and slapping at his face and eyes. I sprang at him. I gave him two fists to the stomach. They burst the air out of him. I launched a left to the side of his big head and a sturdy right directly into his nose.

My right hand went numb with pain. I winced. Rod stumbled, nose bloody. He tripped over his own feet and fell backwards. He hit, rolled, jumped up surprisingly fast, glowered indignantly at me and charged. I waited for him, then dropped. He was not as agile as I'd first thought. As he sailed over me, I punched him hard in the

balls. He crashed into the sand, all head, shoulders and
face. He screamed out obscenities of pain, writhing,
grabbing his two aching misfortunes, rolling and wailing.
I didn't wait. I crossed to him. I kicked him solidly in
the ribs. He toppled over, face stretched in agony.

"Get up!" I yelled. "Get up!"

My right hand was throbbing; my left was swollen and
stinging from the frigid wind.

"I'll kill you!" he shouted. "I'll kill you."

"Then get up!"

I allowed him to rise. He stood off-balance, puffing
vapor, his eyes filled with rage and pain. He blinked
rapidly, glancing about. His eyes changed. A thought
had struck.

I stepped back, panting, pulse racing, waiting for his
next move. My throat was dry, face ice cold, body pumping adrenalin.

Then he broke and ran around me, sand flying from
his heels. Surprised, I watched and my first thought was
that he was running away! Where? But then I saw what
he was after. His parka! The pocket of his parka. The
gun! That damn gun!

I didn't wait. I tucked my shoulder and charged, like a
bull charging a matador, expecting to feel the bullet's
impact. Expecting hammer blows to my chest; expecting
a slow blurring of consciousness; of memory; of life force
and the sudden final mystery of black annihilation.

I saw him squatting in the sand. I saw his hand snake
into the pocket and pull the revolver. I saw him push to
his feet. I saw his hand. I saw the gun rising, aiming,
pointing. I kept driving toward him.

I was just feet away when the bullet struck him. I
couldn't stop. I was in full gallop. I hit him just below
his left shoulder and we sailed, hitting the sand hard and

flat. I tumbled off, rolling right, disoriented, confused. I glanced about wildly, clouds of vapor puffing from my open mouth as I sucked in air. I hadn't heard the shot! Of course not! The ocean was loud. The hollow wind deafened my ears. I looked at Rod. He lay still, legs splayed, his wide dead eyes staring up into the steel gray sky. He did not twitch. He did not move. I saw a red spot in the center of his forehead. One red dot. My eyes found his weapon about 10 feet away.

I searched for a hiding place. I sprang to my feet, grabbed the weapon and, on hands and knees, scrabbled over to a clump of grass at the base of a dune and dropped. I periscoped up, probing. It was utterly desolate. I looked up the beach and down the beach. A mist was rising. There were clay-heavy fat clouds on the horizon. I placed the Ruger in the sand before me. I began to shiver. I folded my arms tightly around my chest for warmth.

What kind of rifle had killed Rod? How far away was the shooter—maybe 200 yards, 100 yards? More? In this wind, maybe it was a bolt-action small caliber high velocity load, maybe a 70 or 80 grain slug? Maybe the .243 Winchester? It's a smaller, lighter rifle and easy to carry. I've seen them. Shot one a couple years back. It can drop a small animal or a deer. Of course I had no idea what the weapon was that took Rod down. It was idle thought—an attempt to cool my agitated mind while I gathered my breath and my courage. My heart was kicking in my chest. I needed to settle, not give way to panic. Who was the shooter? Where the hell was he? Had he aimed at me and hit Rod by mistake?

I waited, watching, rubbing my stinging ears. Maybe it was five minutes, before I saw a dark speck rise from the dunes and approach just above and to my right, about 60 yards away. The dark speck grew in size. I reached for the handgun and crouched down, calculating distance and range. I couldn't hit anything with any kind of accuracy at 25 or 30 yards with the Ruger. Would this guy get closer?

The solemn figure came steadily on, taking sure and purposeful steps. The sand didn't seem to impede his stride or his pace. He crested the last dune and started down the other side. He was only 20 yards away now. My gun was poised. He was dressed in black: long black coat and, as he closed the distance, I saw the black ski mask. Under the crook of his arm, he carried a dark blanket or tarpaulin. My muscles tensed. Surely he'd seen me. He knew I was here. He kept coming. He was short and broad, marching toward me, like a brave soldier. I leveled the gun on him. On he came.

Twenty feet away, he raised a gloved hand and waved me down. "Lower your weapon, Cooper. Lower it and relax."

Who the hell was this!?

He went to Rod. He stood over him and dropped the tarp. He looked at me. "One of my better shots. There's a lot of wind out here. I had you both scoped from the time you hit the beach."

"Who are you?" I called.

I could only see his slitted eyes peering out from the ski mask. He was probably 5'8" or 5'9", with massive broad chest and shoulders, even if the overcoat gave him weight and size.

"You would have taken him," Ski Mask said, in a flat baritone voice. "Even with your bum left leg. By the way, why did you kick him with your left leg? Why not kick with your good leg? Your strong leg?"

I waited, studying the man, shivering. I still had the gun on him. "Because I wasn't thinking too good."

He gave a sharp nod. He didn't seem to notice or care that I had the Ruger pointed at him. "Okay... So go. Get out of here. I'll take care of this."

"Who are you?"

He stood dead still, like a big black piece of black marble. "Paul Callo told me to watch your back."

"Paul Callo!?" I asked, astonished. "You work for Paul Callo?"

"He said to watch your back. That's what he told me. He also said, if I had to take some action then I was to tell you, you owe him. So now you owe him. He'll call on you one of these days."

I lowered the gun and leaned back, feeling the ice cold sand on my very cold ass. "Why?" I asked. "Why would he care about my back or my anything else?"

Ski mask shrugged. "He said something like, chock it up to two guys who'd lost in love."

Ski mask went to work. He gathered up the parka, folded it into a square and moved toward Rod's body. He unfolded the tarpaulin, snapped it out and floated it down, covering the corpse.

I slowly got to my feet. I eased the revolver into my coat pocket. I slapped off sand from my backside and arms and started over to him. We stood there, looking down.

"What are you going to do with him?"

Ski mask didn't look up. "I wire some weights to him and find some deep water. There's a lot of water around here. I used to fish up here when I was a kid. I know this water real good. I got family up here and a couple boats." He lifted his eyes and considered me. "Go, Cooper. You've got one hour with the Elvis kid. Then, I take Paul's kid, one way or the other. Paul said I was to take his kid no matter what. So go. You're wasting time."

What had I told Paul Callo? "In this business things always go wrong." What a great big silly genius I am. I left Ski Mask to his work and trudged off. I glanced back over my shoulder as I left the beach. Ski Mask had the wrapped corpse swung over his shoulder. He was walking as sure and as steady as he had without the load, slowly drifting away in the rising mist, like a dark apparition. I would not want to box that one. I would not like to meet him again. Anywhere. Anytime.

CHAPTER 20

I limped up the road to Main Street, shoulders pulled up to my ears, hands stuffed deep into my coat pockets. The adrenalin was still pumping but I felt that low dragging energy from the combat and from the lack of sleep. Many awful and fearful things go through your mind after a near encounter with death. You think of fate, of luck, of timing. All of the ifs, if onlys and could-have-beens arise, banter, speculate and then die away in "It just wasn't my time." If I'd gone into my father's construction business I'd probably be making a good living, own a house or two and have five or six guys working for me doing all the heavy lifting. If Connie hadn't died in that auto accident maybe I'd have two kids by now. Maybe Connie would have talked me into buying a condo in Manhattan and we'd be living happily ever after.

If I hadn't met Paul Callo, I'd be dead right now. If I'd never met Aleta Fisher, I'd have never met Abner Lipps, Darcy-Lynn or Rod Faulkner. Rod Faulkner would still be alive. If I got into my car right now and drove away, I would never meet Elvis Lipps and, consequently, my life would go off on an entirely different trajectory. Who knows, maybe I'd meet the new girl of my dreams, we'd win the lottery, we'd move to some exotic isle off the gorgeous coast of somewhere and live happily ever after. We'd never have arguments. We'd never grow sick and old and we'd live for ever.

I plodded up the asphalt road to Main Street. Traffic was light. Sun broke through ragged clouds, spilling sunlight onto my shoulders and warming them. I looked left. There it was, the Memory Motel. If I turned left— Elvis. If I turned right—happily ever after on that exotic isle, with the girl of my dreams.

The Memory Motel was a creamy colored single-story 1950's style, time-worn motel. It was surprisingly grungy, when compared to the surroundings. My first thought was it should be somewhere out west in New Mexico or Arizona lying nestled among cactus and desert on Route 66. Maybe an independent film company could use it for a movie about bikers or about lost and angry runaways.

Maybe it had 15 rooms. Maybe more. Maybe you bring a girlfriend here for a breakup, confident she'll take one look at the place and hate you forever. Maybe you bring a ghost buster to purge the place of evil spirits who have been murdered or who died from despair.

I heard a thumping jukebox banging out hard rock. There was a bar in there somewhere. There was an office.

I stood there just staring. I felt displaced, off-centered. I felt time-worn and somewhat grungy myself. Hell, maybe I was just projecting all the crap that was inside my gut outside onto this unfortunate, wayward motel. The Memory Motel. The Living End.

I entered the office, grateful for the enveloping heat. The beefy man behind the desk wore an old gray sweat-shirt that had *Don't Mind if I Do* printed across the chest in white block letters. The man wasn't friendly. He wasn't unfriendly. He radiated indifference. There were photos of rock bands, the smell of aged mold and BO and a fading black and white newspaper clipping hanging lopsided on a back wall, that told of the Rolling Stones' visit to Montauk in the early 1970s.

"Can I help you?" he said, not looking up from his glowing iPhone screen.

"I'm supposed to meet a young couple. Don't remember the room number."

"You can't call them?" he asked, scrolling.

"No, I can't." I said it with an impatient edge.

"Room 19," he said, softly, his eyes reading, his right hand scratching his two-day old beard.

"Thank you," I said, thinking I'd never get a room number from the desk clerk at The Plaza Hotel this effortlessly. There were advantages to The Memory Motel.

As I turned to leave the office, I saw a burgundy Toyota Camry turn in and pull up directly in front of Room 19. My hand was on the doorknob. I paused.

Darcy-Lynn got out, casting furtive glances. Rod had just missed her. Ah, timing, fate and luck. Darcy wore a long gray tweed coat, buttoned to her throat, and black leather gloves. The two inch black heels gave her height and elegance. Her hair was shorter. It had been cut and curled. She reached inside the car and, from the front seat, extracted a black leather attaché case. Then there were more furtive glances.

I decided not to wait. I pulled the door open and walked briskly toward her, across the asphalt surface. She picked me up, just as she started toward Room 19. She froze, eyes wide, first in surprise, then in fear and then in anger. I closed the distance fast and stopped, facing her.

"Hello, Darcy. I like the new hairdo."

"What are you doing here!?" she said, with bold anxious eyes.

"I think you know."

"Well," she sighed with exasperation and annoyance. "Leave. Just go! How did you find me, anyway?"

I ignored her question. I took her arm at the elbow. "We're both going inside."

She tried to wrench away, but my grip was firm, despite my still sore fighting hand. I turned back to her car and looked at the plates. South Carolina. It was a rental. I read the license plate numbers and hoped I'd remember them.

"That hurts," Darcy said.

"Let's go, Darcy."

I wondered if Mr. Desk Clerk was watching. Then I thought, even if his beady eyes were locked to his phone, he was surely watching. Motel clerks see everything— with their ears, their nose and their hair. But this one surely didn't care. After all the things he'd probably witnessed in this seedy outpost, this was just another dreary romance going wrong.

At the big faux oak door, I motioned for Darcy to knock. Reluctantly, she did.

"Hello..." It was a male voice, low and nervous. "Who is it?"

Darcy hesitated.

"Who is it?" the male voice repeated, loudly.

I glared down at Darcy.

"Darcy-Lynn, Elvis. Let me in."

As the door cautiously swung open, I shoved Darcy against it and pushed inside. Elvis, Darcy and me all tumbled in. I recovered and kicked the door shut with my right foot.

There we stood: Elvis, Darcy, Gina and me. Standing like frozen statues, glaring, staring, scowling, probing. Finally, I took a long, appraising look at Elvis.

My first impression was of a tall, well-built kid with a magnetic vulnerability that suggested romance and adventure. He gazed back at me with astonishing sea blue eyes, that took me in fully. His long, thick raven black hair was carelessly styled, and possessed the rich sheen of midnight blue. The shoulders were broad under a straining black T-shirt, the chest wide, waist narrow in tight-fitted jeans. His full lips were parted in surprise, eyelashes long and, as I could easily imagine, devastatingly beguiling to all things female and to those types who wished they were.

Elvis Lipps was born to be gazed at and worshipped by reaching, screaming fans. He was built to strike blows of heart-throbbing pain and pulse-pumping love into a sex-drenched population, who are easily mesmerized by the next movie star, pop star, YouTube star or any eye-popping phantom who dazzles, sun-soaked for a while then, inevitably, shoots away into the night sky of addiction, old age or—the worst hell for the attention-addictive types—forgotten oblivion.

If Elvis Lipps resembled *the* Elvis Presley, and there was a striking resemblance, then there was also a double-dip attractiveness to Elvis Lipps. He had Elvis' unmistakable handsome face and magnetism, but he also had his own particular good-looking individual impact that radiated allure, mystery and the promise of escape to a far away land where this boy would absolutely love and satisfy you—and only you—for all of dreamy eternity.

By contrast, Gina Callo was a thin, petulant, damaged vulgar doll. She gave me an arrogant, dismissive glare. Her bleached red and blond hair was tied up in a half knot and strings of it fell about her face and over her forehead. She wore a baggy, red, long-sleeved sweat shirt, jeans with those stylish rips and holes, and she had a ring in her pug nose. There were two diamond studs on either side of her nose. Her makeup was heavy and her dark eyes were two slits of resentment.

"Who the fuck are you?" Gina said.

I ignored her and turned my attention to Darcy. She gave me a beautiful scowl. Darcy was a very attractive woman, even when scowling. I pushed Rod Faulkner out of mind. I looked down at the attaché case.

"I guess that's the money," I said. "The ten thousand dollars?"

She pulled it away from me, as if I was going to snatch it from her.

Elvis stepped forward. "I need that money!"

Gina flopped down on the bouncing bed. It creaked. "*We* need that money, Elvis!" she stressed. "*We*! Get rid of that prissy little bitch!"

My mind was struggling to disengage itself from the near-death encounter with Rod and the surreal encounter with Ski Mask. I shut my eyes for a moment to erase those images and start with a clear screen. I opened and focused.

"Okay...I don't care who gets the money," I said. "It's Darcy's money and she can do whatever she wants with it."

"Who is this stupid fuck, Elvis?" Gina asked.

Again, I ignored Gina Callo, though it took some effort. I thought, "What a lovely child you have, Mr. Callo. Maybe you want her to stay lost?"

The room was a mess. I saw a half-depleted vodka bottle propped precariously on the edge of the nightstand, tightly wedged between the two unmade double beds. Clothes were tossed in corners or hanging carelessly off the bathroom doorknob. Crunched soda cans stood next to grease-stained pizza boxes and crumbled candy wrappers. Two suitcases were pushed aside, clothes bunched up and spilling out.

"Elvis, I'm Dane Cooper. Your father hired me to find you."

His eyes moved nervously as he shoved his hands into his pockets. His eyes had a slight blur of confusion. His deep, anxious breath smelled of alcohol. "Yeah, I know that. I know all that. He told me all that. And you called me. How did you find me?"

He shot Darcy an infuriated glance. "Did you tell him I was here!?"

"*We* are here, Elvis! *We!*" Gina belched out.

Elvis waved her down. "Okay, okay, we, for Pete's sake. We, okay. Now just shut up about it!"

Gina shot up, with clenched teeth and fists. "I won't shut up. Fuck you, Elvis. Just fuck you and that slut! I know what you're trying to do! You're gonna dump me and run off with her!"

Elvis pivoted toward her, his body a coil spring ready to pop. "You don't know shit, Gina! You're just a stupid little bitch who thinks she knows, but she doesn't know shit! So shut up or God help me, I'll punch you in the face!"

"I'll fuckin' have my father kill you, you son-of-a-bitch!"

"Stop it!" Darcy yelled. "Just stop it!"

Gina threw her the finger. "Fuck you! You had this planned all along, didn't you. All of it!"

Now I knew why this place was called The Memory Motel. There would be so many memories—so many things to remember about the place and the people.

There were so many blemishes, foul smells, ugly expressions and disgusting people and thoughts that I would never forget. These unfortunate scenes, people and impressions would stick in my cerebral cortex Memory Motel for all of time, and nothing, short of a lobotomy, would ever erase them.

Gina went after Darcy and Darcy, surprisingly, sprang after Gina. Elvis jumped between them, arms extended, blocking them. "Cool it! Just cool it! Okay!?

I sighed, audibly.

"Sit down, Gina!" Elvis commanded. "Sit down, dammit!"

Grudgingly, she did.

"Darcy, go over there!" He pointed to the opposite corner, near the front door.

I watched, amazed, as she obeyed.

Elvis slowly lowered his arms. He went to the vodka bottle, unscrewed the cap and drew a long drink. He replaced the cap and bottle and wiped his mouth. He ran a trembling hand through his hair.

I unbuttoned my coat and took a 5 beat. "Elvis, you need to leave... alone. If you do not leave, in the next half hour, you will be killed."

Gina shot up again. "That's bullshit!"

Darcy gave me a savage look. "Don't listen to him, Elvis. Don't!"

I continued. "Aren't you tired of all this, Elvis? Aren't you sick and tired of running and hiding? Aren't you sick of living in rat holes like this? With all your looks and talent, don't you want to do something good with your life? Your father has lined up an audition with some big agent in California. He manages Tom Cruise and... I don't know, some other big guys. Anyway, why don't you walk out of here, call your father and get on

Death Is Lookin' For Elvis

with your life? Why don't you make something of yourself?"

Elvis studied me. Gina scowled at me. Darcy glowered at me.

"Aren't you sick and tired of living like a criminal?" I asked, in a final, reasonable appeal.

Elvis grinned, wryly. He reached for the vodka again. He took another drink. I did not see capitulation in his face. His expression darkened.

"Am I sick of being a criminal? Yeah... I'm real sick of it, but...well, what the hell. That's what I am."

"Elvis... If there's a statutory rape suit, we can..."

Elvis cut me off. "I killed him!" Elvis blurted out. "Don't you know that? Aren't you supposed to know that? What the hell kind of private detective are you!?"

Darcy started toward Elvis. "Stop it, Elvis. You don't need to tell him anything!"

Gina spoke up. "Elvis... let's take the fucking money and go! We don't need her or this stupid detective asshole. Let's just go!"

I fixed my eyes on Gina. My voice was low, cold and threatening. "If you say one more word, young lady, I'm going to tie your young, skinny, vulgar ass to a bathroom pipe and stuff your foul mouth with a wash cloth and duct tape it shut. You got that!?"

Gina tried to defend herself, but her voice lacked conviction. "My father will..."

"I know your father. Paul Callo will shake my hand! He might even send me a very generous check in gratitude for tying you up and shutting you up. Now shut up!"

Stunned and defeated, she dropped, bouncing on the bed. She crossed her arms, pouting.

I focused on Elvis. "Elvis, we are running out of time. You know it and I know it. Now talk to me."

Elvis began to pace on a small patch of frayed, dirty carpet. "I'm sick of it all!" he said. He lifted both hands. "I am, I'm just..."

"Elvis," Darcy said. "We have 10,000 dollars. I can get more. A lot more. I have a lot of money. We'll go to South America. But we need to leave right now!"

Gina jumped up, almost spoke, but stopped. She sat again, fuming.

Elvis faced me. "I didn't mean to kill him." His eyes filled with tears. "I really didn't."

Dread filled my gut. "Kill who, Elvis? Who did you kill?"

"He threatened me, you know. I mean everybody was threatening me. Do this, Elvis. Go here, Elvis. Be this, Elvis or else... or else."

"Who threatened you?" I asked, calmly, evenly. Nerves were beating at my insides. I did not want to have to fight Ski Mask. "Who was it, Elvis?"

Elvis hunched up his shoulders, his eyes pleading. "That porn maker. That awful dude. That fat porn film maker."

My brain locked up. In my normal rested, pre-boxing match, before gunshot and Ski Mask, I would have instantly remembered. Then I did. "Donovan Lassiter!?"

"He said he would contact my father. He said he would put a lot of shit out on the internet about me."

"When did this happen, Elvis?"

"I don't know... about two weeks ago, when Gina and I were still hiding out in New York."

"Tell me what happened, Elvis."

"He just kept pushing me. He pushed me around."

"Did you do a porn film?" I asked.

He turned away. "One... just one fucking, shitty film. It was short. Only like 15 minutes. I hated it. I told him I wouldn't do anymore. I told him I wouldn't finish it. I told him to trash it!"

The vodka was having its effect. Elvis' speech was slurred, body loose, face slackening. Elvis continued on. "He came at me, threatening me. Everybody is always threatening me, wanting me for something. Pulling on me. Jerking me around. Elvis you're so this, Elvis you're so that... The film was only like fifteen minutes... something like that. I said, that's it. I'm outta here. I ain't doin' this no more. He said he'd send it to my father and my mother. He said he'd put it on YouTube...I told him, no, you can't do that! But he just kept yelling at me. He wouldn't shut up! I said, just shut up! But he wouldn't. So I just picked it up. I just reached for that wine bottle that was sitting there next to his computer. I don't know if it was full or empty or what. I just picked it up and swung it at him. I hit him once or twice. I don't remember. But I hit him hard. I knocked him down and... he just lay there. Just..."

Elvis buried his face in his hands and wept.

Darcy shouldered her purse and crossed to him. She gently took his arm. She spoke tenderly, stroking his hair. "It's okay, Elvis. What you did was okay. He deserved it. If you didn't kill him, somebody else would have. Let's go, Elvis. We can forget about everyone and everything now. It'll just be the two of us. Let's just go."

Gina's inflammatory face hardened.

Elvis slowly removed his hands from his face. He looked at Darcy, softly, with swollen, bloodshot eyes. "Can we? Can we go? Can we just leave?"

I took a commanding step forward. "Elvis, I want you to think about something. Just stop for a minute and think about what I'm going to say."

"We don't need to listen to anything you have to say!" Darcy snapped.

"Elvis... I want you to leave with me. Now. We'll return to New York. We'll go to the police, voluntarily. I'll be with you. Your father will hire the best lawyers. We don't want the police to track you down. You need to turn yourself in. Today. We can clear this whole thing up and then you can get back to starting a brand new life. The kind of life you want to live. You should do this, Elvis. Stop running now and face everything. It's the best way to go."

Darcy took Elvis' arm. "The hell with him, Elvis. I have the money. If we leave right now, we can leave the country and they'll never find us. Never! We can make a new start and nobody will ever bother us again. We'll be free from all of them."

Gina leapt up again. "And what about me!?" she barked. She seized Elvis' other arm and yanked him toward her. "You said you'd never leave me. You said you loved me! You did! You did. I can get money. Lots of money. I can get more money than this bitch can ever get you!"

Darcy snatched the other arm and yanked him back to her. "Now, Elvis. Let's go now!"

They jerked him back and forth in a tug of war, like little girls fighting over a rag doll. First Gina. Then Darcy. They heaved and grunted and cursed. Elvis rocked and swayed, teetering carelessly, a helpless desperation building in his weary eyes and on his flushed face.

Then Elvis flexed his arms, jerked and broke free, sending the girls stumbling. He erupted into shouts. "Leave me alone! Everybody just leave me alone!"

His face was a storm of confused emotion. "All of you, just stop it! Stop it! Everybody wants something from me! Old fat women calling for me, grabbing at me..." He mocked their voices. "You are such a darling boy. Get me my towel. Order me a drink. Come over here and fix Momma, pretty boy!"

Elvis stood quivering, fuming. "I'm not going to jail. I'm not leaving the country. I'm not doing anything anymore except what I want to do! Okay!" He slapped his chest. "Me! What I want! I come first now! Okay!?"

He faced both women, and his face got ugly with contempt. "I'm sick of you both! Sick of you! Both of you just... just get the fuck away from me! You both just make me sick! You're like all the others, reaching and clawing at me! Just stop it!"

There was a paralyzing silence as both women, like fluttering moths near a flame, had drifted too close and were singed. Darcy's face crumbled. Gina slumped. Her face twisted in a stunned misery.

Elvis struggled to recover. His eyes dropped to the floor. He held out his hand to Darcy. His voice was flat and lifeless. "Give me your car keys, please. I'm leaving, but I'm leaving by myself... and with the money."

Darcy stood motionless. She looked stricken.

"Give me your keys, dammit!" he demanded.

Darcy slowly slid her slender right hand into her purse, that was still draped over her left shoulder, and drew out a gun. I should have been surprised, but I wasn't. Back on the beach, didn't Rod say that Darcy had a gun and he had taught her how to shoot? Didn't he say she was a better shot than he? I wondered where she'd got the gun. New York? New Jersey? Long Island?

I was familiar with it. Shanahan had bought one for his wife, Jean, for protection. It was a Smith & Wesson Centennial .38 special. Maybe it weighed 15 ounces. It had a good rubber grip. The short barrel made it easier to carry in a purse. It's more powerful than the standard .38. Not as wrist wrenching as the .357 Magnum, but it still carries a lot of punch.

I pulled a breath. "Darcy, put the gun away!"

She didn't move. Elvis stared at the gun with indifference. Gina stepped back, frozen and scared.

I measured the distance to her. It was only five feet. I lowered my voice. "Darcy, give me the gun."

She glared at Elvis. Her chin quivered. Her eyes filled with tears. When she spoke, her voice was low and threatening. "I gave up everything for you: my profession, my husband, my career and my dignity. I have lied and cheated and degraded myself in a thousand ways so that you and I could be together. You are not going to leave me now. We leave together, right now, or neither one of us leaves at all."

Elvis flashed a dark, splendid smile. "So pull the trigger, Darcy-Lynn. I don't really care anymore. 'Cause whether you shoot me or some guy out there shoots me or I go to prison, I'm dead anyway. One way or the other, I'm just dead, so go ahead and finish me off. Please, just finish me off."

I couldn't take the chance of going for the gun. The room seemed to hold its breath.

Darcy slowly turned to me, the barrel pointed at my chest. Watching me, she dipped her shoulder and lowered the purse to the floor. Slightly bent, with her left hand, she carefully drew out the keys, handing them to Elvis. Her eyes were fixed on me, with hatred.

"Go, Elvis... just go! Take the car and the money and go!"

Elvis turned, repentant. "Darcy... I just..."

"Go!" Darcy snapped. "Now! Get away from me! I never want to see you again."

With bowed head, Elvis took the keys, edged past us and picked up the attaché case. He didn't turn back as he opened the door and left, shutting it silently.

We heard the engine grind, then come to life. We heard squealing tires, and then we heard silence.

I stood rigid, staring into Darcy's fixed gaze. "So, Darcy, I guess we're not pretending anymore."

Darcy wavered. Her eyes spilled tears and they ran down her checks. She slumped. Her trembling arm dropped and the gun fell to the floor. The color drained from her face and she wilted and collapsed. I lunged ahead, snatched up the gun and stuffed it into my pocket. I kneeled and checked her pulse. It was strong but erratic. I swept her up into my arms and gently laid her on the bed. I started for the door. Gina came at me, eyes wide and pleading. "You're not going to leave me with her are you?"

"You won't be alone long, Gina. A friend is coming for you."

I left the room, walking briskly across the parking lot toward my car. A thick fog was curling across the road and a fine misty sleet was falling. I knew it was nearly futile to try to catch Elvis, but I had to try. When I saw his contrite expression, just before he left, I saw a spark of hope in his blurring eyes. I had to try to catch the kid. I had to try and reason with him one more time. If I was alone with him, I believed I could convince him to go to the police. Hell, Abner Lipps paid me a lot of money to find and help his kid, didn't he!?

I cranked the engine, blasted heat at my face and swung into a U turn. Out of the corner of my eye I saw him: Ski Mask. He loomed out of the fog, a dim, dark shadow, striding toward me in the same relentless, purposeful way. Gina would be his problem now. Good luck, ice man.

The blowing sleet coated the highway and I eased back on the accelerator. I felt the back tires slide a little and struggle for traction. It would be nearly impossible to catch Elvis in this dismal weather. But then he couldn't make good time either. If I didn't catch him within a half hour, I'd call the highway patrol and have them put out an APB.

I came to a fork in the road. Why is there always a damn fork in the road? Did Elvis turn left on Route 27, Old Montauk Highway, or did he turn right and take the high road that linked up with Route 49? I remembered the map. Route 49 merges into Route 27. I turned left on Route 27.

Visibility was only a few feet, as waves of fog blanketed the road. I switched on the wipers, peering ahead. My thoughts danced images of Ski Mask and Darcy. What would Ski Mask do with her? Snatch the kid and leave Darcy? Yeah, probably. What would Darcy do when she came out of her faint and blinked around the room? She'd be alone—utterly alone. She didn't like being alone. I didn't know her well enough to know how she'd respond. As cold as it sounds, I didn't care. Not much anyway. Okay, maybe I cared a little. Maybe I hoped she'd walk to the nearest restaurant, get something to eat and pull herself out of it. Okay, yeah, I hoped she'd do that. But would she?

Suddenly, I heard a startling noise, a short distance away. It was a crashing sound. A dull, exploding whoosh. I yanked my foot off the accelerator, heart racing. The ghosts of trees and houses appeared and disappeared in fog and mist. I was anxious and disoriented. I slowed to a crawl, looking ahead, straining my eyes.

Then I saw it! Just ahead on the opposite side of the two-lane road. A big burgundy mass of car emerging and dissolving in stringy fog. It was out of place and time. It shouldn't be there. I angled right to the thin shoulder of the road and came to a careful stop. I left the car, stepping cautiously across the wet pavement. I saw a man waving at me, wearing a red ball cap and brown jacket. He stood by the side of the car: Darcy's car.

"Help! Over here! Help!"

I hurried over. Elvis had plowed head-on into a telephone pole.

"Help me get him out," the man said.

I felt a punch of cold wind as I approached the driver's side. The entire front-end of the car had wrapped the pole. The car was crunched and beaten. I gazed tentatively at the shattered windshield and the bloody, crumpled body that lay sprawled over the hood, amid broken glass and twisted steel. Elvis had not used his seat beat and the airbag had only partially deployed.

"We should get him out of there," the kid said.

"No! Did you call 911?" I asked.

"Yeah. He almost slammed right into me! He must have just skidded and lost control!"

I carefully leaned in to Elvis' body and stuck my fingers into the side of his neck. No pulse. Nothing. His face was turned away from me. I was glad about that. Elvis was dead.

The wailing scream of sirens was closing in on us. I stood facing the sea. I couldn't see it because of the fog. I could only hear it, roaring, beating itself against the beach.

I was bone-aching weary, down to the soles of my feet. But I wouldn't be sleeping anytime soon. There would be endless interviews, a coroner's report, an autopsy and statements to be signed. I wouldn't be leaving Montauk today. In New York, there'd be more of the same. After all, I knew who had killed Donavan Lassiter.

Who had killed Elvis Lipps? Perhaps it was death by a thousand cuts. Perhaps he never had the time or the chance to just grow up and find himself. I'd spent all my time trying to find Elvis, and had learned next to nothing about him. Did anyone ever ask him what he wanted to do with his life?

He had been coddled, combed and polished and then roughly handled by the perverted—by the hapless and lonely and by the ambitious, struggling to complete their own empty, depleted lives. Elvis was a shining pop image of hope and salvation through projected fantasy and false idol worship. Thou shalt have no other Gods before me, except this pretty, darling boy, who can help me make it through another long, lonely day and a pathetic, enchanted night. Help me make it, Elvis. You have it all, you ecstatic pretty boy. Dance and sing for me, flutter those long lashes, Elvis, and help me to live my tattered, unfulfilled life through your deathless, magnetic vision. In return, I promise to suck the ever loving life out of you.

As the police arrived, I recalled an incident when I was a kid growing up in Brooklyn. I entered the kitchen one afternoon, where my mother was preparing dinner—fried chicken, mashed potatoes and... let's see, I think it was green beans but it could have been spinach. Anyway, our next door neighbor came bursting through the back door, her face blank with shock. My mother, seeing her expression, dropped what she was doing and wiped her hands on her apron.

"What's happened?" my mother asked. "You look like you've seen a ghost. What has happened!?"

Our neighbor said, "I just heard that Elvis is dead. But how can Elvis be dead? I mean, he's Elvis. He can't just be gone."

EPILOGUE

Spring opened its amorous arms in dazzling sunshine, a roaming warm wind, and glittery flowers that danced victorious, as if thumbing their noses at long, hard perfidious winter. Pretty girls were dancing too: in the parks and on street corners. These are the places you'll find me during this season, because destiny and an inclination to watch pretty flowers and things sends me there. I'm just a helpless man all caught up in the play of fate.

It was a Saturday morning and I was strolling along the carriage path in Riverside Park, up near West 108th Street. Helen had called earlier and demanded I come to her house for dinner that evening to see her new kitchen cabinets. Now let's see, after months of estimates and deliberations, she'd finally decided to nix Home Depot and go with a company that offered her just what she was looking for: solid hardwood panels with a dark rich glaze. I think the company-created color name was Regency Midnight Glaze. Well, Helen devours Harlequin romances and I guess the name just jumped out at her.

So, I'd go to Queens for dinner and Oooo and Ahhh and say, "Helen, these are absolutely beautiful." Then I'd say, "Were they expensive?" and she'd snort and fume and say, "That's none of your damn business!" Which meant, of course, that the cabinets were expensive and she'd already begun to second-guess her decision.

The day before, Friday, Helen had entered my office with a guarded expression, and tossed down a manila folder. Without looking at me she'd said, "I know you'll want to look at this."

After she'd left, I squeezed the two brass pins vertical, opened the flap and drew out three pages Helen had downloaded from one of our many people-search databases. At the top of the page, in bold type, I read

Darcy-Lynn Roberts.

I sighed a little. I had never spoken another word to Helen about Darcy after Elvis' death. I'd seen Darcy only briefly at Elvis' inquest. Our eyes had not met easily, and we had not spoken. Abner Lipps had been there, too. He was a broken man, chin on his chest, sad eyes downcast. I tried to speak with him—tried to find some words, any comforting words—but he'd waved me away without a word. Without any words at all.

I allowed my eyes to slowly drift down the page. Darcy was working for a financial company.

Accounts Payable Manager
San Diego, California

She'd been working there for a little over a month. She was not married. Her address and cellphone number were listed. She had purchased a condominium in downtown San Diego, overlooking Balboa Park. And the price: $559,000. She'd said she had money.

She'd probably meet a banker or hedge fund manager, get married and go sailing on Sundays. They'd have two kids, a sprawling beach house and several dogs, probably Labrador Retrievers, and she'd live the life of her dreams.

The old memories and dreams she had of Elvis would eventually fade and melt away. They'd only reappear on lonely winter nights, years into the future after her kids were grown and gone, and her husband was off on some distant shore struggling to patch up, with strings and Band-Aids, the next financial debacle.

About a month after Elvis' death, his mother, Lucille, had had a massive stroke and died. Abner Lipps contacted me with this news through email. A week before, I'd Fedexed him my final report on his son's case.

In his email, Mr. Lipps informed me that he never wanted to see or speak with me again. In his own florid style, he said he blamed me for Elvis' death and for destroying his family. He said, his hiring me had been the biggest mistake of his life. Fortunately for me, at the end of this communication, he said that he would "keep me in his prayers."

So I strolled Riverside Park, gradually making my way up to Broadway to get a cappuccino at the Samad Deli on West 111th Street. There is an older gentleman who works there, perhaps he's in his 70s, who makes one of the best cappuccinos in the City. Far superior to Starbucks. His name is Lou. He's thin and brown and has a southern accent. It's an open and friendly face, Lou has. It's weathered and round. He always brightens my mood. So I went to the back counter and ordered from Lou.

"Haven't see you in awhile," he said, going to work on the drink, his old hands assured as he tamped the ground espresso into the steel head.

"Are you going to South Carolina anytime soon?" I asked.

"Nah... too hot down there. I go in the fall."

I reached into my wallet, searching for money and saw a business card. As the milk steamed and hissed, I withdrew the card.

It read:

Paul Callo
Manager
The Golden Sunset Hotel and Casino
Las Vegas, NV

So Paul had made manager. He'd sent me the card a few weeks back. No note. No letter. Nothing about his daughter. It was just as well. Maybe he'd forget that I owed him. Yeah, sure he'd forget. That's why he'd sent the card.

Lou poured the steaming foam over the espresso, sprinkled cinnamon and handed me the cup. "So how are the kids?" he asked.

I took the paper cup, grinning, sheepishly. "Oh, they're fine, Lou. They're all fine."

A few years ago, Lou had asked me this same question and for some reason—maybe I was tired or distracted or maybe I was feeling nostalgic and thinking about Connie—who knows why I said it, but I had answered, off-handedly, "Oh, they're fine. Everybody's just fine, Lou."

And so it started, and I've never managed to tell Lou the truth. I should have told him, but I never had. I even avoided the place for weeks at a time so I wouldn't have to face him; because I knew he was going to ask me about the kids, because he always did. But I didn't tell him, and Lou's cappuccinos are delicious. So I'd finally give in and go get one of Lou's excellent cappuccinos.

"The kids must be getting big by now," Lou said.

"Oh, yeah, Lou. They're growing up."

"How old are they now?"

I wrestled with time and dates. "Oh, the girl's seven and the boy's nearly nine now." Had he noticed I hadn't mentioned their names?

"Bring them by sometime. I'd like to see them."

I turned toward the front, quickly removing my guilty expression, and snuck away like a petty thief. "I will, Lou. I definitely will."

I'll tell Lou the truth someday. Of course I will.

On the other hand, after I tell him, what if he refuses to make me another one of those delicious cappuccinos?

The End

CPSIA information can be obtained at www.ICGtesting.com
Printed in the USA
LVOW12s1927190114

370055LV00022B/546/P